RAGE

A SEVENTEEN SERIES NOVEL

BY
SUZANNE LOWE

© SILVERGUM PUBLISHING

First published in 2019
Silvergum Publishing Pty Ltd
www.silvergumpublishing.com

The moral rights of the author have been asserted according to the copyright law
Text © Suzanne Lowe 2019
Cover Design: The Illustrators
Map Design: Fldesigns
Book layout by ebooklaunch

National Library of Australia Cataloguing-in-Publication entry:

Lowe, Suzanne, author.
ISBN: 9780648390824
ISBN e-book: 9780648390831
For Young Adults.
Subject: Young Adult fiction, science fiction/Australia

To Steve, Tahlia and Emilie.
Thank you again for your support and suggestions!

SEVENTEEN SERIES

BOOK TWO

"In the end karma will be a bigger bitch than I'll ever need to be!"

Lexi Valentine

Virus

"An infective agent that typically consists of a nucleic acid molecule, is too small to be seen by light microscopy, and is able to multiply only within the living cells of a host."

English Oxford Dictionary

Australian spelling and slang is used throughout this novel. Contains mild violence and profanity.

PROLOGUE

It has been eighteen months since the KV17 virus was released into our fragile world killing every adult on earth. Throughout Australia, groups of children have banded together to etch out an existence surviving on what food they could scavenge.

In Jasper's Bay located in Western Australia, a cluster of children continued to fend for themselves. As they realised that outside help was not going to be coming their way, they began to plan for the future. However, without the internet, electricity, running water or supermarkets with fresh food, life was increasingly difficult, and many children died.

As two sisters, Lexi and Hadley made their emotional escape from the dying crime-riddled city of Perth, they eventually found sanctuary in the small town of Jasper's Bay. Here they made new friends and a different life for themselves. This wasn't easy, especially with the continual threat of violence from marauding gangs wanting to use the lawlessness of the new world to their advantage. With much at stake, Lexi and Hadley were pulled into a bitter conflict with a gang led by the unscrupulous bully, Broc.

During the conflict, Lexi found herself drawn to Braydon, one of the gang members. Together they formed a friendship, each seeking solace in a world where it was difficult to know who to trust.

Throughout the turmoil, Kevin, one of Jasper's Bays original inhabitants, joined with Broc and his gang in an attempt to take control of the town. Families and friends were betrayed, and a bitter battle left destruction and several lives lost in the fray.

When the battle against Broc and his gang was over, and peace finally ensured, a new unforeseen threat suddenly emerged. The KV17 virus had mutated. Older teens could now be infected, altering their state of mind and emotional control. This raised new concerns within Jasper's Bay as soon after this discovery, Braydon, Lilly and Elisha became infected and consequently exiled from the community.

With several of the older teenagers now banished from town, Lexi found herself appointed as one of the leaders of her new home. Being in charge was not a position she was used to or comfortable with; however, Lexi soon discovered she was an adept leader and began to enjoy the role.

As Lexi, Hadley and their friends endeavour to solve the increasing problem of depleted food supplies and the looming threat of the mutated virus, they are once again harassed by an unexpected source.

The story of the two sisters and their friends in Jasper's Bay continues in this second book; *Rage*.

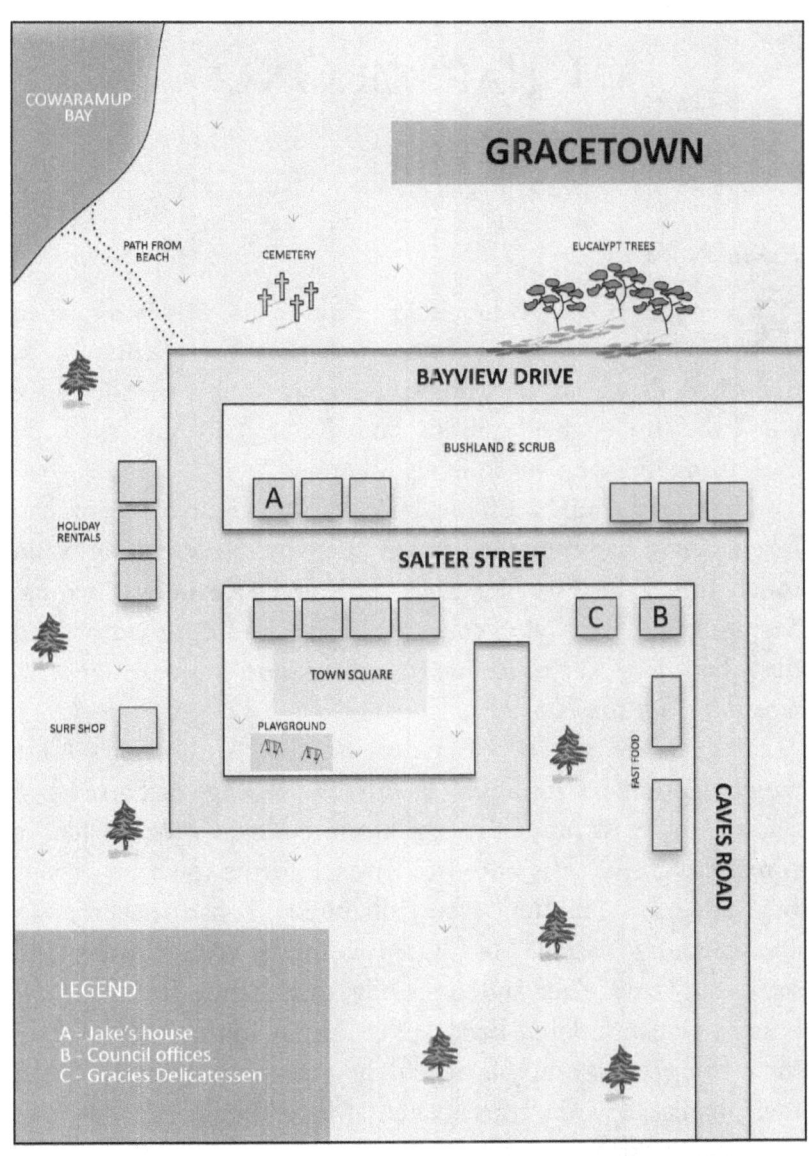

COWARAMUP BAY

GRACETOWN

PATH FROM BEACH

CEMETERY

EUCALYPT TREES

BAYVIEW DRIVE

BUSHLAND & SCRUB

A

HOLIDAY RENTALS

SALTER STREET

C   B

TOWN SQUARE

SURF SHOP

PLAYGROUND

FAST FOOD

CAVES ROAD

LEGEND

A - Jake's house
B - Council offices
C - Gracies Delicatessen

3

CHAPTER ONE

Kevin

Revenge. It was all he could think about. His body ached for it, burned for it like a relentless fire waiting to be quenched. It was all he wanted. Revenge for his friend. There could be no higher calling, and Kevin was going to do everything in his power to make it happen.

Before the night of the bonfire, the night his hero had fallen, Kevin had thought Broc to be invincible. Nothing could touch him - he was like Zeus. However, Kevin was wrong. Seeing Broc's body lying cold and lifeless amongst the dirty red dust had left Kevin feeling nauseous and raw. *How could something like this happen?*

As he had watched Braydon standing with Broc's knife dangling from his trembling hands, the feelings of hatred had started to twist and tighten around Kevin's heart like a constricting vine. His once indifference to the town of Jasper's Bay and the children who inhabited it had become an overwhelming hatred. He wanted to see his older brother and sister Lilly and Zac, and especially that traitor Braydon, the bastard who murdered Broc, suffer. Kevin couldn't wait to see their smug faces crumble when they saw who had facilitated their demise. His mouth salivated at the thought. Very soon it would be his day of reckoning.

As Kevin thought about the destruction of his home town, he realised he needed a plan. While the remnants of Broc's old gang, Cindy and Aaron, were still with him, Kevin knew it wasn't going to be enough. He needed more force. He needed numbers. Kids he could persuade to do what he wanted and bend to his will. When the trio had stumbled across the small fishing community of Gracetown, Kevin knew it was perfect.

After watching the town for a day, Kevin noticed with delight the only inhabitants of Gracetown were a bunch of scrawny children. *Younger* skinny children. This was excellent as far as he was concerned. Younger kids would be easier to persuade. Plus, they all looked as though they could do with a damned good feed, which was ideal. Starving kids would be more vulnerable and open to persuasion. All he had to do now was set the bait and watch them take it, just like a fish snatching a bug.

Gracetown

Out on the ocean that skirted the little town of Gracetown, A young boy stared down into the blue, green seawater. The sun beat down relentlessly on his already parched skin; the thin nylon line cutting into his red, aching fingers. Jake had been up since the early hours of the morning before the sun had even made its appearance for the day. He felt tired and hungry. Fishing used to be fun. It wasn't fun anymore. Not when you had to keep at it all day, every day. And not when others depend on you for their survival.

He carefully pulled the fishing line into the small boat to check the bait. A thin wriggling earthworm remained impaled on the hook. Jake examined the worm before turning to face his companion. "I don't think the fish around here like earthworms all that much anymore. Maybe we should try changing bait?" he said frowning.

A young girl of about ten raised her sunburnt face to stare at him. She nodded her head in agreement, "I think you're right. I haven't had a bite for the last two hours." Kally pulled her own untouched line into the boat. "Let's call it quits. My bums gone numb from sitting in the same spot."

Jake laughed, "Yeah, alright. We've got three fish. That's going to have to do." He shrugged and looked out to sea. "I dunno what's going on? Maybe the fish know we're here. We might have to change spots."

"Hmm, maybe." Kally started to pack the rest of their fishing gear into a blue plastic esky, careful not to tangle the fishing lines. "Listen, Jake. I know you like fishing every day."

Jake groaned in response to her statement.

Kally grinned for a moment enjoying her companion's displeasure. "But I think we're going to have to think of something else besides *fish* to feed everyone," she continued. Kally peered into the esky at the three, silver fish flapping about in the small amount of water. "It's just not enough for the ten of us kids. Anyway, I'm getting tired of only eating a few bits of fish and the occasional bit of damper each day, aren't you?"

Jake looked at Kally and nodded. "Yes, I am. Plus, it takes almost all day to catch enough fish. I don't have time for anything else!" He sighed tiredly. "What can we do, though? Have you got any ideas, because I'm completely blank?"

Kally stared out across the shimmering water. It was such a vast expanse of blue nothingness with no land in sight. After a few minutes, she turned to face Jake. "I know we've already cleaned out the grocer and deli in our town, but maybe other places near us have some food left?" She poked their catch of three fish and one small squid with her finger. They hadn't been able to catch anything at all yesterday, and after a whole morning of fishing, this was all the two of them could provide. "We really need more food. Why don't we find another town to scavenge from?"

Wrestling the cumbersome oars from the bottom of the boat, Jake placed them into their rowlocks, ready to row back to shore. He thought about what Kally had suggested. They were only a small town on the edge of the Indian Ocean, and while it did provide them with a few fish, there weren't any other means of feeding themselves at hand. They had already eaten all the food from the two small shops in town. Unfortunately, there weren't any farms or factories nearby, so the only means of nourishment for the ten children in town was the occasional damper made with flour, and water; plus, the few fish he and Kally could pull from the ocean.

Jake looked down at his scrawny, depleted arms. Just like the other children, he had lost a shocking amount of weight. They were all starving

"Okay, Kally. Let's go and find another town to scavenge from." Jake started pulling on the oars. "I just hope it's not going to get us in trouble."

She smiled sweetly at him, happy to get her own way. "Well, there aren't any adults around anymore, so, who's gonna stop us?!"

Jake grinned at Kally. She was right. They could make their own rules. They just had to decide where to look.

The small community of Gracetown was not all that far from the town of Jasper's Bay. It was situated on the western coast of Australia flanked by the Indian ocean on one side and the Blackwood State forest on the other. There were currently ten children living in Gracetown, their ages ranging from three to twelve. Since the last adult in town had passed away from the KV17 virus six months ago, the children left behind were not doing very well. In fact, like many other children in towns across Australia, having to suddenly fend for themselves was an arduous struggle. In a world now devoid of the indulgences and luxuries once available 24/7, all at the touch of a button, it had become a daily battle to survive.

Jake and Kally, two of the older children in town slowly trudged up the sandy path that led from the beach to the outskirts of their home. Between them, they carried fishing gear, empty water bottles and the three precious fish and squid they had caught that morning.

"Jeeze, it's getting hot already," complained Jake as he wiped his brow with the back of his hand. He immediately regretted his action as his hand stank of fish and bait. He kept walking, dust billowing out behind him.

As Jake and Kally reached the first house at the back of the town, they could see a young boy waiting patiently for them. It was six-year-old Mathew. He was sitting quietly by a row of freshly made wooden crosses, marking the graves of three children who had died over the past few months. Two were young babies who had perished early on, and the last was Mathew's best friend, Tommy. Tommy had succumbed to blood poisoning after cutting his foot severely on a rusty old tin can.

The children had been unable to stop the spread of infection through his young, malnourished body, and he had died only a few weeks ago. His death had hit the children hard and Mathew in particular. Every day he would visit Tommy's gravesite and chat to his lost friend. Today he had brought a little orange toy car with him to play with as he talked to his mate.

"Hi Mathew," waved Kally walking towards the young boy. "Come and see what we've got."

Mathew rose from his spot and ran up to the older children, his dirty face interested and alert.

Jake bent down to Mathew's height so he could see what they had caught. "Have a look. We caught some fish but look what else!" He reached into a canvas bag slung over his shoulder and pulled out a squirming, strange-looking creature.

"What is it!" exclaimed Mathew wiping his nose with his hand and laughing.

"It's a squid!" said Kally, her voice filled with excitement. "Bet ya never seen one of those before, eh?"

"Nooo, I haven't," replied Mathew with wonder. "It's weird looking." He screwed up his nose.

Jake laughed. "Well, it's where calamari comes from. You've had those before, haven't you? We call them squid rings. They used to sell them at the fish and chips shop, remember?"

Mathew's eyes widened in pure delight, and he licked his lips. "Oh, yeah. I've had those with my mum and dad," he started to say before his smile dropped, and he looked down at the ground as he thought of his dead parents.

Kally rested her hand on Mathew's shoulder.

Mathew raised his eyes to look at her. "Squid rings were my dad's favourite."

Kally nodded.

"I like them too," said Mathew with a small smile. "Can we have them for dinner tonight?" he asked, glancing at Jake, his stomach making loud grumbling noises.

"Sure can. They are best when they're fresh," replied the older boy as he placed the squid back in the bag. He ruffled Mathew's hair with his hand. "We'll cook them all up later after we've cleaned them." *The squid was going to be a real treat!*

Mathew clapped his hands in glee before racing off to tell the other kids the good news. They were going to have something different for dinner tonight!

Jake smiled as he watched the young boy skip away. "Come on," he said to Kally, slinging the bag back over his shoulder and continuing up the path. "We'd better get these out of the sun." Keeping food fresh in the Australian summer heat was a real problem for the children. Without any electricity in the town, they didn't have any way of keeping food from going rotten. Anything they caught had to be eaten that day, which meant that some days they feasted and some days they starved. Unfortunately, with ten hungry mouths to feed, unless they caught fish, most days they starved.

After a short walk, Kally and Jake reached the house they were sharing with another boy, Alex. He was one year younger than Jake and perpetually lazy. Alex did little to contribute to the town, yet always had a snide comment or complaint about anything the older children suggested. Even though Jake had a very relaxed and jovial nature, Alex was continually getting on his nerves.

Kally suggested they kick him out of the house and let him find his own place; it was Jake's family home after all, but nothing had been done about it so far. Jake was very unconfrontational and hated any drama.

Walking into the kitchen, Jake dumped the fresh fish on the bench ready to be cleaned and prepared. He pushed a pile of empty food tins and wrappers from the counter onto the floor. "We should really clean this place," he muttered, looking at the filthy table. "At least we won't go hungry today," he smiled in relief. He turned the fish over in his hand. "These are quite a good size too, and I can't believe we actually caught a squid!"

"I know it's amazing! I can't wait to taste it," exclaimed Kally, her eyes growing wide with excitement. The squid would make a nice change from plain fish.

Just as Jake was about to begin cleaning and scaling their catch, he heard a ruckus outside. It sounded like yelling, and he wondered who was getting so worked up.

As the noise outside grew louder, Kally and Jake glanced at each other in surprise. *What was going on?* They quickly covered the fish with dish towels to stop the flies getting to them and ran out to see what was happening.

"Hey! Hello! Is anyone here?" A boy was calling loudly as he and his friends walked down the main street of the town. "Where is everyone!"

As Jake stepped outside, he saw three people wandering along the street in front of his house. Three strangers. He looked at them more closely. The trio weren't adults, that would have been a surprise as he hadn't seen any adults for at least six months. They looked like older teenagers.

"They had better not be here to cause trouble," Jake muttered under his breath as he and Kally marched out onto the street to see what they wanted. There were two boys and a girl, and they looked to be about 15 years old, a couple of years older than Jake.

"Hey, mate. What's going on? Why are you yelling?" Jake asked a little nervously, watching the gang of older kids. He stood up straight and tried to look a little taller, wishing he wasn't so skinny. "Who are you?"

One of the strangers, an Asian girl with a bright pink streak in her hair, turned to speak to Jake. "Well, hello handsome," she smiled, looking him up and down. "We are here to help you out. We're going to be your new best friends."

Kally stared at her and moved closer to Jake. "What are you talking about? Her hands were placed firmly on her hips as she glared at the Asian girl. "Who the hell are you, anyway?"

"Yes. Who *are* you, and what do you want?" questioned Jake walking over to stand in front of the group of strangers. He didn't like the look of these older kids at all.

The guy who had been yelling earlier, a chubby boy with greasy brown hair and a severe acne problem kicked an old coke can out of the way and stepped forward. "I'm Kevin. This is Cindy, and Aaron," he gestured to the other two teenagers with him. "We've just come from a town not far from here, called Jasper's Bay. Do you know it?"

Jake and Kally nodded their heads. "Jasper's Bay sounds familiar, it mustn't be too far from here," whispered Jake. Neither Jake nor Kally had ventured very far from Gracetown for fear of getting lost.

Kevin rubbed his nose as he looked at the two kids standing before him. He brushed his hair back with his hand and tried to appear friendly. Kevin wanted these younger kids to trust him. It would be easier to manipulate them if they believed what he said. "We came here to help you," he stated. "Jasper's Bay has loads of food. You guys look like you could do with some nourishment!" Kevin paused and gave Jake a beaming smile like a car salesman. "Why don't you come with us to Jasper's Bay to see if they'll give you some?"

Jake's eyebrow twitched. He turned to look at Kevin. *Did he say loads of food? God wouldn't that be wonderful.*

Cindy could see Jake was interested, so continued with the story. "Yeah, that's right. They have a whole farm full of food. We've just been there, and they *gave* us heaps of food! Cindy glanced sideways at Kevin, who smirked.

Jake put his hands up in confusion. "Err that's great, but why would they give *us* their food? They don't even know us." He brought his hand up to his mouth and turned his head to whisper to Kally. "I doubt they would give their food away when it's so scarce."

Kally nodded her head slowly in agreement.

Kevin took a step closer to Jake until he was almost touching him, making Jake feel decidedly uncomfortable. "Well, they didn't know *us*, and they gave *us* food."

Peering intently at Jake, Kevin could see he was undecided. "If *you* help us, we will share some food with you, he said, trying to convince him. "You want some extra food, don't you?" His voice had turned steely hard.

When Jake didn't answer, Kevin cleared his throat and closed his eyes for a moment. As he thought about his hometown, his fist curled around the small knife in his pocket. He desperately wanted to go back to Jasper's Bay and seek revenge on his brother and sisters and the rest of the town. How dare they kick him out! He wanted to see the place burn, and he didn't care who got in the way.

He had spent the day watching Gracetown and its inhabitants, trying to see who was running the place and whether they would give him any trouble. As far as he could tell, this boy standing before him was the oldest here, and the rest of them were only little brats. Nothing he couldn't handle. His time with Broc had taught him a thing or two about bullying, and Kevin was determined to make these children in Gracetown help him get his revenge, either willingly or by force. Voluntarily would be a lot easier, of course. However, he was happy to use coercion if it was required.

Jake stood silent, looking uncertainly between Cindy and Kevin. He looked as though he didn't quite know what to make of these newcomers, or if he wanted to get involved with them. He blinked slowly as if unsure of what to say.

When Jake didn't say a word, Cindy walked up to Kally and linked her arm around hers as if she were her best friend. "Come on," she said to the younger girl. "Is this your house?" Cindy pointed towards Jake's home. "Let's go inside and talk about it," Cindy cajoled as she started to pull Kally towards the house.

Jake hurriedly stepped in front of Cindy. He didn't know these kids, and he didn't want them in his home. Once they were inside his house, he might not be able to get them out again! Jake had to think of something quickly.

"Um, listen," Jake blurted out. "There's a little park just down the street and around the corner. It's really nice. It's got seats and shade and stuff. We can meet you there in half an hour." Jake cleared his throat nervously and pointed down the street where he wanted the strangers to go. "We were just in the middle of something. We won't be too long. Then we can talk about your offer."

The trio of strangers turned to peer questioningly at Jake. Kevin had a knowing look on his face as if he knew Jake didn't want them coming into his house.

"Sure," smirked Kevin. "We'd *love* to go to the park. Just don't be too long, or we will have to come back and find you," he said, nodding towards Jake's house. Smiling to himself, Kevin turned away and started sauntering down the street towards the park.

"Yeah, alright. Well, like Kevin said, don't be *too* long," scowled Cindy as she let go of Kally's arm and followed Kevin. The other boy Aaron, who hadn't said a single word, trudged silently behind her like a pet.

Watching to make sure the strangers kept walking, Jake raised his eyebrows at Kally, before quickly pulling her into their house.

"What the hell was with *them*?" asked Kally shaking her head in confusion as she pulled the curtain aside and peered out the front window.

"I know. That was weird. I wonder how those kids got here?" Jake scratched his head. "They must have a car or something because there's no way they could have walked. I think the town they were talking about; Jasper's Bay is inland from us."

Kally closed the sheer curtains and turned to stare at Jake. "Why did you agree to meet up with them later?" she said, her brow creased.

"I don't know, I just panicked," said Jake, his face worried. "I just didn't want them coming in here," he exclaimed, gesturing to his kitchen with his hand. "I didn't know what else to do!" Shrugging, Jake looked down at the fish waiting to be cleaned and cut off its head with one blow of his cleaver. He was obviously upset.

Kally watched Jake angrily cleaning the fish. "It's okay, Jake. Don't worry," she said encouragingly. "It'll be alright."

Jake gave her a half-smile and went on cleaning the fish, only this time a little less aggressively. They needed to be cleaned and salted before they spoiled in the heat of the day.

"I don't think those kids are here to help us," said Jake looking up from the fish and frowning. "And I don't think the people in Jasper's Bay would be giving their food away. I mean, why would they?"

Kally shrugged as she picked up one of the fish. "What are they here for, then?"

"I don't know. I mean, they *seemed* friendly. But I'm just not sure," said Jake turning his knife over in his hands. "There was something about that kid. What was his name? Keith or something."

"Kevin," stated Kally.

"Kevin. Yeah, I didn't like him."

"That girl was annoying too. The way she grabbed my arm!" Kally complained as she rubbed her forearm.

"Maybe we're just not used to having other people in our town." Jake sighed and glanced towards a photograph of his parents sitting on the table in the adjoining room. "What would you have done in this situation? Would you trust these strangers?" he murmured.

He stared at the photograph for a long moment before quickly wrapping his cleaned fish in tin foil, salted and ready to be cooked. Jake then reached over to Kally and grabbed her hand. She stopped what she was doing and looked up at him in surprise.

"Listen, Kally. I think I'd better go and talk to those kids at the park," suggested Jake, his voice serious. "I don't want them roaming the streets and upsetting the younger kids. Can you round up Alex and Martin, then join me down at the park?"

Kally nodded. "Sure, but why do you want the boys to come?"

Jake looked uneasy. "I'd just feel happier with a few more of us around," he said, absently running his dirty hand through his hair. "I'll quickly finish cleaning up, and packing the fish in the esky, then I'll head to the park." He peered towards the front door as if anxious to be on his way and get the encounter over with.

Kally gazed at the fish longingly. "Alright," she groaned. "But, can't we just cook the fish now? I'm ravenous!"

After sitting in the sun all morning, Jake was hungry too. "I know Kally. Believe me, I want to. If we cook it now though, don't you think those older kids are going to want a share?" He stared at the pink and white flesh of the fish, almost tempted to eat it raw. "We really don't have enough to feed them too. We're barely going to have enough to give a share to the ten of us. I can't risk it. We'll have to wait."

Kally took one last look at the fresh fish on the chopping board before turning to go and find the other boys. Her mouth watered with hunger. "Okay, well let's make this quick then," she mumbled as she walked out the door.

About twenty minutes later, the group from Gracetown met with the three gang members who had come from Jasper's Bay. Awkwardly milling around in the children's playground, Jake eyed the strangers suspiciously. He still didn't trust them. All he wanted to do was get back to his peaceful home as quickly as possible and start cooking his precious catch before it went rotten in this incessant summer heat.

"Right, well we're here having this meeting like you asked. What exactly is it you want? I'm kinda busy." Jake wanted to move things along as swiftly as possible.

"What exactly can you be busy with? It's not like you've got homework or anything," Cindy remarked snidely.

Alex, the other young boy who shared the house with Jake and Kally, stepped forward. He had sandy brown hair and a long side fringe, Justin Bieber style, which he constantly flicked from his eyes. He looked at Cindy with a smirk to match hers. "Actually, he's got fish to cook and clean."

Kally and Jake groaned in unison. So much for keeping their fresh catch secret. Alex turned to look at them. "What?" he said, not understanding. He wasn't exactly the brightest of kids.

Cindy grinned at Kally and Jake. "Mmm, fresh fish!" she spoke in an exaggerated voice. "I *do* love seafood. How about you guys?" She turned to Kevin and Aaron rubbing her stomach, her eyebrows wiggling up and down. Both boys smiled at her antics.

Kevin stood next to Cindy with his arms folded across his chest. He wasn't particularly tall or imposing. In fact, he was a little round and plump, but there was something about the look in his eyes that made him intimidating. He looked as if he wouldn't have any remorse for the things he did. He wasn't the kind of guy who would help you if you were in trouble, not unless it was of benefit to him.

"Seafood," said Kevin happily. "Oh, yes, seafood would be nice. I haven't had seafood in a *long* while."

Alex looked guiltily at Kally and Jake. Jake stared back in frustration, and Alex had the grace to drop his eyes in embarrassment. Jake was going to have to say something to these kids now. A confrontation. His shoulders slumped.

Clearing his throat, Jake spoke tentatively. "Err, I thought you said the people in Jasper's Bay already gave you food?"

Cindy's eyes flicked sideways to Kevin. *They had been caught in their lies.*

Kevin smiled coolly. "Yes, but not *seafood*," he replied condescendingly. "Like I said, I haven't had seafood in a while."

"Right," said Jake chewing on the skin of his thumb. "Well, the thing is, we only have a couple of fish, and there are ten mouths to feed in this town already." He shuffled his feet. "We don't really have enough to feed you too."

"What! Are you saying you won't share with us? I thought you were our friends?" Kevin pretended to look shocked. "We came here to help you!"

Kally joined in the conversation, her voice a little shrill. "It has nothing to do with whether you're our friends. We would give you some if we could, but like Jake said, we're starving here." She looked defiant. "This might be the last meal we have for a few days. We have little kids here, and we need to look after them!"

As the mid-day sun beat down oppressively on the group, uncomfortable rivulets of sweat ran down Jake's back. His shirt had become damp, clinging to his body like a second skin. He stared hopefully at the group of teenagers unsure of what else he could say.

Before Jake could say anything further, Cindy sauntered over to him and draped her arm around his shoulders. "We *totally* understand," she declared in an incredibly annoying whiny voice. "That's exactly where we can help you. You see, like we said before, the kids in Jasper's Bay have heaps of food. *Absolutely loads of it.*" She paused to look around at the younger children. They were practically drooling at the mention of extra food. Cindy smiled to herself before continuing. "Like I said, they have tins and tins of stuff and a whole farm with cows and chickens and everything. Just imagine having fresh eggs every morning followed by tinned peaches! How nice would that be?"

Jake took a step away from Cindy, not enjoying her closeness. His fingers twitched, and his mouth salivated at the thought of all that food. "It would be nice," he muttered, shuffling his feet uncomfortably.

A bright yellow butterfly landed on Kevin's arm. He peered down at the insect for a moment before swatting it flat with his hand and flicking its lifeless body away.

Kally gave him a look of disgust.

Kevin smirked at her, then turned to once again move close to Jake. He slapped him hard on the back, wiping his hand across Jake's shoulders. "That's right mate. They have tons of food, and like I said before, we'd like to help you get some." Kevin was sure if he could convince these kids to come to Jasper's Bay, he was confident he would be able to use the food as a temptation to get them to do as he wished.

Jake glanced sideways at Kevin. "And why would you want to do that?" he asked suspiciously, leaning his body away from Kevin.

Kevin laughed. It was a thin laugh that sounded mean. "Well, you're our friends, aren't you?" He placed his arm firmly around Jake's shoulders. "Besides, if we help you now, you can help us later."

Jake looked down at the ground and stared at the little black ants scurrying around at his feet, trying to escape the oppressive heat. "Oh, yes, and what exactly is it you want us to do?" he asked, looking up at Kevin, feeling uneasy.

Not wanting to divulge his real reason for asking Jake and his friends to join him in going to Jasper's Bay, Kevin lied instead. "Don't worry about that now," he said, grinning falsely. "It's simple. If you share some of your delicious seafood with us now, we'll take you back to Jasper's Bay with us." Kevin squeezed Jake's shoulder. "We can get you some extra food from there. Like I said before, they have copious amounts of food. They won't miss it."

Cindy flashed Jake a big toothy smile. "You'd like some extra rations, wouldn't you?"

"Why can't you just bring us some of the food?" asked Kally, her hands on her hips.

Kevin winked at Kally and laughed. "Well, we're not your slaves!" He grinned at her. "If you want food *you* have to come with us to my farm and get it."

"*Your* farm?" Jake questioned warily. He narrowed his eyes at Kevin.

Kevin cleared his throat, annoyed at himself for his little slip of the tongue. He thrust his hand into the pocket of his jacket and felt for his knife, trying to control his anger. He didn't want these kids to know he had a real connection with Jasper's Bay. They might want to know why he wasn't living there. He took a deep breath.

"*The* farm. You need to come to *the* farm with us," stated Kevin coolly. "Like you said, you have a lot of little kids in this town, and I'd hate to see any of them going hungry when they don't have to."

"How do we know we can trust you. We're not going to just drive off into the middle of nowhere with you if we don't trust you," asked Kally reasonably.

Kevin looked at Kally and nodded. *She had a point. He needed something more to earn their trust.* Looking back toward the direction of his car, Kevin suddenly grinned. *He would take a couple of chickens from his home farm. They were rightfully his anyway!*

"Alright, how about this. We could bring you a couple of chickens. I know the farm in Jasper's Bay has some," exclaimed Kevin proudly as though he were giving a speech. "You can have them as a token of our friendship! Then, you can come back to Jasper's Bay with us later and get some more food for yourselves."

Chickens! Jake's eyes widened. He couldn't believe it. Were these strangers really going to get them some chickens! His mouth watered at the thought. He hadn't tasted chicken in so long. If the kids in Jasper's Bay were willing to give this guy their chickens, maybe he was telling the truth? Maybe they were giving away food.

The four younger children from Gracetown huddled together to discuss their options. Deep down, Jake knew something wasn't right. These teenagers were trying to be *way* too persuasive to get them to go to Jasper's Bay with them just so they could all *share* some food. It didn't sound genuine. *But then why were they offering to give them the chickens?* All this talk of food was making him so hungry and confused.

Jake glanced up at Kally, Alex and Martin. They were all staring back at him with miserable looks on their faces, and he knew they must be hungry too. "I don't know what to do," he sighed as he ran his fingers through his sweaty hair. "I don't want to argue with these kids, and I know this is all probably too good to be true. Plus, I still don't exactly know what they want from us." His stomach growled loudly with hunger pains. "But, the thought of extra food, plus the chickens is so tempting." He licked his dry lips.

Kally pulled her shirt up a little way to reveal her hollow stomach and protruding ribs. "I don't think we have a choice, Jake. We're all wasting away. We need food."

Jake twisted his fingers and nodded. He glanced back over his shoulder at Kevin. "Okay. If Jasper's Bay gives you the chickens, we'll believe you. We'll do what you want."

Kevin nodded back with a smirk on his face. His fist was clenched in his jacket pocket, and he had to force himself not to laugh. This was precisely what he wanted. Just like the fish these kids had been catching, they had taken the bait!

Kevin was going back to Jasper's Bay to get his revenge!

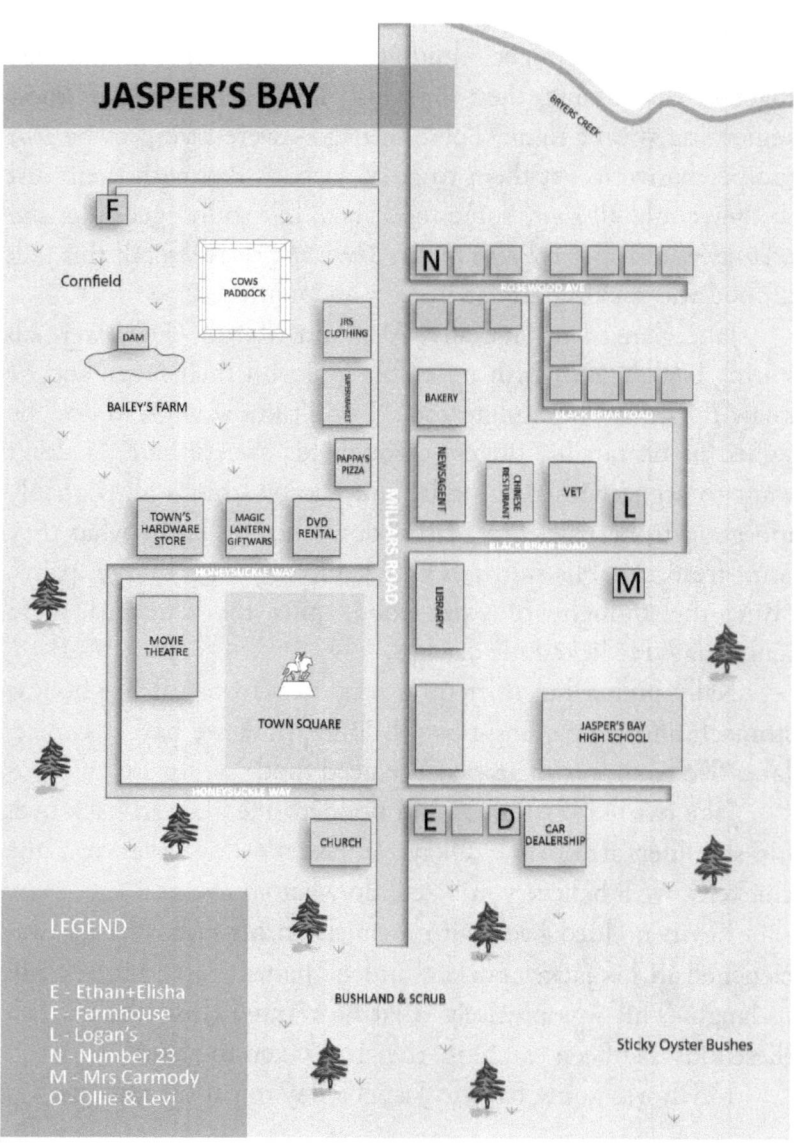

JASPER'S BAY

BAYERS CREEK

F

Cornfield

COWS PADDOCK

N

ROSEWOOD AVE

DAM

BAILEY'S FARM

JHS CLOTHING

SUPERMARKET

PAPPA'S PIZZA

BAKERY

BLACK BRIAR ROAD

NEWSAGENT

CHINESE RESTURANT

VET

L

TOWN'S HARDWARE STORE

MAGIC LANTERN GIFTWARS

DVD RENTAL

MILLARS ROAD

BLACK BRIAR ROAD

M

HONEYSUCKLE WAY

MOVIE THEATRE

LIBRARY

TOWN SQUARE

JASPER'S BAY HIGH SCHOOL

HONEYSUCKLE WAY

CHURCH

E

D

CAR DEALERSHIP

LEGEND

E - Ethan+Elisha
F - Farmhouse
L - Logan's
N - Number 23
M - Mrs Carmody
O - Ollie & Levi

BUSHLAND & SCRUB

Sticky Oyster Bushes

CHAPTER TWO

Jasper's Bay

It had been two months since the *incident* with Broc. Although the children of Jasper's Bay were relieved, they were finally rid of Broc and his terrorising ways, no one wanted to talk about the night of the bonfire when he was killed. Even though that terrible night was still fresh in everyone's thoughts, no one mentioned it. It wasn't as though they had forgotten, you couldn't exactly forget something like that in a hurry. After all, their friend Harry had also been murdered that night, and another two children had succumbed to the KV17 virus and exiled themselves into the harsh, barren Australian bush. It was just that the children weren't used to that amount of violence and fury, and no one wanted to admit they kind of enjoyed the savageness of it all.

Lexi picked up an empty wicker-basket and quickly made her way out the front door of number twenty-three Rosewood Avenue. She, along with her sister Hadley and their friend Jason, were still sharing the house since arriving in Jasper's Bay. Hadley was waiting impatiently for her in the front garden. It was their turn to help at the Bailey's farm.

"What took you sooo long? I've been waiting out here for ages," complained Hadley, scuffing her feet on the path.

Lexi rolled her eyes dramatically. "It hasn't been ages. And I couldn't find the basket. It hadn't been put back in its usual spot!"

Hadley giggled. "Oh, yeah. I was using it to play with Polo." She smiled at the small Jack Russell dog sitting by her feet. "Guess I forgot to put it back. Whoops!"

Not waiting for her sister, Hadley started skipping happily along the road towards the farm. "Come on Polo," she called out beckoning the little dog to follow. "We don't want to be late!"

Lexi glared at her in annoyance. *Hadley could be such a pain sometimes.* "What does it matter if we're *late*," she muttered as she rubbed her wrist where her watch used to be. "It's not like anyone knows what exact time it is anyway." Only a couple of the kids in town had watches with solar-powered batteries. Everyone else had given up using clocks and watches when their batteries had run down. Some had never had watches at all, having used their mobile phones in the past to check the time. Everything was so different now. Time didn't matter as much.

Holding the basket on her hip, Lexi ran to catch up with Hadley. She wanted to talk. The farm was on the outskirts of the town, and without a car, it would take them at least forty minutes to walk there. It was a good chance to chat.

"You've been doing great work with the job roster, Hadley," Lexi praised, slightly out of breath. "It's really been helping to keep things organised in the town, and everyone seems okay with following it so far."

Hadley smiled and nodded. "Yeah, thanks. I like doing it. Plus, I get to boss people around," she giggled.

Lexi smiled too. "Uh, huh. You're definitely good at that!" She stopped walking for a moment and gently grabbed her sister's arm, forcing her to wait. "Listen, Hadley. You know there are plenty of kids in this town you can trust, right?

There's Jason for one. He would look after you. Plus, Ethan and Logan."

Hadley turned to look directly at her sister, her eyebrows pulled together in a frown. "What are you talking about?" she said sharply.

"I just want you to know that you'll be alright if something happens to me." Lexi pulled at the hem of her frayed cotton top.

"What do you mean?" questioned Hadley in concern. "Broc and the gang are gone, and we haven't had any trouble for weeks. Why would something happen to you?"

Lexi ran her fingers loosely through her long dark hair. Her fingers became caught in one of the knots, and she pulled at the tangle distractedly. "I don't know. I just feel really agitated a lot of the time, you know? Pissed off about stupid things. Plus, I am *seventeen* now."

Hadley looked at Lexi anxiously for a moment before giving her a hug. "Don't be stupid. You're practically the town leader. It's just the pressures of having to hold this place together. If you had the virus, you'd be sick by now."

"Hmm, yeah. I suppose so," agreed Lexi, although she didn't sound convinced. She thought about the red rash on her feet that would not go away. *Did she have the mutated virus? She didn't have any of the flu-like symptoms that usually went with it. But then neither did Lilly or Braydon.* Peering out at the hot, dry land around her, Lexi could see the farm in the distance. They were almost there.

"I wonder how Braydon, Lilly and Elisha are coping? It's so barren, and the ground looks parched. No wonder it's difficult to grow anything," Lexi said, shaking her head. She stared out to the horizon, deep in thought. "I wonder if Zac has seen Lilly at all since she left?"

Hadley started walking toward the farm again. "Come on, boss lady. If you stop talking, we will be there soon, and you can ask him yourself."

"Okay. I'm coming!" Lexi took another grim look out to the horizon before trudging on towards the farm. She had so many questions in her head about this virus and no one to answer them for her. No Google, no telephones or adults to ask for advice. It was so frustrating.

The girls kept up a good pace, and it wasn't long before they reached the Bailey farm. As they walked down the long driveway lined with tall pine trees, they could hear cattle in one of the nearby paddocks. The sound of the cows mooing and snorting always made Lexi smile. It was the sound of life, and it reminded her that they had a chance of a future.

Seeing the girls walking up the long driveway, Katie came running out of the farmhouse excitedly. She let the flywire door slam loudly behind her. "Hey! What took you guys so long? I've been waiting all morning to tell you something exciting!"

Hadley ran towards her friend. "It was Lexi," Hadley complained. "She took forever to leave. What's the exciting news?"

Lexi raised her eyebrows at Hadley's comment but didn't bother to retaliate. She was certainly glad that Hadley had made such good friends with Katie. Although she was a couple of years younger than Hadley, they got along exceptionally well. Plus, it meant that Hadley wasn't hanging around Lexi all the time and annoying her with her endless chatter! She was pretty sure that Katie's older brother Zac was happy about it too, as it meant he didn't have to play with Katie.

Katie grabbed Hadley's hand and pulled her towards the side of the house. "Come and see. Our goat Maisy gave birth to two little kids last night! A white one like her and a black one like the dad. They're so cute!"

Lexi watched her sister vanish around the side of the house with the younger girl. She rolled her eyes. *Well, I guess we won't be getting any work out of those two today!*

Tramping towards the field of sweet corn the group had been trying to cultivate, Lexi tucked her empty basket firmly under her arm. The corn had been growing nicely in the hot Australian sun, and she could see that a few of the corn stems already had ears almost ready to be picked. For the past six weeks, the children had been taking turns to water the seedlings with buckets of water from the creek and fertilise them. Fortunately, they had a nice supply of readymade fertiliser courtesy of the farm's cows! They merely mixed the cow patties with water and dug the mixture into the soil. It was revolting smelly work; however, nobody complained as they were all anxious for a food supply. Their canned and dried food stocks had fallen drastically low, with only a few precious cans and packaged items left uneaten.

The corn had grown remarkably fast in the eight weeks since planting, and Lexi hoped they would be able to harvest some of the corn husks soon. The children could then use the cobs to make sweet corn soup, cornbread and have delicious corn on the cob, although without the butter. Her mouth watered at the thought.

Looking down one of the tall rows of corn, Lexi soon spotted Zac, Jason and Ethan. The boys were pouring buckets of water into a trough they had made parallel with the growing plants.

Jason glanced up when he noticed Lexi walking towards them and waved enthusiastically. "Hey, Lexi. Come to help? You didn't happen to bring some food, did you?" Jason was always hungry.

Lexi smiled and nodded. "Actually, I did. It's not much, so don't get too excited," she teased. "We found three old pear trees growing in the backyard of number twenty-nine, a couple of houses down from us. And guess what? They had pears on them!" She dropped the empty basket to be loaded with ripe corn cobs and offloaded her backpack from her shoulders. Reaching inside the bag, Lexi pulled out a few ripe pears, careful not to bruise the flesh.

"Oh my God, that's fantastic!" Jason's face beamed in delight. "It's been so long since I've tasted fresh fruit!" Zac and Ethan looked pleased too.

"Let's go back to the house and wash up," Zac chortled, winking at Lexi. "I stink like cow poo, and we could do with a break!"

"Yeah, you do!" Lexi laughed. She turned to trudge back to the farmhouse. "By the way," she said over her shoulder. "Hadley is going to add tending to the pear trees as part of everyone's weekly job schedule. They look nice and established, so hopefully, they will keep fruiting for a while. We should really look in the backyards of the other abandoned houses too. You never know, there might be other fruit trees or old vegetable gardens we can salvage. I don't know why we didn't think of it before." Lexi shrugged. "I guess we're just not that used to rummaging around in other people's property." She thought of her time at the Robinson's house back in Perth with the black blowflies and dead bodies. A shudder ran down her spine.

Zac nodded his head encouragingly. "Yeah, that's a good idea. It's still going to be a few weeks before this corn is ready. We might have to kill another cow if our food situation doesn't improve." He screwed up his nose at the thought.

Lexi stopped and glanced at Zac. "That must be difficult for you," she sympathised.

"Yeah, it is," he admitted. "Although I've lived on a farm my whole life, and I know exactly where the meat in the supermarket used to come from, it's a completely different situation when you have to slaughter a cow yourself." Zac instinctively turned to gaze at his herd of brown and white Hereford cows grazing in the adjacent paddock. "It's a horrible job."

Jason patted Zac on the shoulder. "Why don't you let one of us help you," he said, rubbing his nose.

Zac started walking towards the farmhouse again. "No, I couldn't do that. They're my responsibility, I'm the one who should do it." He looked at the ground. "I always have a little cry afterwards like a big sook," Zac told them sadly.

"Oh, Zac," said Lexi putting her arm around his shoulders and giving him a hug. "You're not a sook! They're like your family." She glanced towards the cows. "How many cows do you have left?"

"Well, we've got ten cows and one bull," Zac replied with a small smile. "Less than a quarter of our original stock." Approximately twenty cows had escaped into the bushes the night Broc and the gang had let them loose, and Zac had not been able to locate them since. Plus, he'd had to slaughter six cows already to help feed everyone.

Walking up the steps of the house, Zac stopped by a bucket of water sitting by the front door and proceeded to wash his hands and arms with a half bar of soap. "I really don't want to kill any more cows until it is absolutely necessary," he continued looking grim. Zac wanted to keep the cattle for as long as he could, just in case the situation became desperate, and they ran out of all their other food. "Unfortunately, our cows aren't dairy cows, so we can't use them for milk; however, I am hoping I can try breeding them and rebuild the herd," he declared excitedly.

Lexi listened to Zac talking about the cows and began thinking about the corn they had all helped plant. *Cultivating the corn had been an excellent idea, but it wasn't enough. Not to feed the twenty-one hungry children of Jasper's Bay.* The younger kids were always hungry, and while the older children were doing their best to manage the situation, Lexi knew the difference between calm and upheaval in the town, was a full stomach. *They were going to have to come up with another food source.*

Even though the children of Jasper's Bay were always thinking of ways to try and create something sustainable, they were continually having to use their quickly diminishing tin food stores. Several children had managed to plant small vegetable gardens in their backyards using seedlings from the local Farmer Jack's supermarket. Some were thriving, and some were not. Plus, it was going to take a few weeks of growing before the vegetables would be of any use, and a few weeks could be a long time when you didn't have a lot of food.

"Can you throw that water onto the plants by the side of the house when you've finished washing," asked Zac, nodding his head at Jason and Ethan. "I'll get some more from the dam later."

"Have you had any luck devising a filtration system for the dam water?" asked Lexi as she and Zac made their way into the house.

"No. Not yet," said Zac pulling up a chair and sitting at the small round kitchen table. "I'm still using the chlorine bleach to get rid of any nasties. How about you?"

Lexi sat next to him and started taking the pears from her bag. "Well, we've been boiling the water we collect from the creek and then using bleach too, but I'm not sure what we will do when that runs out. We'll have to think of something else."

Zac nodded his head and stared at the ripe pears.

By this time, Ethan and Jason had also made their way into the kitchen and sat down.

"I've been using iodine," said Ethan joining in on the conversation. "It gives the water a foul taste, but I read it's effective for killing micro-organisms, so…" He shrugged.

"Right," said Lexi. "Good to know." She leaned forward and cut up the yellow pears with her pocket-knife. Her mouth watered at the thought of biting into her share.

Folding the knife and placing it back in her pocket, she took a piece of the fruit. Ever since Broc had terrorised her and Hadley in their home, Lexi had taken to carrying the pocket-knife at all times. Besides making her feel more secure, it was a handy tool to have.

Zac winked at her as he shoved a whole slice of pear into his mouth. He grinned in delight. "Mmm tastes so good. You forget how nice fresh food tastes when you haven't had it for a while."

The others nodded in agreement. Lexi thought about all the times she and Hadley had ridden their bikes to the local shops in Perth, to purchase an afternoon snack; usually Malteser chocolates or Tim Tams! She remembered the rows and rows of fresh fruit and vegetables in the fresh produce aisle and how they had taken them for granted thinking they would always be there. Oh, how she would love a fresh banana or mango! Yum. Lexi doubted that she would ever get to taste a fresh mango ever again.

Jason looked at Lexi's melancholy expression. "Hey, what's wrong with you? Isn't the pear any good?"

Lexi glanced up quickly, not wanting to seem ungrateful for the food. "Oh, no. It's fantastic. I just wish we had more like it. I can't believe I used to complain when the shops didn't have blueberries, and I had to have strawberries instead!"

"I know. We certainly took all that fresh food for granted. Actually, the pear has given me an idea. What if we went scouting in the bush to look for native berries and stuff? Didn't the Indigenous Australians eat native fruits?" Jason scratched his head. "I wish I had the internet to look this stuff up. God, I miss it!"

Ethan, who had been very quiet up until now gave a huge belly laugh. "Ha ha ha. Yeah, the internet would be fantastic, plus electricity, television and McDonalds," he grinned at the others. "Heck, I'd even settle for a Mr Whippy soft serve ice cream right now, and I'm lactose intolerant! Guess I don't have to worry about that anymore!"

Lexi gave Ethan a concerned sideways glance, his voice sounded strained, and she wondered how he was coping without his sister Elisha. "Umm, Ethan I meant to ask you. Have you seen Elisha around at all?" She looked around hopefully at the others. "Have *any* of you spotted Elisha, Braydon, or Lilly since they left town?"

"No," Zac shook his head sadly. "I really hope they're okay. I'd like to see Lilly." Ethan hadn't seen Elisha either.

"Yes, and it would be good to see if the virus is progressing," suggested Jason as he helped himself to the last piece of pear.

"Well, yes. But also, to know if they are alright. They've been on their own for two months now." Lexi thought of Braydon, she would like to see him again too. "We could go and look for them out in the bush."

Ethan looked at Lexi and nodded in agreement. Jason, however, didn't look so confident.

"If we kept our distance, I'm sure it would be fine," reassured Lexi. She knew it was a risk; however, it was a risk she was willing to take if it meant she could speak to Braydon again.

"We'd have to be careful," frowned Jason picking at his thumbnail.

"I agree. We would have to be careful." Lexi stood and walked to the window, looking out towards the bushland. "Only a few of us should go so that we don't freak them out."

The others nodded in agreement. Everyone wanted some news of how the exiled trio was coping on their own and the extent of their infection from the virus.

"Maybe we should take a few weapons with us," suggested Jason quietly. "Just in case."

"I don't think that will be necessary." stated Zac, his voice rising in alarm. "We are talking about my sister, not someone like Broc." He glared at Jason.

Jason gave Zac a grim look. "Yeah, I know mate. But I was thinking of *his* sister," he said, jerking his head towards Ethan. "She was *insane* last time we saw her!"

Ethan flinched at Jason's harsh words.

"I'm not using any weapons against my sister," replied Zac shaking his head. "I can't stop you taking some, but I won't let anyone hurt Lilly." He gave Jason a steely glare.

Jason held up his hands. "Fair enough, mate. I was just saying we should be prepared. They've been in the bush for weeks. They might not be the same as when we last saw them." Jason rose from his chair and went to stand by Lexi. His back was turned to the other two boys.

"I don't know about you, but I'm taking a weapon," he murmured quietly under his breath.

Lexi looked at Jason and subtly nodded. She would take one too.

Ethan and Zac remained seated for a while longer. It had been hard for them, having to see their sisters exiled from the town and left to fend for themselves just because they were sick. *That wasn't how society operated, was it? Weren't you supposed to look after the sick?* Both boys had struggled with the situation and had gone looking for the banished trio several times before, to no avail.

Zac looked furtively at Ethan, who nodded slightly. They hadn't mentioned to the others that they had already unsuccessfully searched for their sisters. "Err, well we should probably tell you we've already tried looking for the girls," Zac said sheepishly. "We couldn't find them."

"Huh. What do you mean, you already looked for them?" questioned Lexi. "Why didn't you say something? We could have helped you."

Ethan shrugged. "Well, we thought everyone else would be too afraid to go, and we couldn't leave them out there in the bush without knowing if they needed help. Have you seen the bushland? It's so dry and inhospitable out there. I don't know how anything survives!" He looked down at the remains of his portion of pear unhappily, as if he felt guilty eating it.

"I would have helped you!" said Lexi, her voice full of emotion.

"Me too," added Jason.

Ethan gave him a dirty look.

"What? I would have!" said Jason with his hands out in front of him. "Just because I want to be prepared doesn't mean I don't care about them. I do." He looked offended.

"Anyway," said Zac in a weary voice. "We looked all around the outskirts of town and here on the farm, but we couldn't see a single sign of them." He lowered his gaze sadly and stared at the table. "I guess they don't want to be found."

Lexi walked over and reached her arm around Zac's broad shoulders. "Listen, how about we look again but out in the bush this time. Jason and I will help. You never know. More eyes might just spot something. Plus, we can take some food out with us," she said encouragingly giving Zac a hug. "Maybe the smell of food cooking will draw them out. I'm sure they haven't left the area."

Zac slowly nodded his head; thankful they were going to try and find Lilly. He missed her terribly, not that he would ever admit that to her, of course!

"It's a good idea to look out in the bush. We can definitely help," said Jason watching Zac. "And I'm really keen on looking for some bush food while we are out there," he said excitedly. "I'm going back into town to ask Levi and his brother if they know what to look for." His face beamed with enthusiasm. "They caught a couple of rabbits yesterday. And considering they are only 5 and 9 years old, it was very impressive!" Jason waved and walked towards the door. "I'll see you guys later."

"That *is* impressive," agreed Lexi. "Maybe they can help us too." She looked at the other two boys sitting at the table. They were grinning eagerly. "Right, well let's make this official. Let's plan on going in two days Agreed?" suggested Lexi taking charge. "That will give us time to finish our work on the farm and collect what we need for the trip."

The two boys looked at her blankly.

"We can't just go wandering around in the bush un-prepared," stated Lexi with her hands on her hips. "We need to take some water and food and stuff with us."

Zac laughed.

"What's so funny! Lexi scratched her nose self-consciously and stared at him.

"Nothing," said Zac continuing to laugh. "It's just that you're a city girl, telling us country boys how to go camping!"

"Oh, ha-ha," Lexi replied good-naturedly clipping Zac over the head with her hand. "Enough lip from you! Now, get outside country boy and water your crops!"

Zac and Ethan laughed as they all made their way back out to the paddocks, ready to start work on the cornfield again. Zac raised his hand to his eyes and peered out towards the bushland. "With all of us looking, maybe we can find our sisters," he smiled at Ethan, who nodded back.

Zac picked up his spade and dug into the soft earth. It was bone dry and would need watering. Turning his eyes upward, Zac noticed the sky was a perfect robin's egg blue, there was not a hint of rain clouds anywhere in sight. Any water for the crops was going to have to come from their own hands. He dropped the spade and picked up a bucket.

"I'll fetch some water," called Lexi, seeing Zac holding the bucket. She'd rather tramp to the dam for water than dig in the dry, dusty earth!

Lexi thought about their planned camping trip as she picked up an empty container and took the bucket from Zac. The three of them could work all day at the farm today, and tomorrow they could find some camping gear and pack provisions. Lexi began to feel excited. It would be wonderful to get out of town and the usual chores for a day or two. Plus, the prospect of seeing Braydon again made her feel more than a little delighted.

Lexi hummed happily as she made her way to the farm's dam to collect the water. This camping trip was a great idea, and she didn't feel guilty about leaving Hadley behind one little bit!

CHAPTER THREE

Later that afternoon, as Lexi and Hadley walked along the hot bitumen road back to their house on Rosewood Avenue, the feeling between them was tense. It was as if someone had pricked their skin all over with sharp pins leaving them raw.

"That's a stupid idea!" ranted Hadley when Lexi informed her of the plan to seek out the exiled Lilly, Braydon and Elisha. "What if they attack you?"

Lexi glanced at her sister in frustration. "It's alright, Hadley. We've thought of that. We're going to keep our distance. We just want to make sure they're okay. Besides, it's important to see how far the virus has progressed."

Hadley frowned in annoyance. "Hmm, I suppose so," she said begrudgingly. "Well, I'm coming with you."

"Oh no, you're not! Lexi replied firmly, shaking her head adamantly. "We're only taking a few kids. Remember how Elisha was when there were too many people around her; she freaked out. The smaller the number of people, the better."

Scuffing her feet along the ground as she walked, Hadley pouted. "It isn't fair! I don't know why I can't be one of the people going."

Lexi stopped walking and grabbed Hadley's arm. She was fed up with her whining. "Listen, Hadley, while we will be careful, it could still be risky. It's better if we take people Lilly, Elisha and Braydon know, with us." She glared at Hadley impatiently. "Understand?"

Hadley pulled her arm away from her sister and kept walking.

After a while, Hadley turned back to face Lexi. Her hands were placed firmly on her hips. "Alright, I get it," she sighed. "I just wish I could go camping too. It's so dull here. All we do is work!" She waved a fly from her face in frustration.

Lexi nodded her head, the tension between them subsided for the moment. "Uh, huh. I know." She looked at Hadley thoughtfully. "Listen. When I get back, why don't I look after baby Sarah for a night? Then, you and Katie can camp out at the Bailey farm in one of the tents."

Lexi tucked a stray piece of her hair behind her ear. "I'm sure Zac will help you make a campfire and everything. Might even find a ripe ear of corn you could roast in the coals. Fancy some popcorn?" Lexi laughed.

"Ooo yes! That would be fun," exclaimed Hadley brightening noticeably. "We could stay up all night and tell ghost stories!" Hadley clapped her hands and started skipping down the road towards their house.

Lexi stared after her sister. *Sometimes I feel like I'm a parent.*

When she reached the front door of their home, Lexi sat down on the front porch step. It was thick with dust, like Sleeping Beauty's castle, only much less pretty! No one bothered with appearances anymore. Absently drawing a smiling emoji face in the thick dust, her thoughts drifted once again to Braydon. She thought about the little scouting trip they had planned. *Would Braydon talk to her? Would he still recognise her?* She wondered if he looked the same. *They must have all lost weight; they would be eating much less than the kids in town.*

"I must remember to bring extra food for them," she said quietly to herself. *I hope Elisha doesn't attack us. Or the others. We don't know how sick they've become.* She drew a sad face in the dust next to the happy one.

Her anxious thoughts were soon interrupted by Jason and Levi wandering up the little stone path towards her. The two were chatting together merrily as they walked.

Lexi stood and stretched her back feeling stiff after her long trek from the farm. "Hi, Levi," she waved. "I haven't seen you for a few days. Has Jason been chewing your ear off?"

The young boy squinted at her while pulling at his ear. "Huh?"

Lexi smiled a little sadly, "Oh, don't worry, it's just an old expression my dad said all the time. It means has Jason been talking to you a lot."

Levi nodded his head before giving Jason an uncertain sideways glance, unsure how Jason would react to Lexi's comment. He needn't have worried. Jason was grinning happily, so Levi relaxed and smiled too. Even though Jason, Lexi and her sister had been in Jasper's Bay for a few weeks now, Levi couldn't help but think of them as outsiders. Especially as they were all originally from the city.

"You should try living with both Jason and Hadley in the same house," Lexi joked. "It's impossible to get a moment of silence!"

As if on cue, Hadley came bursting through the front door singing loudly, her arms stretched wide as if serenading someone. She looked straight at Levi, reaching her hand out towards him. "Can you feel the love tonight!" she sang off-key.

Levi froze looking a little hesitant. Lexi rolled her eyes at her sister before pushing past Hadley and opening the front door wide. "Come on in Levi. Don't worry about her. She's just showing off. Come inside and have a drink. We've got Milo," she said, noticing his anxiety.

Levi followed Jason up the stairs and into the house, while Hadley continued to sing loudly and twirl about on the front porch not realising that everyone had gone inside! The little dog Polo stood on the porch watching her.

"I hate not having any electricity," griped Hadley dancing around Polo. "I want to listen to some music." She cocked her head to the side and listened. A few birds were calling to each other in a tree nearby; otherwise, it was quiet.

Ever since the solar power cells were smashed by Broc, Jasper's Bay no longer had the comfort of electricity. And that meant they couldn't use their iPods, game consoles, DVD players or computers. As soon as they ran out of power, all those electrical devices the children had become so used to, had become useless. The town had become *silent*. It was as though they had gone back to the dark ages, and Hadley hated it. Being a child of the Millennium, all she had ever known was technology. Adapting to a life without it was proving to be a challenge. Like many of the others, when she wasn't helping with the town work roster or doing jobs of her own, she didn't quite know what to do. There had always been her parents, a teacher or another adult around to direct her. Now that she could do whatever she wanted; Hadley didn't know what it was she wanted to do! Sure, she could sleep in for as long as she wanted, wear whatever clothes she chose, wear make-up, or go bare faced. Whatever took her fancy. However, unfortunately, the fantasy wasn't as good as reality. She soon became tired of trying on clothes and make-up. It wasn't much fun when there wasn't anywhere special to wear them to. Life without her parents and even her teachers wasn't half as much fun as she thought it was going to be. The world had changed too much. It was hard work every day just to survive, and she missed her parents and even school terribly.

Hadley frowned as she looked up at the endless blue sky. "I wish it would rain," she muttered, bending to pat Polo's head. "You'd like that too, wouldn't you, boy?" She scratched under his chin, and the little dog wagged his tail. "At least it would be a change, and I'm tired of having to go down to Bryer's creek for water. I wish we had a water tank like some of the other houses," Hadley moaned looking distastefully at the plastic bucket sitting on the veranda waiting to be filled. She angrily kicked it down the steps before storming inside. *Lexi or Jason could get the water for a change!*

Stomping into the living room where Lexi, Jason and Levi were sitting and talking, Hadley stood and stared at them wondering what they were discussing. She watched as little Polo jumped to sit on Levi's lap, and the young boy reached down to stroke him behind the ears. Hadley pouted in annoyance. "No one asked *me* to join in the conversation," she muttered.

"I'm just going to make a hot drink if you want one?" asked Lexi, glancing at Hadley as she slumped down into one of the cosy lounge chairs.

Hadley looked through to the kitchen where she could see a pot of water boiling on their little camp stove. Since the electricity had stopped, they had taken to cooking on the old stove which was fuelled by bottles of LPG gas. Lexi had found a stash of full bottles at the hardware store and Jason and Hadley had helped her carry three of them back to their house. They weren't sure how long the bottles of gas would last, so were making good use of them while they could.

Hadley looked away from the boiling water. "No thanks," she answered sullenly, not happy at being left out of the conversation.

"That's the last of our water by the way," said Jason smiling at Hadley.

Hadley glared at him and groaned.

Jason looked confused. "What? You're the one who made up the roster. It's your job. At least you're not digging the toilet trench!" He grinned at her, hoping to make her laugh. She didn't.

Hadley groaned again. "I'm going to my room," she said, rising from her chair. *Bloody water*, she muttered to herself as she trudged out of the room.

Lexi watched her sister walk away and slapped her hand on her thigh. "I'm not your mother! I shouldn't have to remind you to do your chores!"

Hadley ignored her.

Lexi sighed, she had bigger things to worry about right now than Hadley's laziness. Turning her back, Lexi faced the others. "So, anyway, Levi, as we were saying before. Our food situation is getting to be serious," Lexi explained. "There are only a few cans of beef stew, soup and baked beans left, plus about ten small bags of pasta and rice. I think we also have a couple of packs of flour and sugar too."

Levi shook his head, grimly. "That's not going to last very long."

Lexi nodded and stood to turn off the boiling water. She wanted to make hot, sweet black tea. They had all become used to drinking tea, coffee and milo without milk. Fortunately, they had a small supply of sugar to sweeten the tea and coffee.

After making the tea, Lexi carefully carried the three hot drinks into the sitting room. "Zac told me his ten chickens are still laying eggs at the farm, so thankfully we can all have a ration of those." She placed the steaming mugs on the table in front of the boys. "Unfortunately, that only provides one egg per person every few days, and the corn and vegetables we have planted at the farm are nowhere near ready."

Jason scratched his chin in irritation. He had started to grow a coarse stubble, which was annoying. "We're going to run out of food very soon unless we think of something else to help supplement what we've got," he stated bleakly looking at Levi.

Nine-year-old Levi looked at Jason, wondering why they were telling him all this. His hands were clammy, and his heart was thumping. Levi wiped his hands on his pants. "Um, don't you older kids usually work all that stuff out?" he asked timidly.

Jason took a sip from his drink; his eyes were shining in excitement. "The thing is Levi; we think you and your little brother might be able to help save the town!"

Levi looked a little stunned at this comment.

Jason chortled to himself. "What I mean is, you can help with our food situation. Sorry, I get a little over-excited sometimes."

"Just tell Levi what you want him to do," exclaimed Lexi rolling her eyes at Jason. "The poor kid looks like he's going to have an anxiety attack."

Jason wandered over to Levi and put his hand on his shoulder. "Don't stress, it's nothing bad. I just want to know if you can help us find some bush food. Ethan said your mum taught a class on native plants at the school. Did she ever show you any bush foods growing around here we might be able to eat?" he asked excitedly.

Levi visibly relaxed, his shoulders dropped, and he smiled. "Bush tucker. Yeah, I think so. We never ate any ourselves, but I remember my mum showing me some plants in the bush. She used to eat them when she was a little girl. My grandparents taught her."

Lexi looked out the window towards the bushland. "Do you think there would be any now?" she asked her voice rising with excitement. "It could really help our food supply if we could find some." She smiled encouragingly.

"I don't see why not, but we might have to walk a little way out of town where the bush is thicker." Levi was excited too. He felt proud to show the others part of his heritage. He hoped he could remember what his mother had taught him.

Lexi continued to stare out the window deep in thought. *If they could supplement their dwindling food supplies with native bush food. Combined with the eggs from the chickens and the vegetables from the gardens, they might be alright. Everyone would still be hungry, but at least they wouldn't be starving.* She turned to face the two boys.

"We've decided to go out bush in two days. Are you okay to come with us then, Levi? Your brother Ollie can join us as well if he wants to."

"Okay. I'll ask him. He loves the bush, so I'm sure he will want to." He stood to leave, placing Polo on the floor. "Thanks for the tea."

Jason walked with him to the door. "I'll come with you," he grinned. "I want to go and see Logan. He might have a couple of tents and gas lanterns we can take with us."

Lexi looked at Jason and smiled, knowing that wasn't the only reason he wanted to see Logan. Each boy enjoyed the others company greatly, however, both were too shy to take it any further.

"We have one pear left," said Lexi digging into her back-pack. "Why don't you take it over to Logan's. You two can share it."

Jason cleared his throat bashfully. "Thanks, Lexi, he'd like that. Logan's been a bit down since the death of Harry."

"Um, we've got a tent and a lantern at our house" suggested Levi helpfully as he waved goodbye to Lexi. "We can take that."

"Fantastic! You've been such a terrific help!" Jason smiled and clapped Levi on the back. "It's amazing how people from the country are so much more prepared than us city folk! We never had lanterns or anything like that at *our* house. My parents always had to race to the shops for candles whenever the lights went out," grinned Jason.

As soon as Jason and Levi left the house, Hadley came storming into the room to confront Lexi. "So, how come Levi and his brother can go on the camping trip and I can't! They're younger than me!" she yelled furiously.

Lexi placed her empty mug on the coffee table. "Calm down Hadley." She held up her index finger. "Firstly, it's not a camping *trip*. We're not going out there for fun. We're trying to find another source of food so that we don't all starve!" Lexi glared at Hadley and held up a second finger. "Secondly, the two Indigenous boys are coming because they know more about the bush than we do, and they can teach us! Do *you* know where to find bush food?"

Hadley put her hands on her hips in defiance. "No, I don't, but neither do you. Why are *you* going?"

The temperature that afternoon had reached an uncomfortable 37 degrees Celsius, and the heat in the room was even hotter. Without the use of electricity, the house couldn't be cooled with air-conditioning or even a fan. Lexi could feel her face becoming flushed, and she pulled at the collar of her shirt uncomfortably. She couldn't believe she was having this conversation with her younger sister. *Why was Hadley so annoying?* Taking a slow, controlled deep breath, Lexi tried to calm down. She could feel herself becoming aggravated, and it wouldn't help to grow annoyed.

"Listen Hadley. You know we're going to look for the exiled group while we are out there. I'm probably the person Braydon became closest to over the few days he stayed in Jasper's Bay and I …"

"Oh, right. *Braydon*," Hadley interrupted rudely, smirking at her sister. "I suppose this is just some elaborate plan to spend time with your *boyfriend, Braydon.*" She said his name slowly as if she didn't know how to pronounce it correctly. "You probably just want to kiss him again."

Lexi snatched the empty cup from the table and threw it against the wall in anger. The white china smashed loudly into the solid wall falling to the floor in sharp shards that looked like shark's teeth. Lexi's eyes widened, and her mouth dropped open in surprise at what she had just done. She had never thrown anything in anger before, although she had often wanted to.

Quickly sitting back down on the couch, Lexi muttered, "I don't want to kiss him, Hadley. I just want to talk to him and Lilly. I need to know what the virus is doing to them. It's important for all of us. We know the mutated virus doesn't kill teenagers like it did the adults, but that's all we know."

Hadley was staring at her in shock, her own anger drained away. Lexi's outburst was entirely out of character, she was usually so in control.

Watching Hadley's face turn white, Lexi closed her eyes not wanting to look at her or the broken cup any longer. She breathed in deeply through her nose and out through her mouth. After a few moments, she became calmer and opened her eyes once more. Turning to face her sister, Lexi tried to explain. "Hadley, I'm seventeen now, and you know what that could mean. I'm probably going to get the virus if I haven't already got it." She glanced again at the broken shards on the floor before quickly looking away. "I need to know what the virus does. I'm always thinking about it. Yes, I want to see Braydon, but that's not all. I want to see if he, or any of them, are still affected by the virus. The uncontrollable rages and all that. You understand, right?" She looked at Hadley for support.

Hadley came to sit on the arm of the chair beside Lexi. She was relieved to see her sister had returned to her usual calm self. "Geez Lexi, calm your farm. You can go and see your boyfriend if you really want to!"

"Hadley! I told…"

Hadley poked her sister in the ribs with her finger making Lexi squirm. "I'm joking! You're right, someone needs to see how they're doing. I'd be too scared to talk to Elisha if I saw her anyway. She was completely feral last time we saw her. Do you think she's still like that?"

"I don't know Hadley. That's why I want to talk to them."

"Right." Hadley stood and walked over to where the broken cup lay and nodded her head towards it. "You might want to clean that up before Polo walks on it and cuts his paws. I'm going to get some more water." She walked out the front door without another word.

Lexi watched her sister leave, unable to fathom Hadley's changing moods. "I guess I can't talk about emotions," she whispered to herself, staring at the broken cup. Lexi sighed and rubbed her hand across her forehead before moving to clean up the mess.

CHAPTER FOUR

L exi looked above her and saw tall walls reaching high over her head in a dome configuration. As she ran her hand across the wall with her fingers splayed, she tried to feel for an opening. The surface of the wall was solid rough brick, the edges raw and uneven.

Lexi watched with growing fear as the final brick was laid in place. *What was going on? Why was she here?* It was so dark, and her pulse quickened. The air around her was rapidly becoming stale in the closed environment. Feeling increasingly uncomfortable, an intense pressure built in her chest as she struggled to breathe. *Was she going to have a heart attack?* As the temperature in the tomb-like structure rose as if she were in the middle of a desert, she could feel rivulets of perspiration running down her back in between her shoulder blades. *She was going to bake if she stayed here. She had to get out!*

Lexi pressed hard against the walls in a panic, a feeling of claustrophobia overwhelming her. Using all her strength, she tried to push against the unrelenting walls. They would not budge even a little.

"Help!'" Lexi shrieked loudly. "Somebody help me!"

A loud noise made Lexi turn her head quickly, causing her to bang her head on the wall. The pain made her open her eyes. Feeling confused, she looked blindly around her. It took Lexi a few moments to realise she was still in her bedroom. She banged her head on her own bedroom wall! She had been having a nightmare! A very curious and disturbing nightmare, but only a bad dream.

Lexi rubbed the side of her head. *Did the dream mean something?* It had seemed so real.

Untangling her legs from her twisted bedsheets, she placed her feet on the tiled floor. It was wonderfully refreshing on her hot feet, and she wiggled her toes for a moment, enjoying the sensation.

Taking an elastic-band she kept around her wrist, Lexi pulled her long hair into a rough ponytail. Her hair was sweaty and limp, and she screwed up her nose in distaste. She looked down at her t-shirt and pulled the damp material away from her chest. Her whole body felt hot as though she had just run a marathon. *If only I could have a long refreshing shower and wash my hair*, she thought wistfully. Showers were now a thing of the past. A luxury people took for granted before the KV17 virus. If Lexi wanted to wash her hair, she would need to traipse down to Bryer's creek and bring back a bucketful of fresh water.

Feeling very unsettled from her nightmare, Lexi wandered into the kitchen to find a drink. Her throat was dry and parched as if she had actually been screaming. Making her way over to the kitchen laminate bench where they kept the buckets of fresh water, Lexi took an empty glass from the sink and tried to scoop some water from one of the buckets. The glass hit the bottom of the plastic bucket with a dull thud. It was empty! Frowning irritably, she looked in the second bucket. It too was dry. Lexi angrily thumped the glass onto the bench. *Hadley had forgotten to fill the buckets again!*

Licking her dry lips in irritation, Lexi stared at the empty glass. She was going to have to walk down to the creek herself. Parting the curtains in the kitchen window to look outside, Lexi could see that it was still dark. Glancing at her watch, she noticed that it was only 4 a.m. The sun wouldn't be up for another hour. Not feeling safe to be walking to the creek in the dark, she slumped onto the sofa in the adjoining room instead and contemplated her dream. *What did it mean? Was it her subconscious trying to tell her something?*

Being the oldest person now in Jasper's Bay, Lexi had enjoyed her role as one of the town leaders. It was something she would never have wanted or even thought she could do in her old life. However, lately, the responsibility was really bugging her. There was always something that needed solving or doing. While Lexi knew surviving was an ongoing challenge, there were times when all she wanted to do was run away and read a book or go to the beach. Anything where she could be by herself and enjoy being a teenager.

Sitting in the darkness contemplating the future, Lexi's thoughts drifted to Braydon. She wondered if she would ever see him again. She thought about what Hadley had said about wanting to kiss him. *Was she right, did she want to kiss him?* If Lexi was honest, she did like him, and she really missed talking to him about movies, tv shows and the distractions from their past lives, but did that mean she also wanted to kiss him?

Lexi thought about his red curly hair and deep, infectious laugh. The thought of him gave her butterflies in her stomach.

Lexi smiled. *Okay, she did want to kiss him!* Not that Lexi would ever admit it to her sister. Hadley would be intolerable if she knew she had been right! *So what if she did want to kiss Braydon? Everyone needed a little love in their lives, right?* She couldn't just think about growing food and getting fresh water all the time! *Fresh water.* Lexi groaned and looked over her shoulder back at the two empty buckets sitting in the kitchen. She really needed a drink. Well, she thought rising to her feet and grabbing a torch from the cupboard under the kitchen sink. *If I'm going to get the water, even though it's Hadley's job, I'm going to wash my hair with it. It feels so greasy and foul!* Lexi pulled the band holding her hair tighter before grabbing both buckets and stamping out the front door.

Although the sun had not yet fully risen, its imminent appearance cast a faint orange glow in the sky signalling the start of another hot day. Using the torch to light her way, Lexi trampled through the bush towards the creek. Luckily the bushland was quite sparse, and she was able to make her way easily without getting lost in the darkness. As she walked, Lexi could hear the noises of the Australian wildlife filling the air. Crickets and cicadas were chirping loudly, motorbike frogs made their distinctive call, and in one of the Eucalypt trees overhead, a Kookaburra let out its laughing song. As the sky gradually lightened and the sun slowly rose in the east, the sky lit up with colours of vibrant pink. Lexi stopped for a moment to gaze at its wondrous beauty. It made her happy to see such splendour.

Making her way down to the edge of the creek, Lexi scoured the banks for any suspicious dark lumps. She was sure Jasper's Bay was too far south for crocodiles, but she figured you could never be too careful. Her imagination was fuelled by watching Australian horror movies like "Black Water" and "Rogue". Plus, everything looked eerie in the early morning light.

Smiling at her folly, Lexi took another wary glance around her before bending down to scoop fresh, clean water into her mouth. It felt so wonderful to drink. She turned the empty plastic buckets on their sides and let the creek water run into them. They didn't take long to fill, and she placed them on the sand beside her ready to carry back to the house.

Undoing her hair from the tight ponytail, Lexi reached down to the creek and splashed cold water on her face and neck washing the remnants of her bad dreams away. She let the water run through her hands for a while enjoying the peacefulness of the surrounding nature. Breathing in deeply, she closed her eyes and listened to the wildlife. It was nice just to sit for a moment and not have to think about anything. Just 'be'.

A disruptive noise that didn't seem to fit the environment suddenly forced Lexi to open her eyes and scan her surroundings. At first, she couldn't see anything out of the ordinary. Then, not far from where she crouched Lexi could see a person stomping towards the water. The tiny hairs on the back of Lexi's neck bristled. *Who was that?*

Standing slowly, Lexi tried to get a better look. In the early morning light, it was still relatively dark, making it difficult to see. Her heart was hammering in her chest. Lexi peered into the dimness, quietly watching the person, not wanting to draw attention to herself. As her eyes became more accustomed to the dark, Lexi could see someone squatting by the creek, noisily splashing water over themselves and drinking thirstily. Lexi narrowed her eyes and peered more closely. *Was that Ethan's sister, Elisha?* She was extremely skinny, and her hair was a large knotted clump on top of her head as though she hadn't brushed it for weeks; however, Lexi was sure it was her.

"Hey, Elisha!" Lexi called cautiously. "How are you. Are you alright?"

Elisha abruptly stopped splashing water from the stream and stood as though ready to run. Her face held a mean-looking scowl with her eyes narrowed into slits. The sides of her mouth were pulled downwards.

Lexi waved her hand in a friendly manner. *Maybe Elisha didn't recognise her in the dim light.* "It's me Lexi from number 23 Rosewood Avenue. Remember? You let my sister Hadley, Jason and me, move into the house." She smiled hesitantly not sure if Elisha could even see her, or what her temperament was. The last time Lexi had seen her, Elisha had been acting crazy, and Lexi didn't want her to start acting like that again. Especially not while Lexi was here on her own with her. Plus, she hadn't brought anything to defend herself with except for the two plastic buckets which wouldn't be any help at all!

As Lexi spoke to her, Elisha didn't say a single word. She remained motionless as though rooted to the spot and stared straight at Lexi with unblinking eyes.

The two girls remained staring at each other for a few moments and soon the sky began to lighten in the early morning, turning the water in the creek pink and purple. It would have been beautiful to look at if Lexi weren't feeling so afraid. She cleared her throat and wiped her hands on the sides of her pants.

"Umm, Elisha, why don't you let us help you. You must be hungry?"

Elisha remained silent. She looked tired. Her eyes moved from side to side as if she were having difficulty focusing.

Lexi wasn't sure what she should do. She could tell from Elisha's stance that she wasn't pleased to see her, and she felt somewhat relieved that Elisha was on the other side of the river from her. Elisha had obviously *not* recovered from the effects of the virus.

Just as Lexi were about to try and speak to Elisha again, Elisha unexpectedly started to emit a strange low, almost growling noise. Lexi's eyes widened. *Was that peculiar noise coming from Elisha? She sounded like an animal!*

Glancing at the creek, Lexi wondered how deep it was. It was difficult to tell in the low light. She wondered if Elisha would be able to cross the creek over to her side. Lexi hoped not. She had seen first-hand what Elisha could do when she was enraged. She remembered how Elisha had stabbed one of the gang members and killed her, for merely being annoying.

Not wanting to anger Elisha, Lexi quickly took hold of the heavy buckets of water and dragged them away from the stream. "Um. I'm going now Elisha," she called out in a fake chipper tone. "No need to worry. I won't disturb you any longer." Lexi lowered her head a little and tried to look non-confrontational as she slowly backed away, unsure whether Elisha could even see her expression in the darkness.

Not waiting for an answer, Lexi turned and made her way back through the bush. She walked towards the house as best she could while carrying the two heavy buckets. Even though her arms ached, she tried to hurry along as fast as she could without spilling the precious water. Once she reached the edges of the bushland, Lexi took an anxious glance behind her just to make sure that Elisha hadn't crossed the creek and followed her into town. Scanning the bush for any signs of the girl, she couldn't see or hear anything out of the ordinary, so either Elisha was excellent at hiding, or she hadn't followed her. Lexi hoped it was the latter.

It wasn't long before Lexi reached number 23 Rosewood Avenue and she wondered if the others were awake. She wanted to tell them of her encounter with Elisha. Without the luxury of electricity, the children had become accustomed to rising when the sun rose and sleeping when it set.

Lexi carefully carried the water up the front porch steps before nudging the unlocked fly screen door open with her bottom. Hadley and Jason were sitting in the kitchen sharing a tin of baked beans they had heated on the little gas camper stove.

"Hey, there you are! I wondered where the water buckets were," grinned Hadley cheekily.

Lexi gave her a dirty look but decided not to comment, she wanted to tell them her news. Lifting one of the heavy buckets onto the bench, Lexi poured some water into a big metal pot ready to boil.

"You'll never guess who I just saw?" she said, lighting the gas camp stove and sitting with the others at the table.

Jason shrugged as he shoved food into his mouth.

Hadley stared at her. "I dunno, who?"

"Elisha!" said Lexi raising her eyebrows.

Jason dropped his spoon with a clatter. "What! Where? Is she in town?" His eyes darted to the front door. "She didn't attack you, did she?"

Lexi shook her head. "No, she didn't. I saw her down by Bryer's creek. She was on the other side." Lexi took a gulp of water before continuing. "She didn't look too good. Very thin and dirty from what I could see." Lexi's eyebrows furrowed in concern. "It looked as though she had red sores and scratches all over her face. It was kinda freaky being there with her watching me. I tried to talk to her, but she didn't say a single word. She just kind of growled at me."

"Growled?"

"Yeah, like an animal."

"That *is* freaky," stated Jason standing from the table and placing his breakfast bowl in the sink. "Were Braydon and Lilly with her?".

Again, Lexi shook her head. "Not that I could see. Unless they were hiding deeper in the bush. She looked like she was alone." Lexi rose to tend to the boiling water. "I'd better go and tell Ethan I saw his sister. He'd want to know."

Hadley reached forward and placed her hand on Lexi's arm. "Did she look any better? You said she was growling!"

"No, she didn't look better. From what I could see, she hasn't recovered from the virus at all. I think she looked worse."

"That's not good news," commented Jason shaking his head.

Hadley stared at Lexi with a worried look on her face. She bit her lower lip.

"It's okay Hadley, she didn't hurt me. She didn't even come near me."

Hadley nodded, however; she still looked unsettled.

"Listen," said Jason turning to face Lexi. "I'm going over to see Logan this morning. He said he wanted to talk about something important. Do you want to come along with me before you see Ethan? I think we should all walk in pairs from now on. Just to be safe."

Lexi nodded as she looked at Jason. "Sure, I'll come along. Although I really don't think Elisha will come into town. She seemed as though she wanted to be away from people."

Lexi watched Jason straightening his shirt and smiled. She knew he liked Logan and could tell he was making an effort to look nice. "Do you know what Logan wants to talk about?" She pulled her hair back into a ponytail. Washing her hair would have to wait.

Jason walked towards the front door. "He said it's something about the virus," he explained. "I know he's been spending a lot of time in the town library and doctor's office reading medical books."

Lexi raised her eyebrows in interest before grabbing her blue Avengers cap and walking after Jason. "That's interesting. I wonder what Logan has found out?"

Closing the screen door behind her, Lexi was glad to be back outside. The temperature in the house was already rising. *It was going to be another scorching hot day.* She swung her arms as she strode after Jason trying to catch him up.

Hadley, who surprisingly hadn't said much all morning, suddenly blurted out, "Wait! I'm coming too!" as if she didn't want to be left alone in the house. "I'll just get Polo; he could do with a walk." Hadley quickly went around the side of the house to release Polo from the back garden. "Come on little fellow," she said in a high-pitched voice. "We don't want to be here in case Elisha comes back!" Hadley glanced towards the bushland before she scampered after Lexi and Jason. The little dog trotted happily by her side, grateful for the company.

Lexi stopped and waited for Hadley at the end of the path leading to their house. The grey stone pathway had numerous weeds springing up between the stones and was beginning to look quite rundown, as was the rest of the front yard. The once green grass had turned a pale yellow as it baked in the hot sun and tall dead weeds languished everywhere, waiting for a shower of rain to revive them. Lexi crumpled a dead flower in her palm and thought about the owners who must have lived here before the world turned to shit. Everything was so different now. Nobody gardened for pleasure. Growing flowers and having a beautiful garden was a thing of the past, a hobby no one had the time or energy for anymore. Lexi herself never enjoyed gardening in the first place and certainly didn't have the inclination to do it now. Besides, they could not spare the water on frivolous things like flowers.

Pulling a shrivelled weed from the front path, Lexi wondered what condition their house back in Perth was in, and if she and Hadley would ever see it again. The garden would be dead for sure. She only hoped that vandals hadn't broken in and trashed the place. Trying not to think about it too deeply, she put her arm around Hadley's shoulders, and they quickly walked to catch up with Jason, who was already half-way down the street.

Over in the centre of town, Logan Bartley sat waiting in the front room of his house. After the death of his best friend Harry at the hands of Broc, Logan had lost some of his spark. In the past, Logan had done everything with his friend, and now he was gone. It had been such a violent and sudden death that Logan still felt shocked whenever he thought about his mate. No one was supposed to die at age sixteen. It was such a waste. The two of them had made all these plans for their future lives, and now that was all gone.

Logan looked sadly at the chipped cup in his hand. *He supposed those plans wouldn't have worked anyway.* No one was going to travel the world on a surfing trip or open their own mechanic business anymore. Everything had changed.

To take his mind off the loss of his friend, Logan had taken to spending his time at the town library and local doctor's office looking through books and journals on the human body and mind. Books about physiology, anatomy and psychology. They all interested him. Logan wanted to see if he could find out more about the virus, especially the mutated version that was now affecting the older children. He knew he wasn't a scientist or anything like that, but he figured that if he could at least learn about the human body, maybe he could try and understand why the mutated form of the virus might be affecting only the older kids.

Not far away, Jason, Lexi and Hadley made their way through the quiet streets to where Logan lived. A few of the younger kids were riding up and down the road on skateboards and bicycles, but in the hot summer sun, most of the town's children were indoors. Logan's home was a single-story, cream brick house with a peaked silver tin roof. It was attached to the back of the veterinarian centre his Father used to run. Many of the antiseptics, bandages and other medical supplies in the vet practice had been useful to the children of Jasper's Bay, and they often came to see Logan when they had scrapes and minor injuries. He hadn't minded helping them at first, however, now his attention and time were focussed on finding out about the virus. It had become an obsession.

"How long has Logan been doing all this study?" Lexi asked Jason as they walked around the back of the property and through the little side gate that led to the main house.

"I think he started about a week after the night of the *incident*," replied Jason. Meaning Broc's attack. "He doesn't want to see anyone else hurt." Lexi nodded her head in understanding. She didn't want to see anyone else getting hurt either.

Jason looked a little sheepish. "I think he's also worried about me," he murmured, blushing. "I *am* almost seventeen."

Lexi stared intently at Jason for a while lost in thought, her eyes glazed over. Waving his hand in front of her face, Jason chuckled. "Lexi, hello. Anyone in there?"

Lexi gave him a shaky smile. "Oh. Sorry, Jason. I was just thinking about something." Not wanting to explain her thoughts, she turned and walked briskly up to Logan's home, knocking on the brown wood door. Lexi had only just turned seventeen herself, and she was increasingly worried whether she was infected with the virus. *Had she become a walking host to this disease that either killed people or turned them into raging timebombs?*

She needed to find out what Logan had discovered. Not wanting to wait any longer, Lexi turned the handle on the unlocked door and went inside.

The trio found Logan sitting cross-legged in his living room surrounded by piles of books and medical journals. Some were tagged with little coloured plastic strips as if he had been gathering information for an assignment. Other books were discarded upside down in an unwanted pile.

Logan, deep in concentration, glanced up in annoyance from the book he was reading when he heard the others enter the room. "Oh, hi Jason," he smiled happily when he saw who it was. "Hi Lexi, Hadley. I thought you were one of the younger kids wanting a band-aid or something," he laughed.

"We wondered why you didn't answer the door," questioned Hadley, flumping down onto one of Logan's armchairs. Polo immediately jumped onto her lap, and she began tickling him behind his ears.

Logan continued to flick through the book he was reading. It was dusty and gloomy in the room, and it was a wonder Logan could see anything at all in the subdued light. Lexi walked over to the window and opened the thick curtains letting in some sunlight, brightening the room. Logan blinked.

"So, Logan. Do you want to tell us about what you have discovered?" Lexi prompted raising her eyebrows as she spoke.

"Huh?" Logan had been up half the night trying to read by dim candlelight leaving him with a slight headache forming behind his eyes. He gazed at the particles of dust floating in the air, brightened by the sunlight streaming in through the window.

Pointing at the pile of books on the floor, Lexi asked again, "Logan, have you learnt anything about the virus?" her voice was tense.

Logan turned his attention from the dust particles to Lexi. He quickly turned the corner of the page in the book he'd been looking through, marking the section, before pushing himself up from the floor. He shuffled through a pile of medical journals on a small side table until he found a notebook, he had been writing in. Logan gestured to it excitedly with his finger. He had been making copious notes about anything that could provide them with some answers about the virus and had come to a few conclusions. It appears children's brains were wired and organised differently to those of adults. While adult brains used long-distance networks, children's brains used more localised ones. This meant children's brains hadn't matured yet.

"Well, obviously there's not really any information on the KV17 virus in any of these medical journals," Logan stated, pointing to the piles of journals face down on the floor. "And we don't have access to the internet, so I'm just making assumed guesses about how *our* virus might work based on other viruses. Plus, any information I've found in all these books on the human body and mind." Logan glanced up at the others and pulled at his ear.

"It's okay Logan," said Jason smiling at his friend. "We know you're not a scientist. Just tell us what you think is happening."

Logan took a breath and straightened his shoulders. "Okay. Well, from what I can work out, children's brains and in particular *young adult* brains, are in a process of change," explained Logan looking down at his notes. "Particularly the Insular Cortex regions," he stated, pointing to the side of his head.

Lexi stared at Logan, trying to understand what he was talking about. She shook her head slightly feeling confused. "But what does that mean? Are you saying that our teenage brains are more mature than younger children? But still less mature than adults?"

Logan nodded his head vigorously, his eyes becoming excited. "Yes, that's it exactly. I think older teenagers are becoming infected with the mutated virus because their brains have matured more. However, the virus isn't killing them like it did with the adults." He looked at the others briefly before continuing, flicking through his notebook to find the right page. "I think instead of killing the teenagers, it's just changing them. Apparently, the Insular Cortex is where emotions and thoughts are integrated." Logan looked up at Jason for a moment. "What if the virus is inflaming that area of the brain?"

"I don't understand," said Jason rubbing the side of his head wondering if his brain was becoming inflamed. It didn't exactly sound appealing.

Logan went to sit next to Hadley and Polo, balancing his notebook on his knees. "Well, again I'm no scientist, so I'm just guessing. But if the virus *is* infecting the Insular Cortex, which controls emotions and thoughts, that would explain while the *Devs* like Elisha, have increased incidents of uncontrollable emotions like anger."

Lexi sat in one of the other chairs and looked excitedly at Logan, finally understanding. "And younger children are not affected by the virus yet because that part of their brain hasn't matured enough."

Logan clapped his hands, causing his notebook to fall to the floor. "I'm not sure about the other symptoms like the sore throat and red rash though. I suppose they're just a side effect." I don't think whoever engineered this virus was expecting it to affect teenagers like us. I guess they wanted to use it for warfare, and it was released before it could be perfected.

"So? Why hasn't Zac got it? After all, being Lilly's twin, he is the same age as her," stated Lexi.

"Well, he's pretty immature!" piped up Hadley, laughing to herself.

Logan bumped his shoulder against hers playfully. "Yeah, he is sometimes," he agreed, smiling. "But I don't think that's it. Maybe he has some sort of immunity to the virus."

"Or maybe it affects people differently like most viruses and diseases. Some people get it worse than others, and some people have no symptoms at all." Lexi shrugged and stared into the distance. Logan had certainly given them all something to think about. If they had some idea of what this virus was doing to them, maybe they could work out a way to manage it in some way.

Lexi absently scratched at her feet and the red rash that wouldn't go away. She thought about Elisha and her encounter with her down at the creek. Her eyes had been wild. She didn't exactly look like someone who could be *managed*. Still, if there was any chance of controlling this virus, they had to give it a shot. If the children of Jasper's Bay were going to survive without them all becoming feral, they had to try.

Feeling determined, Lexi stood and faced Logan. "I can't believe you figured that all out Logan," she said with praise. "It's really great."

Logan cleared his throat and bent over to retrieve his fallen notebook. "Thanks, but like I said. I'm only guessing."

Jason smiled broadly at him and winked. "Yeah, mate, we know. At least it's given us some ideas though, and it all sounds legit to me."

Logan blushed bright red, his cheeks and neck turning crimson.

Walking over to the stash of books scattered across Logan's floor, Lexi stooped to pick one up It was a large, heavy leather-bound book entitled, *The Effect of Pharmaceuticals on the Human Brain*. "Hey, Logan. Can I borrow this book from you for a while?" Logan had inspired Lexi to do a little research of her own.

Logan smiled and nodded. "For sure. They're not mine anyway. I sort of *stole* them from the library!" he nudged Hadley again, and she laughed.

"I don't think that matters anymore. Mrs Thompson's not going to rip you to shreds for having a late library book!" Hadley giggled at the thought.

Logan, Lexi and Jason joined in the laughter too. It was funny how they still clung to their old way of life, even with all that was happening around them. Overdue library books, paying for food you take from the supermarket, not snooping in people's houses uninvited. It was difficult to let go of those habits and normalities of their old lives.

Logan's face suddenly fell, and he looked at his fingernails. "I miss Mrs Thompson. She was actually cool for a teacher." The death of the adults in the children's lives was continuing to hit them hard. Every one of them felt the loss.

Lexi noticed Logan's melancholy. "So, Logan," she said, walking close to him. "Are you coming out to the bush with us tomorrow?" She held the heavy book close to her chest.

From the corner of her eye, Lexi noticed Hadley glaring at her and turned her body away not wanting to see Hadley's face. Lexi heard Hadley give an exaggerated sigh and was about to turn back to face her, however, she changed her mind, pursing her lips and focusing her attention on Logan instead.

Logan smiled at Lexi and shook his head. "Ah no, I'm not. I want to do some more reading. I did find my dad's old tent you can use. Jason mentioned you needed one," he said, casting an eye in Jason's direction, who nodded. "It sleeps three people. Plus, I found a solar-powered lamp too."

"Oh, that's fantastic, Logan," grinned Jason. "That will be a real help. Do you go camping a lot?"

Logan stood from his seat and went to fetch the lantern and tent from the next room. "Actually no, not anymore. I used to go camping with my dad up to Bluff Knoll all the time when I was younger. But I haven't been up there in years." He handed the lantern to Jason. "We would spend the day fishing in one of the local waterholes and cook our catch over an open fire. In the morning, we would get up early before the sun had fully risen and start our climb to the top of the steep knoll." Logan's face had turned peaceful. All the worry had gone as he remembered the fun times he experienced with his dad. "The view from the top was terrific."

Jason smiled broadly. "That sounds amazing, Logan. We should all go up there one day."

Logan shook his head. "Nah, it's too far away from here. We wouldn't make it." He leaned over and straightened Jason's crooked cap. "Still, it's nice to remember it."

"Are you sure you don't want to come with us, Logan?" asked Lexi, looking between the two boys.

Logan chuckled. "No, it's okay. You have enough people going. I'll go next time."

"Yeah, Logan, you can come with me," remarked Hadley, grinning at him. Logan didn't look interested.

"Well, your Dad's tent is going to be very helpful," said Lexi ignoring Hadley. Things were looking up for the camping trip. "At least we won't be sleeping out in the open, and with two tents now, we won't be cramped either." Lexi was looking forward to the trip. A day out of town might be fun. It would certainly be a break from the monotony at least.

Leaning forward a little, Lexi cradled the heavy medical book in her arms. She looked down at the book and wondered if it would provide her with any information. Lexi wanted to know what drugs could be used to control emotions and if there were any natural alternatives

"You guys be careful out there," said Logan glancing at Jason. "From what you described Elisha sounded as though she has deteriorated, and you don't know what state Braydon and Lilly are in either." He shook his head sadly. "They could be dangerous."

Jason nodded. "Yeah, we'll be careful. If we see them, we'll keep our distance."

"We just want to talk to them," said Lexi as she patted Logan on the arm. She started to walk toward the front door before turning back to face Logan. "But you're right, Logan. They could be dangerous. Don't worry, I'll keep an eye on Jason. We'll all be careful." She knew Jason could be reckless sometimes.

Lexi made her way to the front door and left Logan's house and the others behind. Jason and Hadley could bring the tent and lamp back with them. She wanted to get back to Rosewood Avenue before the others and read a few chapters of the text she had borrowed from Logan. Lexi had the urge to make a few notes herself before tomorrow's outing.

As she walked down the street towards her house, she thought about what Logan had said and wondered if Braydon and Lilly had deteriorated to Elisha's level. *Would Braydon still recognise her?* She gulped uncertainly.

Pushing the front door to the house open, Lexi welcomed the quietness and solitude. With Polo, Jason and her sister in the house, it could be extremely noisy and abrasive. Pushing a pile of Jason's dirty clothes onto the floor, she flopped into one of the big comfy leather armchairs and began to flick through the pages of the medical book. Thinking about the forthcoming camping trip had given Lexi an idea, and she hoped to find some information that would crystallise it. Tomorrow the group would head into the bush and Lexi wondered what they would find.

CHAPTER FIVE

J ason, Lexi, Zac, Ethan, Levi and Ollie made up the scouting party. While technically there should have been a town meeting about the plan to go into the bush, Lexi, Jason and Zac, the three older children, had decided to keep it a secret for now. Well, not exactly a secret, but they hadn't made it public knowledge either. It would only upset some of the younger children and inflame an already anxious town if they knew they were planning to try and speak with the *"Devs"*. After Elisha's outburst and violent behaviour in the town square, everyone was afraid of her and what she might do. And while most of them had not witnessed the actual murder of Broc by Braydon. They had all heard about the stabbing, making them frightened of him too. If the group found out any vital information or saw anything unusual, they could inform the rest of the town later.

Each member of the scouting party carried a backpack with a few essential supplies. Ethan and Zac each carried a tent, Lexi carried the solar lantern, camp stove and matches. Jason had volunteered to bring the group's food and cooking pot. Levi and Ollie carried the medical supplies, just in case someone was injured. Snakes were common in the Australian bush during the summer. As were blue tongue goannas and frilled neck lizards, not dangerous, however, they could leave you with a nasty bite. Each person also carried their own sleeping bag, ground mat and water.

Not having an exact plan of where they were going, the group slowly picked their way through the scrubby bush looking for signs of Braydon, Lilly and Elisha. Levi and Ollie, the two young Indigenous Australian boys, scouted the area looking for any native food they could collect. It was going to be a challenge as the bushland around the townsite was mostly sparse and dry.

It hadn't rained in quite a while, and although a few of the mature trees such as the tall Eucalyptus with their shiny green leaves, and the Grevillia filled with bright red and yellow flowers were growing, many of the younger plants were withering in the never-ending heat. Ethan wiped sweat from the back of his neck with a red paisley bandana and wondered if there would be any native fruits left alive for them to find. It looked as though most of the bush was dead or dying. He pulled at the annoying strap of his rucksack, digging into his shoulder. The weight of the tent he was carrying was heavy, and his back hurt already. Without school and its compulsory sporting activities such as football, cricket and basketball, Ethan had become a sloth. His forehead was covered in beads of perspiration, and his face had a pink sheen indicating the beginnings of sunburn. He didn't feel so good.

"Geeze, it must be 40 degrees out here!" he complained, swiping at a fly buzzing around his face. Another one was crawling on his shoulder, itching his skin. Ethan took a sip of water from the canteen slung to his belt. The water was warm, but at least it was wet. Chewing on the side of his fingernail, Ethan peered around him. "Do you think we will see Elisha?"

"I'm not sure Ethan," replied Lexi, shifting the weight of her pack into a more comfortable position on her shoulders. "I hope so. She looked like she could use our help when I saw her."

Ethan nodded. He wasn't exactly sure how he felt about seeing Elisha. Of course, one part of him wanted desperately to see her. The other part was a little reluctant. The last time he had seen his sister, the whole episode had been horrible. Elisha had been wild and uncontrolled, like an animal that had been cooped up for too long. Ethan had become afraid of his sister, and he was sure the others were as well. After all, she had broken Zac's nose and plunged a knife into Debbie. Lexi had told him Elisha seemed agitated when she ran into her at the creek yesterday, and he hoped there wasn't going to be a recurrence of violence.

Re-attaching his flask to his belt, Ethan glanced over at Zac and wondered if he was nervous about meeting Elisha again. Without the luxury of having a doctor available anymore, Zac's nose had remained crooked from being broken by Elisha, and he now snored quite loudly. Ethan watched him walk. Zac's backpack was just as heavy as Ethan's, however; he was walking effortlessly, as though the weight didn't bother him at all. *All those years of manual labour at the farm,* Ethan thought to himself, a rue grin spread across his face. *Not like me, a church minister's son.* He scuffed the dry ground with his dirty shoes and kept plodding along, making sure to create enough noise to deter any snakes.

Walking a few steps away from Ethan, Zac hadn't given Elisha much thought at all. He was more concerned about how his twin sister Lilly, had been surviving. He couldn't imagine how she had been able to find any food in this desolate landscape, and it worried him greatly. Zac was grateful that Lexi had organised a small amount of food to be left for the exiled trio every couple of days, but it was such a meagre amount that he knew it wouldn't have been enough to sustain them all. Feeling guilty, Zac tried not to think of his own rumbling stomach and licked his parched lips. They were cracked and split from his many hours of work outside in the sun. Although the work on the farm was physically demanding, especially for a boy who had only just turned seventeen, he loved it. Apart from the constant hunger, Zac was enjoying in this new world where he didn't have to go to school or complete assignments. His dyslexia made it difficult for him to read, and he would much rather be outside planting crops or attending to the animals. Since the KV17 virus had struck, the Bailey farm had become a real focal point of the town - its primary food source. Zac was proud his family's farm was helping to sustain the town. He felt like he had a real purpose, a future, something Zac never had when he was at school where he was always looked down on as the dumb kid. The other kids in town now looked at him with a kind of respect. *If only Lilly were there to be part of it.*

Zac stared at his sunburnt, rash-free hands as if wondering why the virus hadn't affected him like his twin sister Lilly. *Was he immune?* Zac glanced at Lexi walking silently beside him. She noticed him watching her and gave him a happy smile. *She didn't seem to have the virus either.* Zac smiled back before continuing to look around for any signs of Lilly. He didn't think he would ever say it, but he couldn't wait to see his sister.

It was just at that moment that Levi let out a joyous cry of discovery. His excited hollering scattered a company of galahs nesting in a nearby Silvergum tree. They flew into the air like a pink and grey blanket.

Levi was pointing animatedly at a tall bush with large green leaves while bouncing excitedly from one foot to the other. Hidden amongst the large shiny leaves were clusters of small, lime green orbs. They looked a little like figs. Levi and his brother Ollie gave each other an excited high-five before they both sprinted towards the tree. Reaching the bush first, Levi bent over and placed his hand on the trunk for balance. Ollie quickly scampered onto his brother's shoulders, using his back as a ladder!

"Oww, watch my head!" Levi exclaimed as Ollie's bony knee knocked painfully into the side of his face.

Ollie laughed. "Sorry bro, can't you stand a little taller? I can almost reach them." His fingers stretched towards the tempting green fruit, tantalisingly just out of reach.

Ethan stopped and stared at the two younger boys wondering what they were doing. His mouth hung open as he watched Ollie trying to balance on his brother's shoulders. "What are you two doing?" He laughed heartily. Ethan liked the two boys, even though they were much younger than him. They were carefree, and nothing seemed to bother them that much. They both enjoyed coming to work on the farm when it was their turn, and Ollie was especially good with the cows. The cows liked Ollie, and he often sang quietly to them when he came to visit.

Ethan wandered over to the younger boys to see what they were up to.

Unable to reach the lime green fruit, Ollie groaned and jumped from Levi's shoulders. Levi breathed heavily, "Geeze, you're heavy for a little bloke! Ollie grinned broadly.

Turning to face Ethan who had joined them, Levi pointed towards the middle of the tree. "It's a Billygoat tree, and those green things are fruit. Bet you haven't had one of those before have ya?! You won't find those in a supermarket."

Ethan smiled and shook his head. "No. Actually, we won't find *anything* in a supermarket these days!" he poked Levi in the ribs playfully making him laugh.

By now the others in the group had joined them. Everyone was standing peering up at the fruit in amazement. *They'd found some bush tucker!* Two rainbow Lorikeets had flown into the branches and were watching the children down below. Their orange, green and blue feathers looked majestic in the sunshine. Levi hoped the birds weren't going to eat the precious fruit before they could pick some for themselves.

"A Billygoat tree, huh?" said Lexi in wonder. "I wouldn't even have known to look for fruit up there."

Levi nodded at her. "That's because it's a native tree." He clapped his hands in joy at being able to find the tree on his own. A smile spread across his face in happiness. "My mum showed them to me a few times. I think she said they have a lot of vitamins in them. You eat them to keep you healthy."

"That's so cool. Let's try and reach some." Lexi's stomach gurgled with the thought of food. Some fresh fruit to eat straight from the tree would be fantastic.

Ollie shook his head in disappointment. "I can't reach. My arms are too short." He raised his arms over his head to show the others and wiggled his fingers in the air for emphasis.

Standing by the base of the tree, Zac linked his hands together in the shape of a stirrup. "Come on, Lexi. Why don't you climb on my shoulders and have a go? You're tall enough."

"Yeah, okay," Lexi laughed as she walked up to Zac and placed her foot in his hands. He hoisted her upwards, and she clambered awkwardly onto his shoulders. She felt his shoulders sag a little under her weight. Peering up into the centre of the tree, Lexi reached her hands towards the fruit. They were growing in clusters of ten to twenty fruit per branch. Stretching her fingers upwards, she managed to grip onto one of the clusters and snapped the stem with a satisfying crack. The two rainbow lorikeets screeched in fright at the sudden noise before flying away. Slowly lowering the fruit to the waiting hands below, Lexi was careful not to lose her balance on Zac's shoulders. Levi and the others let out a cheer at the sight of the green fruit.

Lexi managed to harvest four more bunches of the Billy-goat plums, giving the group about sixty plums in total. It was a nice haul. Other fruits were growing on the tree, however; they were too far up. They would need a ladder to reach those.

Jason helped Lexi pack the fruit she had collected into his bag ready to eat when they set up camp. Having never eaten bush food before, he wondered what they would taste like.

Once Lexi climbed down from the tree, Zac pulled a roll of bright orange plastic tape from his backpack and proceeded to wind some of the tape around the tree's grey trunk. He wanted to make sure they would be able to find the tree again. It could be a handy addition to their food supply in the future, especially if Levi were right about the fruit's vitamin content. That would be a bonus particularly as medical supplies were starting to run out in the town.

They would have to learn to become more self-sufficient and live like people had in the past. Zac fastened the tape around the tree with a knot to stop it blowing away in the strong westerlies that often blew up in the afternoons.

"Great idea, Zac!" encouraged Jason, patting him on the back. The orange really stood out in the green and brown bushland, making it easy to spot from far off. "We just have to remember how we got here. We'd better mark a path or something."

The others agreed, looking around for rocks and logs to mark the area. There was a lot of old fallen tree branches and sticks lying on the ground. A drought had hit Jasper's Bay and the whole of the south of Western Australia a few years before, leaving a great deal of death in its path. It was nature's way of evening out the population, not unlike the KV17 virus that had swept the Earth, decimating the human population in a matter of months. Except nature had not created this virus. The KV17 virus was a man-made creation, and it could just as well be their demise. Could any species live without their adult population for very long?

While the others continued to pile rocks by the tree to make a kind of marker, Lexi pulled a large notepad from her own pack and started drawing. "We could make a rough map of where each important tree we find is," she suggested helpfully. "Just to give us an idea of where to look for them next time." Lexi glanced up at the others for confirmation.

They were all nodding their heads in agreement. A map of the area would be a good idea, and hopefully, they would find some more native plants and foods to add to the sketch.

The afternoon sped by quickly as the little group continued to scour the area for any signs of native foods they could harvest, as well as keeping an eye out for the exiles. Once they spotted a small grey rabbit which would have made an excellent addition to their haul, however, it had seen them way before they could come close to it and was much too quick for them to catch. It bounded away across the landscape before scuttling down a hole somewhere in the scrub.

Ollie, who had become skilled at catching rabbits, perched nearby for a while. He sat silently watching and waiting, hoping the rabbit would make a reappearance. Unfortunately, it didn't, and the group soon continued with their search.

The blue sky stretched above them like a vast painting with only a few wispy white clouds breaking up the endless blue. A flock of little grey and white finches with bright red beaks and flaming orange circles on their cheeks bounced playfully from branch to branch as they watched the children pass by. Their joyous chirps filled the air, and Lexi observed them for a while as they feasted on the many insects inhabiting the Australian bush. *At least they're not going hungry,* she thought.

Lexi decided to call the others together and end the search for the day. They had been walking for hours, and in the hot sun, it was draining. Plus, none of them had eaten properly since leaving the townsite. It was time to set up camp for the night and take stock of what they had found. Lexi swung her pack onto one shoulder and carefully folded the makeshift map she had been drawing before placing it securely in her backpack. She did not want to lose it after all the effort she had made to draw it. *Braydon would be proud of my drawing attempt.* Lexi wondered if he still thought about drawing, or if the virus had taken that away from him.

Watching Lexi, Jason soon came up to join her. "What are you laughing about?" he asked before dropping his heavy pack on the ground. "God, I'm starving!" He began rummaging around in the pack, pulling out items of food.

Lexi squatted down next to him, offloading her own pack onto the hard ground. "I was just thinking of a joke I have with Braydon about my drawing abilities. It's strange we haven't seen any sign of them. I wonder where they are. You wouldn't have thought they would move too far away from the townsite." Lexi undid the rolled ground mat strapped to the bottom of her pack and lay it flat on the rough ground. Little pieces of rock and rubble covered the soil, and she was relieved that she had remembered to bring a mat to sleep on. Sitting on the mat, Lexi watched Jason pull food from his pack.

"You know, not to be bossy. But you might want to wait until we set up camp before pulling all the food out," suggested Lexi with a broad grin. "There are lots of ants around here. You wouldn't want them getting into those gingernut biscuits." She pointed to a packet of sweet biscuits Jason had laid on the dirt. "That's the last packet of those. We'll probably never get to eat them again."

Jason looked startled. "What! Oh, right. Ants." He quickly snatched the biscuits and shoved them back into his pack along with the other food he had offloaded. Lexi laughed. *Jason sure did love his food.*

"Make sure you share those biscuits with everyone," Lexi reminded Jason as she pointed at his bag. "That's the last packet of those. We'll probably never get to eat them again." There were very few *luxury* items such as biscuits, chocolates or potato chips left in town, and it was an unwritten agreement between the children that if any were found, they would be shared with others. Lexi had found this particular packet of goodies tucked away in a back cupboard of one of their neighbour's abandoned houses.

Pushing herself up from the ground, Lexi wandered over to help the others put the two tents up. "Besides," she called over her shoulder glancing back at Jason. "We should try the bush foods first. I want to know what a Billygoat plum tastes like!"

Jason zipped up his pack and raced over to join her. "Hell, yes! That's a great idea. Billygoat plums for me too!"

Meanwhile, Levi and Ollie had laid out the collection of bush food the children had managed to collect from the different plants in the area, while the older children finished setting up the campsite. They had two tents between the six of them, plus a couple of solar lamps and each had their own sleeping bag. If they could light a campfire, which shouldn't be too difficult with the amount of dry wood lying around, they would be quite comfortable.

Levi smiled at his brother. The two boys were enjoying their time out in the bush with the older kids. It had been a struggle ever since their parents had died from the KV17 virus, and Levi had found it particularly difficult. Being just nine-years-old, he wasn't ready for the responsibility of looking after his younger brother. He wanted to ride his bike and kick the football with the other kids. He wanted to play on the computer and go fishing with his dad like he used to. He didn't particularly like this new world where he had to do everything himself. It was hard work, and there wasn't much time for play.

Levi watched Ollie as he placed the fruit in a line on one of the unrolled sleeping bags and puffed out his chest. "I'm glad we could show the older kids where to find the bush food," he said proudly, picking up one of the fruits. "You did a great job

76

finding them," he winked at Ollie, who smiled. Both boys were pleased to share their indigenous culture.

In addition to the Billygoat plums, Ollie had also found bush tomatoes which were yellow rather than red in colour, golden yellow gooseberries nestled in their paper-thin pods and native sage with its tall purple flowers. Plus, some wild bush passionfruit.

"We can't eat the passionfruit yet," warned Levi pointing to the bright lime green fruit. "They're not ripe. I remember Mum warning us never to eat the passionfruit unless it's bright orange."

"Oh, why?" asked Jason sitting next to Levi. "Are they bitter?"

Levi shook his head. "No, they're toxic!"

Jason stared at him and raised his eyebrows. "Oh, right! Geeze that's something good to remember!"

"Wow, Ollie nice job," praised Lexi walking over to join the boys. She had helped erect the tents, and everyone's packs were placed securely inside. "Fantastic work today Levi, these were a real find." She smiled at them both encouragingly, and they beamed back at her.

"I didn't realise we had managed to find so much!" said Zac thinking that the bush food was going to make a nice addition to the town's food supplies. It would certainly help to ease the pressure off the farm. Plus, it meant that they could spare the cows for a while longer if they could find food elsewhere. Zac really wanted to keep the remaining herd for breeding.

"Can we taste some?" asked Jason, his stomach rumbling for the umpteenth time that day.

Levi looked up and realised Jason had been asking him permission to try the food. His cheeks flamed red, and he coughed in embarrassment. He wasn't used to the older kids asking for his advice or permission on anything. "Go right ahead," he said shyly.

Just before Jason could grab a whole bunch of food, Lexi held out her hand to stop him. "Make sure you leave some for tomorrow!" she suggested smiling at him. "We still have a whole day ahead of us, and there's no guarantee we will find more food."

Lexi stared at the unusual food lying on the ground before her. "We should probably take some back to Jasper's Bay with us too. I'm sure the other kids would like to try some bush foods," she said with a half-smile. The thought of facing Hadley without bringing her any food they had found filled Lexi's mind, and it wasn't a happy thought. Especially not with the mood Hadley was in now. Lexi did not want to deal with Hadley's sulking for a week!

The others agreed with Lexi's suggestion, although it was tempting to scoff the whole lot, then and there!

The oddly shaped Billygoat plums were Lexi's favourite of the bush food. They tasted both sweet and slightly tart, a little like dried apricots. She wondered if they could dry some of the native fruit like they used to with grapes, peaches and plums. It might be something to investigate for the future. A way of preserving the fruit if they ever found they had too much at a particular time.

Ethan and Zac had managed to get a fire started by laying thin, dry twigs in a pyramid shape over a mess of dry spinifex. The small group of campers sat around the comforting flames, chatting and laughing. Even though it had been a hot day, the sound of the wood cracking in the campfire and the sight of the warm flames flickering was both soothing and mesmerising.

Not far off, a butcher bird warbled, and the constant thrum of insects filled the air. It wasn't long before the children started reminiscing about their lives before the KV17 virus had hit Australia. It was difficult for them to know precisely how much time had passed since the virus had hit, as the electronic watches and mobile phones they used to rely on no longer worked. Even the wall clocks in the school, the library and some of their homes no longer functioned as the batteries had run down. Time had begun to stand still. It really didn't matter what day of the week it was or even which month. There was no school to get up for, no homework deadlines and no rules to follow. Only the ones they made to suit themselves and their town. Life had slowed down.

Leaning forward and throwing a dry stick on the fire, Jason went to sit by Zac. "Did you ever play that game *Sims?*" Jason asked. He had a big smile spread across his face at the memory of playing computer games.

Zac laughed. "Oh, yes. I loved that game! I used to trap my *Sims* in one room with one toilet and one bed and make them all compete. Ha-ha. Did you ever do that?"

Jason laughed raucously. "Ha-ha yeah. I used to do that all the time. Do you ever think that we could be in a *Sims* game and there's someone up there making us play?" Zac and Jason all looked up towards the sky and stared at the first sprinkling of stars scattered across the coming night.

"Well, I hope you find us some more food," shouted Jason tilting his head backwards and looking up at the sky. "Uga Uga," he said, pointing at his mouth, which meant I'm hungry in *Sims* language.

"I could really do with a Maccas run!" laughed Zac loudly. "Remember having a big, juicy double cheeseburger with fries and a large coke!" Everyone groaned in pleasure at the memory.

"Or a packet of chocolatey Tim Tams. They were my favourite," recalled Lexi as she reached over toward the fire and carefully placed a branch on the smouldering flames, its heat keeping them warm in the cool night air. Now that the sun had gone down for the day, the temperature was no longer scorching hot and had become quite cold. The children clung to the fire for both warmth and light.

Lying back on her sleeping bag, trying to find a comfortable position where the small hard rocks from the ground didn't dig into her side, Lexi peered out into the blackness of the night. As there was no moon out tonight, it was dark around them. Now there were no longer electric lights to cast a glow over the environment, it was especially dark. The night was as black as the inside of a cave, and Lexi wondered if she would be able to see anything at all if they didn't have the light of the fire.

As Lexi peered out into the inky blackness and her mind began drifting into thoughts of the past, she suddenly heard a distinct sound directly behind her. Quickly sitting, Lexi twisted around trying to focus on where she thought the noise had come from. She was sure it had sounded like a twig snapping. In fact, it sounded exactly like someone stepping on a dry branch. A person and that meant they weren't alone.

CHAPTER SIX

"There's someone out there," Lexi whispered urgently as she gestured to the others to be quiet.

"What are you talking about?" laughed Jason. "There can't be anyone else out here. We are too far from town. It's probably a snake. There's lots of Western Brown's out here. Better be careful one doesn't try and slither into your sleeping bag!" He laughed again when he saw Lexi shiver at the thought.

Lexi shook her head at him and put her finger to her lips wanting him to shut up. *It wasn't a snake.* Lexi was sure she had heard a person walking around not far from their camp. *It might have even been more than one.* It was difficult to tell in the darkness. She strained her ears and tried to hear above the crackling of the fire burning. Lexi heard the noise again. *There was someone or something out there,* she was sure of it now.

The others all stood, quickly scampered from their sleeping bags as the sound of someone approaching became louder. The noise of dry sticks and leaves crumpling and crunching under the intruders' feet could be heard distinctly in the still night air. Zac and Ethan both grabbed one of the flaming branches from the fire and Jason pulled his slingshot from his back pocket, ready for action.

Lexi was tempted to hiss *I told you so* but restrained herself and quickly went to stand by the two youngsters, Levi and Ollie instead. Ollie shyly took her hand in his, looking up at her with his big brown eyes. She smiled at him reassuringly and squeezed his hand.

The little group from Jasper's Bay peered out into the blackness of the night. They had become used to having to defend themselves after Broc and the gang's attack on the town. Through the weak light thrown out by the fire, two figures could be seen approaching their camp. They looked gaunt and tall, not like anyone the children knew. *Or maybe it was just a trick of the fires' light.*

Suddenly, Zac dropped his flaming branch back into the fire and took a few steps closer.

"Lilly! Is that you?" Zac rushed forward to greet his sister in surprise as she walked nearer into the light. She looked very different from the last time he had seen her. Her exile in the harsh Australian bush had taken a toll on her body, and she had lost a lot of weight. Zac could see her collar bones protruding from her shirt like two thin rods, and her cheeks looked hollow and gaunt. He noticed that her hair hung past her shoulders limp and greasy as if she hadn't bathed in weeks, but it was Lilly.

She gave Zac a little smile and nodded her head to say *hello*, before sitting cross-legged a little way from the group. Lilly abruptly held up her hands in a stop gesture as Zac moved to continue towards her. She didn't want him coming any closer.

Zac turned his head to look back at Lexi and the others, his face a mixture of happiness and uncertainty.

Lexi dropped Ollie's hand and went to stand by Zac, smiling hopefully at Lilly. Slowly turning towards him, Lexi whispered encouragingly into his ear. "It's okay Zac, just give her a little space. We don't know how much the virus has affected her. She might be like Elisha, or she might be even worse!"

Zac cocked his head towards Lexi. "Yes, or she *might* be better." Lexi nodded her head in agreement. *It was true. There was a chance Lilly might be less affected by the virus than Elisha had been*. From this distance, her eyes didn't look as wild and feral as Elisha's, but it was difficult to tell until they talked to her.

"Why don't you give her one of the Billygoat plums. She must be hungry. You can roll it toward her," suggested Lexi going back to the campsite to retrieve one of the bright green fruits.

Zac took the plum from Lexi and rolled it over the bumpy ground towards Lilly. "Here Lilly, have one of these fruits. You must be hungry," he said as he gave Lilly a big welcoming smile wanting her to feel at ease.

Zac watched his sister intently. Her body looked so emaciated! He blinked rapidly, shocked to see her looking so terrible. Lilly's face was hollow, her hair lank and her once vibrant eyes were dull. She looked tired. Ethan could see that his sister had not been having an easy time of things out in the bush, and he wondered where Elisha and Braydon were.

Watching the bright green plum roll towards her, Lilly began to laugh. Her voice sounded strained. The plum stopped about half a metre from where she sat. Unable to reach it, Lilly stood and moved closer to the fruit, picking it up in her hand before flumping back down onto the ground. Her long legs folded to one side as she sat. Lilly turned the fruit over and over in her palm before taking a bite. She grinned lopsidedly at the group.

"We've been eating these lovely fruits for the last few weeks," hiccupped Lilly as she chewed the delicious plum. "These and the occasional yabbies from the creek. It's the only food we've been able to find besides the food you guys leave for us." She nodded her head at the others still smiling as she finished eating the plum. "Thanks for that by the way." Lilly's voice slurred as she spoke.

Just as Lexi opened her mouth to say something, Braydon stepped out from the darkness and staggered up beside Lilly.

He slumped down on the ground next to her and peered up at the group. Like Lilly, his face was very drawn. His cheeks now hollow and thin were covered in a scraggly beard. Braydon's once red curly hair now sat plastered to his face, limp and mattered. Lexi wondered when the last time either Braydon or Lilly had washed.

Retrieving another one of the precious fruits, Lexi took a step closer to Braydon. She was about to roll the food to him when Jason abruptly strode toward Lexi and grabbed her hand. She turned to look at him, and he mouthed silently for her to be careful. Lexi nodded. *She wouldn't get too close.* Just like Lilly, they didn't know what state of infection Braydon was at. *He could be dangerous.* Though she hoped not. Lexi really wanted to talk to him. She had just been getting to know him and enjoy his company when he had made the shocking announcement the night of the town bonfire that he was infected with the virus. He had kissed her for the first time that night before he had stumbled off into the dark and it had made Lexi feel alive. She hadn't been able to stop thinking about that kiss ever since, and she wanted to do it again just to see if she had imagined the feeling, or if it had been real. She wasn't stupid, Lexi knew their way of life was never going to be the same as it had been in the past. The times of *going out on a date* or even having *boyfriends* or *girlfriends* were long gone. That wasn't what she was expecting or even thinking about. She just wanted closeness with someone her own age. Someone she could reminisce with about things from the past. Movies, TV shows, books, heck she'd even be happy to talk about computer games, anything to take her mind off the hardships they now faced. She knew it was a very *21st-century kind of problem*, but that was who she was, what they all were. 21st-century kids suddenly thrust into a world more like the past than any future they had been expecting. The world they had grown up in hadn't prepared them for this new life. Just occasionally, especially when she had a hard day, or her sister Hadley had been particularly annoying, Lexi just wanted to remember those frivolous days. It wasn't easy to let go of the past and those much easier times.

As Lexi took a step towards Braydon and Lilly, the fruit held in a kind of offering in her outstretched palm, Braydon held up his hand just as Lilly had. His blue eyes met Lexi's. "Wait, Lexi! Don't come too close. We only came because we saw the light of the fire and could hear you guys talking." He glanced up at the others with a rueful smile. "We just wanted to see who it was." Like Lilly, his voice sounded slurred.

Were they drunk?

Lexi glanced sideways at Jason before taking another step forward. She could see Braydon and Lilly immediately tense as if they wanted to flee or fight. She wasn't sure which it was. Lexi thought Braydon looked just like an athlete on the starting line. The muscles in his legs taught and his arms bent at his sides with his fists clenched. His body was full of adrenaline. She could hear him whispering to himself to keep calm and stay in control.

Not wanting to upset either of them, Lexi slowly lowered herself to the ground and squatted on her haunches. She was ready to turn and run if she had to. Trying to remain calm even though her own heart was beating fast; Lexi placed her hands on the ground to steady herself. Now she knew exactly what it felt like to be a deer stalked by lions! She took a slow controlled breath in and out. She knew it was risky, but she didn't know how long Braydon and Lilly were willing to stay, and Lexi wanted to find out how they were. She wanted to know more about how the virus was affecting them.

Lexi scratched distractedly at her arms. When she had woken this morning, she had noticed a red rash similar to the one on her feet, now formed on her forearms. *Was the rash a sign she was infected?* She pulled at her sleeves making sure her arms remained covered.

Watching Lexi closely, Braydon gave her a knowing look. He seemed as though he wanted to say something privately to her. There was a sadness in his eyes that Lexi hadn't seen before and she wanted to speak to him too.

Then, just as Lexi was about to risk taking a step closer to Braydon, Ethan pushed past her. He had his hands out in front of him in a pleading motion. "Have you seen Elisha? Is she here with you?" Ethan peered around him wildly. He looked as though he wanted to run up to the pair and shake the answers from them. "Where is she?" he yelled in exasperation. Ethan had not seen his sister for eight weeks.

Feeling alarmed, Lexi quickly stood and pulled at Ethan's arm, trying to hold him back. She could see that Braydon and Lilly were already on edge and she didn't want him to inflame the situation. "Slow down, Ethan," she whispered urgently in his ear. "We don't know how much control they have. We don't want them going feral!"

As Lexi held Ethan back, Lilly abruptly stood and shook her head, her face was flushed. "I'm sorry, Ethan," she said in a shaky voice. "We haven't seen Elisha for a few days. We've only ever seen glimpses of her." Lilly shrugged, sadly. "She never responds when we call out to her, and if she does see us, she runs away. It's as if she wants to be on her own."

Ethan stared at Lilly for a moment as if he wanted to question her further. From the corner of his eye, he could see Lexi, subtly shaking her head. Eventually, Ethan sighed and went to sit by the fire. He stared out into the darkness; his face blank.

Lilly remained where she stood and looked over at Zac, her mouth turned downwards. "We've all been doing it tough," she slurred. "This virus changes a part of you. Most of the time, you feel normal." She paused for a moment and examined her filthy fingernails as though she didn't want to talk about the next part. She shrugged as if resigned. "Then, just when you think you're okay, something will upset you, or frustrate you. And that's when you go a little crazy. It's a feeling of overwhelming wildness and anger." Lilly looked upset as she glanced at Braydon, who had come to stand beside her. They both looked weary, and their eyes appeared glazed.

Braydon suddenly gave a ragged cough from deep within his lungs. It sounded wet. Sleeping on the cold hard ground had brought on the beginning of a chest infection.

Taking a small, tentative step towards Braydon, Lexi gave him an encouraging smile. "Are you able to control the rages at all?" she asked while discreetly pulling her jacket sleeve a little up her arm to show him the start of the red rash that had begun to form. Braydon's eyes flicked upwards to meet hers, and he gave her a subtle nod of understanding. After a moment, Lexi quickly tugged the sleeve back down. She didn't want the others to know about the rash just yet.

"Well, you can't always *control* them because you don't always know when the rages are going to hit," explained Braydon, his eyes sad. "Like Lilly said. One minute you feel fine, totally normal in fact like now, and then it just hits you. It's like a sledgehammer to your head, and suddenly you feel as though your whole body is on fire. There is an overwhelming feeling of heat and irritation like it's consuming your whole being. Then, before you know it, you're in this state of uncontrolled rage like an animal." Braydon ran his fingers through his unkempt hair. "I don't really remember anything that happens after I reach that point. It's all a blur. Once you reach the raging state, there's no going back. You just have to go with it and hope you don't do anything too disastrous." Braydon looked down at his feet sadly. He was thinking of his cousin Broc and the violence that besieged the town on the night of the bonfire. "Eventually it subsides," he mumbled quietly.

Scuffing his feet in the dirt, Braydon stirred up little clouds of red dust. He looked awkward. Lexi watched him in sympathy, grateful that he and Lilly had revealed the extent of their infection. *It must be humiliating for them to admit their inability to control their own bodies.* Her fingers twitched at her sides as she had an overwhelming desire to hug them and tell them it was going to be alright. But was it? There had to be some way she could help them. They couldn't just stay out here in the bush until they died! That wasn't humane! Lexi covered her eyes with her hand for a moment, unable to look at either Braydon or Lilly.

After regarding the small group before him for a moment, Braydon sighed as he reached into his coat pocket and pulled out a half-empty glass bottle. Taking a long drink of the amber coloured liquid, he then wiped the top of the bottle before handing it to Lilly. She took a sip, grimaced at the taste and hiccupped.

Zac, who had come to stand by Lexi, gave his sister a quizzical look. He nudged Lexi in the ribs with his elbow. "Is that *Bundaberg Rum* Lilly's drinking?" he whispered, trying not to laugh. "I thought she sounded wasted."

Braydon took the bottle back from Lilly before having another long drink. He saw Zac and Lexi watching him. "Don't judge us," he murmured. "This is how we've been keeping the rages at bay. We found some bottles of this stuff in a few abandoned houses." He tapped the bottle with his finger. "Tastes disgusting, but it dulls our senses, which seems to have an effect on the rages."

Lilly nodded her head in agreement. "If we constantly stay tipsy, our emotions stay dulled. I don't know how it all works, but it seems to keep everything a bit muted. The less sensory input we have, the less our body is overloaded, and the fewer times we *blow up* in anger." Sensing the others watching her, Lilly looked up at all the faces staring at her and blinked.

Even though she knew all these people, Lilly was beginning to feel overwhelmed.

"Being around people exacerbates the feelings," added Braydon glancing sideways at Lilly. He could see she was struggling. "It's not that we don't want to be around you or see you. It's just that when we're with other people, we feel more emotional." Braydon looked at Lexi, hoping she understood what he was trying to say. "It's not that I don't want to be with you. It's just that I can't," he mouthed silently.

Lilly waved her bottle of alcohol in the air. "Yes, and the only thing we have found that can mute the emotions so far is alcohol. The problem is, we don't have a lot left. Maybe four bottles including this one and that's not going to last very long."

Braydon continued to focus on Lexi. She had a worried look on her face.

"The thing is, we don't know what's going to happen when the alcohol runs out, and our bodies go into sensory overload. How do we stop the rages then?" he said, quickly taking a step back from the group. "I hate feeling this way, and I don't want to put anyone in danger." Braydon's voice sounded miserable. He glanced back over his shoulder toward the safety of the bush behind him. Just as he turned his body getting ready to flee, Lexi's voice suddenly pulled him back.

"What if we can find something else to dull your senses?" suggested Lexi, her voice determined. "Something more natural. Something we can make." The others stared at her in confusion.

"What do you mean?" asked Lilly, her face brightening for the first time since her arrival at the campsite. "Have you got an idea?"

Lexi glanced uncertainly towards the young boys Levi and Ollie who were standing quietly at the back of the group. "Well, I'm not entirely sure yet. I was thinking of a natural food or drink." She looked once again at Ollie and Levi. "Do you guys know anything that could help?" she asked the boys.

Levi and Ollie glanced at each other. Both boys' faces went red. Neither were accustomed to having all the attention focused on them.

Levi scratched his head. "I remember Mum bringing me to the bush to teach me about native Australian plants." He shook his head. "I can picture her talking and pointing to bushes and seeds. She was smiling," he said happily. "But I can't remember what she was saying." Levi shrugged. "To be honest, I don't think I was paying attention to what she was telling me. I was probably thinking about playing my computer games," he said, giving a sheepish grin before looking at his brother for inspiration.

Ollie stepped forward, his face cheerful and proud. "What about the Sticky Oyster bush? Mum said people used to boil the seeds and flowers to make a drink when they had body aches or wanted to relax."

Levi's mouth dropped open, and he stared at his younger brother in wonder. "Well, apparently *you* were paying much more attention than I was," exclaimed Levi laughing. "Just as well!" Levi placed his arm around Ollie's shoulders and grinned. Ollie was bouncing up and down on his toes in pleasure.

"Do you think that will work? Have you seen any Sticky thingy bushes around here?" asked Lexi, feeling excited at the prospect of finding a remedy.

"Yeah, I think so. I'm sure I saw some on our way here," said Ollie. "They grow quite plentiful around the town. They don't need much water you see, so they don't mind the dry sand." Ollie scuffed the dry red dirt with his sneaker scattering a nest of black ants.

"We can collect some in the morning as we make our way back to town," suggested Lexi walking over to Ollie and patting him fondly on the shoulder. The young boy looked up at her and smiled. He didn't have any idea how to prepare a *remedy* like Lexi wanted, but at least he could help her locate the plants. It would be up to his brother and the older kids to work out how to use them.

Braydon and Lilly, who had been listening to the others talk, suddenly stood. They both seemed agitated, and Braydon's face was particularly flushed as if he were holding his breath.

Lilly was also looking anguished, and she peered sorrowfully at her brother Zac. "I'm sorry Zac, but we'd b-better get going," she stammered. "It's getting hard to stay in control." She abruptly turned to leave before Zac could argue with her and try to convince her to stay. Braydon was by her side.

"Wait!" cried Lexi, running towards Lilly and Braydon momentarily forgetting about any risk.

Braydon's head whipped around sharply to look at her, the expression on his face causing her to skid to a stop before she reached them. She quickly raised her arms in front of her. "It's okay. I won't come any closer. I just want to know if you'll be alright?"

Braydon's eyes met hers and lingered as if he wanted the moment to last as long as possible. "I hope so Lexi. I hate being like this."

Braydon looked over at the others briefly before glancing again at Lexi. "I wish I could kiss you again," he whispered, his voice cracking. "Just work on that remedy as soon as you can, okay?"

Lexi relaxed her stance and blushed hoping the others hadn't heard. "We will," she said, nodding her head slightly. "We can collect some of the seeds from the bush Ollie was talking about in the morning and then head back into town. Logan might have some idea of how to use the plants, he's been doing a lot of reading. Don't worry, we haven't forgotten about you." Lexi gave him an encouraging smile. "Meet us on the outskirts of the farm tomorrow night. Where the bushland is."

Braydon reached to grab Lexi's hand in his before hesitating. His hand hovered awkwardly in mid-air before he shoved it deep into his pocket. With the virus swirling around his body, increasing his emotions and keeping him constantly on edge, touching Lexi could be risky. Braydon coughed self-consciously and looked down at the ground.

"Are you okay?" asked Lexi taking a small cautious step closer to Braydon.

Braydon glanced up at Lexi, his face full of pain. He nodded quickly before turning and running into the night with Lilly close behind him. *Would he ever be able to kiss Lexi again? Would it always be too risky to be around her?*

The remaining children watched their two friends run into the darkness, feeling both elated and discouraged by the chance encounter. While they were all happy Braydon and Lilly were still alive, what kind of future did they have? And where was Elisha? One thing was for sure, the children of Jasper's Bay had to help them in some way. They had to find a way to control the KV17 virus. Lexi pulled at the sleeve of her jacket subconsciously. *The future of the older kids depended on it.*

CHAPTER SEVEN

The meeting with Braydon and Lilly had spurred the others into action. The sight of their withered bodies and obvious distress had been shocking, and the group was determined to help in any way they could. As more children turned seventeen, the problem was only going to grow, and if Jasper's Bay and its inhabitants were going to survive, they needed to find a remedy for the virus. Some way of controlling its effects on their young minds.

After a restless night with little sleep, the children rose early and quickly packed away the campsite. The mood around the camp had turned sombre, and everyone decided it was best to head back into town.

Ollie and Levi took the lead, scouring the surrounding area for signs of the Sticky Oyster bush or any other native plants as they walked. The children wanted to make it back into Jasper's Bay as quickly as possible as their water was running low and the air in the bushland was already blisteringly hot. Overhead, as if to mock them, jet black crows cried out dolefully to each other as the children passed by. Caw caw caw.

Eventually, not far from town, Ollie found a cluster of Sticky Oyster bushes clumped together in a little clearing. There were about twenty bushes, all covered with shiny green leaves and winglike purple flowers holding the precious seeds. The children hoped they might be able to use them to make a remedy or tonic.

At the sight of the bushes, Levi clapped his hands excitedly and jumped up and down. His brother had done a fantastic job locating the precious plants. Placing his arm around his shoulders, Levi gave Ollie a quick hug. Ollie blushed, but he let him hug him anyway. When Levi finally let go, Ollie looked up at the sky and smiled. He liked to think that their mum was looking down at them and smiling too. *She would be proud at just how well the two young brothers were dealing with this new life they had all been thrown into.*

After quickly gathering the seed pods and carefully placing them into Ollie's backpack, the group decided to continue their trek back to Jasper's Bay. While it had been fun camping out, now all everyone wanted to do was to go back home and show the others in town what they had found. The native bush fruits would make a welcome change to the tinned food the children had been living off.

As they reached the outskirts of town, Lexi could see the familiar shape of the church steeple in the distance. She remembered driving down the main street of the town with Jason and Hadley towards that church, not that long ago. A lot had happened to the trio in the few short months they had been welcomed into the town. She couldn't quite believe they had been so lucky to have found a group willing to let them live with them. She knew that many other communities wouldn't have.

Lexi glanced over at Ethan. He had been their main supporter, allowing them to stay in town, and she would be forever grateful to him. She watched him as he trudged along. His posture was a little slumped as though he were carrying much more on his shoulders than the backpack. Walking over to join him, Lexi asked, "are you doing okay, Ethan?" She nudged him with her shoulder in a friendly manner. "I'm sorry we didn't see Elisha."

At the mention of his sister's name, Ethan twisted his head to look at Lexi. His mouth was turned downwards. "Yeah. I'm okay. I just wished we had seen Elisha." He sighed. "I really wanted to see her."

Lexi rested her hand on Ethan's shoulder. "I know you did. It must be tough to be without her."

Ethan bit his lip and looked as though he wanted to cry. He thought about his sister out there in the bush all alone. "I just feel so awful not being able to help her," muttered Ethan.

"Were you two close?"

Ethan looked at Lexi, the corner of his mouth twitching. "Not really. I always thought she was a bit of a pain in the ass. Always bossing me around. I suppose that's what big sisters do" he laughed winking at Lexi.

Lexi laughed too. "I'm sure Hadley would agree with you. She always tells me I'm too bossy."

Ethan looked out to the dry bush ahead of them as they walked. "The thing is, she always had a good heart," he said quietly. "When all the adults died, and us kids were left alone, it was chaos for a while. The young kids were hysterical, and nobody knew what to do." Ethan looked at Lexi and gave her a sad smile. "It was Elisha who brought everyone together. She became a pillar of strength for our town, giving the kids guidance and support, and now she's nothing more than an outcast!" Ethan gulped and shook his head in dismay. "All the young kids, *plus some of the older ones*, fear her!"

"Don't give up hope, Ethan," Lexi said encouragingly. "I know it's bloody hard. But you will see her again. I know it." The pair trudged on in silence the rest of the way into town, each deep in their own thoughts.

* *
*

After about half an hour, the group reached the main street of Jasper's Bay and stood together outside Logan's house. Jason wanted to show his friend what they had found out in the bush, and the others agreed to join him before going back to their own homes.

They found Logan in his backyard playing with his dogs, Max and Sheba.

"Hey, Logan!" called out Jason joyfully at the sight of his friend. "How good are you at cooking?"

Logan stood from his crouched position where he had been rubbing the belly of his sheepdog Max and raised his hand to his forehead shielding his eyes from the sun's glare. "Terrible," he laughed in response. "Why? Did you catch a kangaroo?"

Jason shook his head sadly. "Unfortunately, not." The thought of fresh kangaroo meat roasting over a pit fire made his mouth water. "We have a challenge for you." He grinned playfully at Logan.

Logan looked at him quizzically. "Oh, yeah. What's that?" Jason and the others went on to describe their meeting with the exiled kids, the poor condition they were in and Lexi's idea to use the Australian bush foods as a tonic.

Ollie stepped forward and showed Logan the purple seed pods from the Sticky Oyster bush. The winglike flowers looked a little like butterflies lying in his outstretched hand.

Logan took one of the flowers and peered down at it. He nodded his head. "Well, that's a fantastic idea, and it could work. But what do you want *me* to do? I don't know anything about native plants."

Jason put his arm around his friend's shoulders. "Well. We know you've been doing a lot of reading, so we thought you, Levi and Ollie might be able to come up with something," suggested Jason. "Braydon mentioned they've been using alcohol to dull their senses and keep the rages under control."

Logan picked up a stick and threw it for Max. He watched the big dog chase after it for a moment before returning his attention to Jason.

Jason nodded towards Ollie and Levi. "Ollie says the Sticky Oyster bush was used to help headaches and relaxation. Do you think it could work as an alternative?"

Logan screwed up his nose and shook his head. "How the heck would I know," he laughed. "I'm not a chemist!" He glanced once more at the little flower resting in the palm of his hand his brow furrowed in concentration. "I suppose we could try grinding the seeds?" He looked up at the others and shrugged.

Lexi patted Logan's shoulder. "Yes, or we could boil them to make a kind of tea. I'm sure I've read about people using herbs for remedies for sickness in the old days. This virus is a sickness, isn't it?" she said. "We might not be able to cure it, but maybe we can control it," Lexi spoke excitedly, and her eyes glimmered with hope. "If we could control the virus, then maybe Braydon, Lilly and Elisha, can come back into town." Lexi licked her parched lips. "Or anyone else who develops it," she added.

The others looked at her uncertainly.

"Well, okay. Maybe not directly into town, but maybe on the outskirts?" she suggested. "That way, they could still be part of our community, without being a threat."

Zac nodded his head in agreement. "Yes. That could work. We could give them the camping tents, so they at least have some shelter from the elements. And we can keep an eye on them. I know Katie and Sarah would be thrilled to see Lilly again." The thought of Lilly returning to live close by gave him a warm feeling in his stomach.

"So, how about Jason and Logan look in the school library for any books on native plants or herbal remedies," suggested Lexi. "Ollie and Levi, you can either go home if you're tired or help Jason and Logan." The two young boys agreed that they wanted to stay and help. Lexi nodded fondly at them.

"Zac and Ethan, you can come with me to look in people's houses for books." She cocked her head at Zac. "Someone in town must have been into natural health. Do you know of anyone?"

Zac scratched his head thoughtfully. "There was Mrs Carmody. She was always talking about health and stuff. I remember her coming to the school to give a talk on *the benefits of healthy living.*"

"Excellent," Lexi grinned. "Let's start at Mrs Carmody's house. You lead the way, and we can all meet up here later."

Lexi waved at the others as she followed Zac and Ethan back out through Logan's gate and down the road. She hummed as she walked, trying to keep calm. The condition of Braydon and Lilly had left her feeling anxious and unsettled. The hot morning wind blew her hair around her face, and she watched the trees rustling. If only she could scatter her feelings like the dried leaves that were blowing about in the wind. She was sure she could feel the virus growing inside her, she was almost certain of it now. Her fingers clenched into fists by her sides, giving away the tension Lexi felt inside. *They had to find a way to control this virus. Then she would have a chance of staying in the town with Hadley.* If not, she would be exiled like the others. And while the thought of being with Braydon was a happy one, the idea of having to leave her sister after everything they had been through made her feel nauseous. Hadley would crumble, and so would she. While Hadley could be extremely annoying at times, they had grown close since their parents had died. Besides, Hadley was the only family Lexi had left, and family had to stick together.

Reigning in her thoughts, Lexi ran to catch up with Zac and Ethan, who were walking up the path of a white-bricked house with an olive-green wooden door. The house was unlocked, and Zac turned the front doorknob and walked straight in. Lexi smiled to herself, *you would never have found a house unlocked like that in the city.* It seemed people from the country were much more trusting.

All the curtains in the house were closed, and a thick layer of dust covered everything, as if they were entering Sleeping Beauty's house, sealed shut for a thousand years. Flowers sat dried and brittle in vases now devoid of water and spiders had made their homes in webs in the corners of the ceiling. The air smelled old and musty.

Zac reached for the light switch on the wall beside the door before realising his mistake. He chuckled to himself. *Old habits die hard.*

Throwing back the curtains to let in some light, Lexi spotted Mrs Carmody's bookcase straight away. It was a large structure made of dark walnut wood, positioned in a place of prominence in the front living room. The shelves were loaded with books and magazines. Some were stacked high on top of each other and looked as though they might topple over at any moment. *Mrs Carmody obviously enjoyed reading.*

Striding over to the bookcase, Lexi began scanning the books hoping to find the answers they needed. A thick layer of red dust covered the books that were lying flat, evidence of their disuse in the now abandoned home. Using her finger to wipe away the grime, Lexi red titles that included books on horses, children's rhymes and the history of bushrangers. *Nothing of use.* She picked up one book entitled *The five day fast. How to lose weight quickly.* She laughed and showed it to Zac.

"We absolutely don't need that one," he chortled, raising his eyebrows.

Eventually, they found something that might be useful in a section that housed books on all manner of health, including one on using herbs for common ailments. Nothing on Australian bush foods, but at least this would give them some ideas on how to prepare herbal tea. For example, did they have to dry the herbs first or could they use them fresh?

Leaving the boys to continue browsing amongst the shelves, Lexi walked into the Carmody's bathroom with the intent of washing the dust from her hands, before remembering there was no longer any water in the pipes. Instead, she opened the bathroom cupboard feeling a little sheepish at looking through other people's things. Scanning the items, Lexi salvaged a tube of toothpaste, dry hair shampoo and a bar of unopened soap that lay amongst the other *hygienic* necessities. Lexi left other items such as hairspray, mascara, nail polish, and hair remover on the shelf. These were things that were no longer needed. Nobody needed to look fashionable or chic anymore.

Slowly closing the cupboard door, Lexi gazed at the reflection of the girl looking back at her in the mirror. She ran her finger over the small red scar on her right cheek. The cut was a souvenir from her encounter with Broc and the gang a few months ago. It reminded her she could be brave and do whatever needed to be done. Not something she knew Broc would have intended. Lexi smiled to herself.

Leaning in closer to the mirror, Lexi peered at her image. She knew she had never been a beauty, far from it. Lexi had always considered herself quite ordinary, but right now, she looked atrocious. She laughed, turning her head this way and that. Her hair was a tangled mess, her green eyes were bloodshot, she had a black smudge of dirt across her cheek, and a pimple was forming on the end of her nose. "Oh well," she sighed. "Lucky there's no Facebook or Instagram anymore," she said to her reflection before poking out her tongue.

"Hey, Lexi! Are you coming?" called Zac from the other room, anxious to meet back at Logan's house and start brewing the concoction they planned to make.

"Coming," she said as she started to walk from the room. Pausing in the doorway, Lexi strode back into the bathroom, opened the cupboard door and retrieved the bottle of nail polish from the shelf, sliding it into her pocket. Bright pink! Hadley would love it. Maybe it would cheer her up for a while.

*
*   *

After reading through the natural remedies book they had *borrowed* from the Carmody's house, the group decided to make a *tea* using the Sticky Oyster bush flowers and seeds. Lexi had also discovered that sage was often used for anxiety and to promote calmness in people. She thought that the *native sage* Ollie had collected could possibly have the same effect, and so the native sage was added to the brew. The idea was to boil the leaves, crushed seeds and flowers for a couple of hours over a fire making a kind of tea. Hopefully, the *tea* would have enough medicinal properties to have some effect on Braydon and Lilly.

The children gathered together and watched on excitedly as Ethan heaved the heavy cooking pot now filled with water and herbs onto the open fire. He had helped build a circle of large rocks in Logan's backyard for an impromptu fire pit and now stood gazing at the flames. "I can't believe I didn't see Elisha," he muttered to himself in disappointment. Ethan had kept a lookout for her all the way back to town in the hopes that she would try to contact him just as Braydon and Lilly had. "How can I help her if she doesn't want to be found?"

Ethan watched Lexi stir the water with a long-handled spoon. She saw him watching her and nodded to him. "Ethan, you know some of this brew is for Elisha too. We can save some of it in a bottle and you can give it to her if…" She stopped when she noticed his glum face. "*When* you see her. You might want to start by looking near the river. That's where *I* saw her."

Ethan tried to smile. "Of course. You're right. Sorry to be so glum."

"I totally understand. Just remember we're all in this together. Okay? We look out for each other," Lexi reminded him as she continued stirring the pot, her face becoming pink from the heat of the fire.

"Come on, Ethan," nudged Zac. "Come and play football with us while we wait for the brew to cook." He pulled Ethan to his feet and was about to run out onto the road to play football when he saw his younger sister Katie trotting towards the house with baby Sarah perched on her hip. She was calling out to him and waving her other arm, trying to get his attention. Lexi's sister Hadley was with them, and she was calling out too. Their voices were high and full of alarm. *Something must be wrong!*

He dropped the football and ran to meet them. "What's the matter?" he asked, looking at Katie and Hadley's red faces. "Have you run all the way from the farm?"

Katie nodded without saying anything for a moment as she tried to catch her breath. She handed baby Sarah over to her brother and wiped the sweat from her eyes. By this time, everyone had gathered in the road to listen to what she had to say.

"Someone's been on the farm! She cried in dismay. They've stolen half the chickens and trampled the corn!

CHAPTER EIGHT

L ogan and Ethan agreed to stay back in town and look after the brew while Zac, Jason and Lexi ran with Katie and Hadley back to the farm. It was hot and uncomfortable running in the burning sun, and by the time they arrived, everyone's face was red and sweaty.

"How do you know it wasn't foxes or dingoes?" questioned Zac striding towards the chicken coop.

Katie glared at her brother angrily. "I'm not stupid, Zac. The coop had been unlocked, the doors were swinging open, and there was no sign of any disturbance at all. It wasn't a dingo."

Zac peered into the cage. "Hmm. I think you're right. There would have been feathers, and hay scattered about if a fox or dingo had found their way in there. Are you sure you didn't leave the door unlocked?"

Katie rolled her eyes in exasperation. "Yes Zac, I locked it like always. Besides the chickens aren't the only thing missing. Like I said, there's a whole lot of corn gone too."

Zac turned to look at the paddock where the corn had been planted. "Shit, that's right. I remember you said." He groaned and ran over to where the others were looking at the trampled mess. Rows of corn plants had been pushed into the ground, and precious ears of corn lay discarded in the dirt.

Jason and Lexi started to pick up whatever corn cobs they could find and throw them into an empty basket. The green corn was inedible, but maybe they could dry it and use it for seed. It seemed such a waste to leave it to rot in the ground.

Lexi's face was flushed in anger. "Who would do this? No one from *our* town, it must be outsiders!" With food supplies running low, plus all the hard work to grow the corn, the blatant waste of perfectly good food made her feel sick.

"They stole five of our chickens too. We've only got four left now, plus our rooster," said Zac sadly. He hoped they hadn't mistreated them.

"Well, that's it!" yelled Lexi slamming a corn cob into the basket. "We need to set up a guard roster to keep a lookout in case they come back -whoever they are. I hope it's not another bloody gang of wankers like Broc and those idiots!" She kicked her foot out viciously, sending the basket of corn flying.

Hadley stared at her sister with wide eyes. "Lexi!" she exclaimed, biting her bottom lip anxiously.

Lexi's face was bright red as she stomped back and forth. Her arms were rigid by her sides, and her hands clenched into tight fists. Picking up the scattered corn husks lying on the ground, Lexi began angrily throwing them at the overturned basket.

Running over to Lexi's side, Hadley tried to comfort her. "Hey, Lexi it's alright. We'll work something out. Don't worry about it."

Lexi looked down at Hadley's anxious face and took a deep breath trying to control her fury. It wasn't easy. Lexi was usually quite even-tempered, but right now she felt like she wanted to explode. She wanted to raise her head to the skies and scream out loud. It was like an irritation burning under her skin that could only be released by physical action.

From the corner of her eye, Lexi could see the others anxiously watching her, waiting to see what she was going to do. She took another long slow calming breath, gently taking Hadley's hand in hers. "I'm okay. I just feel so frustrated.

Why can't these dip-shit people leave us alone? All we're trying to do is find a way to survive this crappy mess we've been landed in! If it weren't for the bloody scientists and Governments messing around with viruses, we wouldn't be in this nightmare in the first place!" Lexi gulped. She could feel herself starting to fume again, the heat burning inside of her. *What is wrong with me?* She sat down on the ground amongst the trampled corn stalks with a heavy thump.

Walking over and squatting down in front of Lexi, Zac's deep brown eyes looked at her for a moment holding her gaze. When she didn't say anything, he reached forward as if to grab her wrist and look at her arm.

Lexi pulled her arm away before Zac could see and quickly stood up. She smiled tentatively. "I'm okay, just tired and feeling emotional after seeing Braydon and Lilly yesterday." She wiped her dirty hands on her pants and linked them behind her back. "I really want to focus on helping them, and now we've got this new problem to deal with."

Zac stood too. "Yeah, it really is a pain in the butt, and I know it is extra work, but I agree with you. We should set up a guard straight away. We can't afford to lose any more food or animals." He motioned his head towards the farmhouse. "Want to help me keep watch tonight? Just in case the people who did this, decide to come back again." Zac looked towards his sisters. "Hadley can stay and have a sleep-over with Katie. She'd love the company."

Not waiting for Lexi to answer, Hadley raced over to where Katie stood with Sarah, grabbing her hand excitedly. "Oh, yes! It will be such fun to have a sleepover. If only we could still watch TV and play music all night like I used to with my old friends."

"We can play board games, and read old gossip magazines," suggested Katie jumping around happily.

"Ooo, yes, that could work!" giggled Hadley. She smiled over her shoulder at Lexi before skipping happily into the farmhouse with Katie.

Lexi raised her eyebrows. "Well. I guess that means we're staying! Looks like I'm on guard duty tonight."

Zac laughed. "I'll get a couple of chairs and warm blankets for later. It becomes surprisingly cold out here at night. Thanks for staying." He gave her a friendly wink before striding into the house after the girls.

Jason had been watching Lexi intently. He had barely known her for a few months, and in all that time, he had only seen her lose her temper a couple of times. Most of the time, she was calm and rational. That's what made her a great leader in the town. He knew she would say they were all a team, and they were, but she was definitely their leader. She made smart decisions, and unlike him, she didn't let her emotions rule her head. Right now, Jason could see that she wasn't herself. Something was on her mind.

He wiped the sweat from his forehead and sniffed his dirty t-shirt, screwing up his nose at the sour smell. This hot weather and not being able to shower was undoubtedly having an impact on his hygiene! Jason ran his fingers loosely through his dishevelled hair and looked back at Lexi.

She was staring off into the distance over the cornfield. She had a faraway look in her eye, and her face looked troubled.

"Hey, Lexi. You sure you're alright? You know you can talk to me."

Lexi blinked her eyes and turned to look at her friend. "I'm fine," she said dully, her arms crossed defensively across her body.

Jason wasn't sure what to say. She didn't *look* fine, but if she didn't want to talk about it, what could he do. He couldn't force her. Feeling worried, Jason sneaked a look at her again.

Lexi stared straight back at him with her green eyes before letting out an exasperated sigh. She reached her hand up to place it comfortingly on his shoulder. She wished everyone would stop asking her how she was. "*I'm fine!* Let's just deal with this stealing problem alright?" Bending down to pick up the basket she had kicked over, Lexi swiftly scooped the corn back inside.

Jason gave her one last doubtful look before nodding in agreement. He would focus on the stealing problem for now, however; he was determined to keep a closer eye on her. Lexi and Hadley had helped him when he was stuck out on the road in the middle of nowhere. They could have driven away and left him, but they didn't, and he would never forget that. Besides, Lexi was his friend, and he wanted to make sure she was alright.

Jason threw the remaining broken corn cobs into the basket. "I'm going to help Logan and Ethan bring those tents over to that bushland on the edge of the farm. Lilly and Braydon can stay in them if they want to. Do you want to help?" asked Jason.

"Definitely," said Lexi, her face brightening visibly. "The bush brew should be ready by now too. Let's give it a taste. We can bottle some and give it to them later today. That's if they remember to meet us. Do you think they'll come?"

Jason shrugged, "I hope so, and I hope the brew works. It might give them some relief."

"I hope so too," said Lexi as the two of them started the long walk back to Logan's house. "Some relief would be good." She scratched absently at her wrist as she walked, trying not to think of her own future.

* *
*

Later that day, Zac helped Jason string up a red flag they had cut from an old sheet to the top branches of a small Silvergum tree. The group hoped that Lilly and Braydon would spot the bright red material in amongst the green and browns of the Australian bush. The plan had been to meet in the bushland on the northern outskirts of the Bailey's farm, although no one had said precisely where. Plus, they couldn't even be sure that Braydon and Lilly would remember the plan to meet at the farm. They had seemed a little drunk last night.

After tying the makeshift flag, Zac shimmied down from the top of the tree being careful not to fall. Deprived of doctors and hospitals, nobody could afford to be seriously injured without dire consequences anymore. So far, most of the children in Jasper's Bay had remained relatively unscathed, however; it would only take one outbreak of measles, a severe case of gastroenteritis or a broken leg to change all that.

Walking over to where the others stood, Zac pointed to the wicker basket sitting by Lexi's feet. They had loaded the basket with whatever food supplies they could spare and four large bottles of the now cool specially brewed bush tonic. Lexi had added a bottle of cough syrup Logan had given her for Braydon's cough. It wouldn't help his situation if it developed into a chest infection or pneumonia.

"Do you think we should try some?" asked Zac, pointing to the bush tonic. "I wouldn't mind seeing what it tastes like."

Lexi reached into the basket and pulled out one of the sealed bottles. "Good idea. I'd like to see what it tastes like too." She opened the screw top lid and slowly brought the glass bottle to her lips. Lexi paused for a moment before taking a sip of the golden amber liquid. She immediately screwed up her nose. The drink was bitter and tangy. The others laughed at her reaction.

"That good, huh?" smirked Jason reaching for the bottle.

Lexi took another drink before handing it over. "Actually, it's not too bad once you get over the initial taste. It's very bitter, but I'm sure they will be able to handle it."

"Handle what?" said a deep voice behind the group.

Lexi and Jason turned swiftly to see Braydon and Lilly standing a little way off from the gathering. The duo had seen the red flag and followed the voices towards the meeting spot. They looked almost the same as they had the night before, perhaps a little worse in broad daylight.

Zac grabbed the bottle from Jason, who was just about to take a swig and walked cautiously towards Lilly, the bottle thrust out in front of him. "Drink this Lilly."

Lilly looked uncertainly at her brother and took a small step backwards, feeling on edge. "What is it?" she asked, cocking her head to the side slightly.

"It's the natural bush tonic. We brewed it this morning from the native flowers and seeds Ollie found."

Lilly looked at the bottle suspiciously.

"It's supposed to help relax you. Remember we were talking about making it last night. It might help you." Zac thrust the bottle hopefully at Lilly.

"I've tried it, Lilly. It's a little bitter and tangy, but otherwise, it's fine," said Lexi reassuringly.

Lilly looked between Lexi and Zac before nodding in agreement. She gestured for Zac to leave the bottle on the ground where she could retrieve it.

Zac took a couple of hesitant steps towards Lilly before placing the full bottle in the soil, carefully positioning it so the contents wouldn't tip over. He walked back to stand by Lexi, who was watching Lilly intently.

Lilly carefully pulled the bottle from its resting place in the dirt and carried it over to where Braydon was standing. He looked quite comfortable leaning his body against the Silvergum tree. Anyone looking at the group would think that he was entirely at ease, only his eyes gave him away. They darted around, betraying his nervousness.

When Braydon's eyes found Lexi's, he smiled, his eyes crinkling at the sides. He was really pleased to see her. "What does the drink do?" he asked, wanting to know more.

"Well, we're not sure yet but, like Zac said, it's all natural, so it's got to be better than the alcohol you've been drinking. We brewed some leaves and flowers to make a tea. We're hoping it will help to calm you." Lexi nodded her head reassuringly at Braydon, encouraging him to take a drink. "If you take it regularly throughout the day, it might help keep you settled." She shrugged. "It's worth giving it a try. It might just work."

"Sounds good to me. I'll give anything a shot," said Braydon, winking at Lexi. Keeping his eyes firmly fixed on her, Braydon took the bottle and had a long drink. "Urrg, that is going to take some getting used to," he grimaced before handing the bottle back to Lilly. Braydon hoped Lexi was right and the tonic worked to help keep them calm. They could sure do with a little luck. He pointed towards the two green tents the others had erected in a clearing not far from where they stood. "Are those for us?' he asked, nodding his head towards the impromptu campsite.

"Yes," said Lexi, stepping forward. "And so is this food and a couple more bottles of the brew. If it works, we can make some more. Maybe a little stronger next time." She placed the basket of goodies close to where Braydon stood.

Braydon watched Lexi carry the basket towards him. She was smiling brightly and looked so pleased to see him. He tapped his hands on his thighs before he suddenly stepped towards her and grabbed her roughly in his arms. Braydon held her tightly to his chest and breathed in the musky smell of her hair. The sweet scent of boronia flowers and lemon myrtle from the bush was on her skin.

Being this close to Lexi brought on a surge of emotion. He could feel the burn beginning to smoulder in the pit of his stomach. Although surprisingly, it didn't feel as intense as usual. The KV17 virus usually heightened every feeling he had. Anger, hate, sadness, even lust. *Could the bush tonic be working already?* Even if it dulled his emotions just a little, he felt that could be enough to control it. At least for a short period.

Would the tonic mute every emotion he felt? Not only the anger and rage but also happiness, joy and love? Was it worth it? He supposed so. If it meant he could be with Lexi and part of the community again, it was worth it to him.

After a moment, Braydon reluctantly pulled away from Lexi. She looked at him wide-eyed and obviously a little shocked at his actions. He grinned cheekily at her, and she smiled back.

Lilly quickly stepped towards them and handed Braydon the glass bottle. Braydon took another drink. "I wonder how long the effect will last," he murmured, as his eyes once again found Lexi's. Braydon laughed happily for the first time in weeks. "If we can control the impact of this virus, maybe Lilly and I can have a future. One where we don't have to be out of control and a danger to everybody." Braydon gave a sheepish smile.

"I'd like that," agreed Lexi pulling at her necklace.

"Me too," said Braydon winking at her.

Lilly looked between them both and cleared her throat. "Let's hope so because the alternative isn't so great."

"How do you feel Lilly?" asked Zac as he hovered close by not sure whether to embrace his sister. He ran his hand over the stubble on his chin.

Lilly took another drink of the bush brew and smiled at Zac. "Actually brother, I feel a little calmer. My emotions are still heightened, but they don't feel as intense." She carefully placed the bottle by her feet. "I think it might be having an effect. It's the same sort of feeling you have when you've just walked out of an exam room. Your anxiety is still strong, but not as much as when you first walked in."

Zac laughed. "Right. Well, not being a big fan of exams, I've never had those feelings, but I get what you mean." Zac nodded towards the campground. "Listen, you guys can stay in the tents as long as you want. There are sleeping bags and solar lanterns in there for you to use. I'll bring Katie and Sarah over to see you later. They'll be so happy to see you."

Lilly placed the bottle on the ground and looked sadly at Zac. He was trying so hard to make everything seem normal, and she didn't want to disappoint him, but she wasn't ready to meet with her two younger sisters just yet.

"The tents and stuff are really great Zac! We really appreciate your help. It's been bloody cold out here at night." She glanced over at Braydon, who nodded vigorously.

"Yeah, bloody cold," he agreed.

Lilly glanced at Zac again, her face determined. "Don't tell the girls I'm here. I don't think I… "

"What!?" interrupted Zac. "Why not? You know they will want to see you!"

"No, Zac," stated Lilly firmly. "I know the girls want to see me and believe me; I want to see them too. I just don't think it's a good idea. At least not until we know for sure this tonic helps and how long it lasts."

"But surely they can come over for a short while. Just to say hello."

"No, Zac," Lilly repeated sadly. "There's no guarantee I can control myself yet even with this tonic." She bent to pick up the bottle by her feet and peered at its golden contents. "It's too soon. We don't even know if it will work and I don't want them to see me in a rage if I lose control. I don't want them to remember me like that." Her voice had become quiet.

Zac slowly walked over and sat by his sister, who had let her body sink down at the base of the Silvergum tree, her head resting against the white trunk. Her eyes were firmly closed as if she were embarrassed to look at anyone.

Lilly didn't try to move away. She was tired of hiding from the others and always being ready to run. She just wanted to come home and be with her family. However, she wasn't stupid, and she knew that was not how things were going to work out. They might be able to control the virus with this native bush brew, but they'd never cure it. Without a cure, there was no way she, Braydon or Elisha could live among the other kids. They would always be on the outer.

Taking his sister's hand in his, Zac gently squeezed it reassuringly. "You know none of this is your fault, right?"

Lilly opened her eyes and turned to look at him. "I know. It's not that. I just want them to remember me as their cheerful big sister who used to play dolls and tea parties with them. The sister who always wanted to go to university and become a nurse. The one who loved riding our horses and playing practical jokes on their brother Zac. Not some crazy person with crazy eyes that would scare them and haunt their dreams. I don't want them to remember me like that!" Lilly's voice quivered with emotion as she spoke. A single tear rolled down her pink sunburnt cheek.

Looking distressed himself, Zac put his arm around his sister's shoulders to comfort her. "I hate seeing you so upset," he murmured.

Lilly hurriedly pushed him away. "Don't touch me, Zac. I can't stand anyone touching me right now! It feels like hundreds of ants are biting my skin!"

Quickly getting up, Lilly strode over to where Braydon was standing and grabbed the glass bottle from him. "I can't stand it!" she said again. Her voice breaking.

"The thought our family and the life I once had and probably won't ever have again is freaking me out!" cried Lilly with tears in her eyes. She looked at the bottle of remedy held tightly in her hand. "I feel like I'm always on the verge of losing control, and just one little thing will push me over the edge." Lilly took a long drink, feeling the bitter fluid slide down her throat. She turned to look once more at Zac who was still sitting at the base of the tree. His face was a picture of confusion.

"I have to go Zac," Lilly sighed in frustration. She wiped her hand across her eyes. "I'm sorry, but I have to be on my own. I really wish it wasn't like this and I hope it gets better. I don't want to hurt anyone!" Turning to leave, Lilly looked as though she was going to break down.

"Wait!" yelled Zac, running to her. "Take this." He held out his hand, opening it to reveal an ugly small black plastic spider. It was the one he used to scare Lilly with only a few months before, back when everything was normal.

Lilly looked at the spider with its black hairy legs and laughed heartily. She sniffed and wiped away her tears. Lilly had always hated that spider, but right at this moment, she loved it. Taking it from Zac's outstretched hand, she briefly hugged him and nodded to the others before racing towards the tents.

Braydon's gaze followed Lilly. He walked briskly over to the wicker basket containing the food and extra bottles of bush brew. "I'd better go too," he said, picking up the basket and making his way over to Lexi.

Wanting to leave on a happy note, Braydon smiled at her. "I don't have any plastic spiders to give you," he winked playfully.

"That's alright," chuckled Lexi. "I'm not a big fan of spiders."

Braydon stood close to Lexi and took her hand in his. It was warm and comforting. "Listen, Lexi," said Braydon quietly leaning a little towards her. "You might want to make some more of the bush brew. And make sure you keep some for yourself," he suggested meaningfully. Braydon tapped her rash covered forearm now concealed by her clothing.

Lexi nodded her head in agreement. She could see him peering at her intently with his bright blue eyes. Coughing subconsciously, Lexi looked away. Tomorrow she would gather the remaining seeds and flowers the camping party had collected and make another pot of the tonic. The others could go back out to the bush in a few days and collect some more of the ingredients.

Knowing he had to leave, Braydon bent down and kissed Lexi on the mouth. It was a brief kiss, a mere touch of the lips that he wanted to last longer. *If only they were alone, and the circumstances were different.* He took her face in his hands. "Look after yourself, Lexi. I'll see you soon." And with that, he turned and walked briskly away.

Lexi watched him go, her feelings a mix of emotions. She really liked Braydon, however; she knew that now was not the time to be forming romantic relationships, not when she didn't know what her future would hold.

As if nature were mocking Lexi and her turbulent feelings, a fierce willy-willy suddenly arose, blowing leaves and debris around in a mini tornado, whipping her hair sharply across her face. Lexi quickly raised her hand to shield her eyes from the flying sand and sticks.

It wasn't long before the wild wind petered out, lasting only a matter of seconds, leaving her standing amongst the debris. The fierceness of the wind matched her own inner turmoil, and she wondered how much time she had before the virus really took hold of her, and she would have to leave Hadley and the others behind. She thought of her sister and the disorder her leaving would cause. Pulling sticks and leaves from her tangled hair, she sighed deeply. Things weren't going so smoothly at home at the moment, and Lexi wanted to make peace with Hadley just in case she did have to leave the group. The girls had constantly been arguing, and every day brought about a new disagreement. Lexi just wanted to get on with helping to run the town, and Hadley seemed determined to complicate matters.

Just yesterday, Lexi had caught twelve-year-old Hadley smoking in the backyard of their house. When Lexi had raised her concerns at the stupidity of starting a smoking habit in the middle of an apocalypse.

"*What did it matter, it wasn't as if they were likely to grow old enough to get cancer!*" Hadley had screamed at her in anger.

What was Lexi supposed to say to that? Hadley had a point. With such an uncertain future ahead of them, why not just do what you wanted? Still, being the older sister, Lexi had felt obliged to suggest that Hadley was *being an idiot*, before throwing her hands up in the air and walking back into the house. Hadley hadn't spoken to her for the rest of the day.

Lowering her hand, Lexi pulled at the sleeve of her jumper to cover the ever-growing rash. She wouldn't be able to conceal it for much longer. Lexi was going to have to tell Hadley and the others soon. First, she wanted to settle the problem of the thieves, then she could focus on her own issues.

Lexi took a deep breath and turned to face the others. "Come on, Zac," she urged. "Let's head back to the farm. I have a feeling you're right about those thieves returning, and I want to be there when they do."

CHAPTER NINE

Gracetown

Jake and Kally were sitting cramped and uncomfortable in the back seat of the old Holden, squeezed next to Aaron. It wasn't somewhere they particularly wanted to be, but the enticement of extra food had weakened their judgement. Driving away from their home in the late afternoon with a bunch of strangers wasn't exactly something they would normally do. However, the lack of food and the threat of starvation had made them desperate.

The newcomers, Cindy, Aaron and Kevin, had returned to Gracetown last night with five chickens. Five chickens! How wonderful. The town kids had promptly barbecued two of the birds over an open pit fire, gorging themselves on the tender meat. It had been a long time since any of them had tasted chicken, so when Kevin had revealed that he could bring back more, plus the promise of a goat if only Kally and Jake would help him, they couldn't say no. The look of craving and need on the other younger kids faces had made it difficult for Jake to refuse. Now, stuck in the back of this cramped car with virtual strangers, heading to *god knows where* Jake hoped he had made the right decision. He didn't really trust Kevin or Cindy. They were always bragging about how they could make things better in Gracetown as if it were *their* home. The other kid Aaron was strange too, he never said a word. Two of them wouldn't shut up, and the other sat there, mute. Jake couldn't wait for them to be gone. He just had to figure out a way to make them leave without causing any trouble.

The closeness of the children's bodies in the car, the smell of stale sweat, and the increasing heat were beginning to feel claustrophobic. "How much longer until we get to this town? What did you say the name was?" asked Jake peering into the front at Kevin who was driving.

Kevin looked back at Jake in the rear vision mirror. "It's called Jasper's Bay, and we'll be there in about half an hour."

"And how did you find out about this place?" asked Kally who had wound down the window trying to let in a little fresh air. The temperature in the car had now reached a sweltering 40 degrees Celsius, and the oppressive heat was becoming intolerable.

"I've been there before," said Kevin smirking at Kally, before turning his head to wink at Cindy who was fanning herself with an old, thin paperback book.

Kally frowned. "But how did you know where to get the chickens?" she questioned, not happy with Kevin's answer.

Glaring at Kally in the mirror, Kevin's eyes narrowed meanly. "Like I said, I've been there a couple of times before. Now, shut up and enjoy the view," he hissed.

Kally sighed and sat back. She looked outside at the landscape whizzing past them. "Yeah, sure. Enjoy the view! What view?" The more they headed inland, the more the land became barren and dry. There was nothing much to see except red dirt and spinifex bushes. Most of the trees were dead or dying, and large red termite mounds dotted the landscape. It all looked so hostile. Kally wrinkled her nose. "I prefer the coast," she muttered.

Shifting his eyes away from Kally, Kevin glanced at the petrol gauge on the Holden. They had three-quarters of a tank left. It should be enough to get them to Jasper's Bay and back to Gracetown without too much of a problem. It was the last of his fuel, so he was going to have to make the most of this trip. He might not make it back to Jasper's Bay, for a while and he wanted to cause as much trouble as he could while he was there.

"How dare they kick me out of the town," he whispered to himself. "I have as much right to be in that stinking town as they have if I want to." Not that Kevin actually wanted to live in Jasper's Bay, he hated the place. But he wanted the *right* to live there if he wanted to!

"Were you talking to me?" asked Cindy, turning her head to look at Kevin.

"Nope," muttered Kevin, continuing to stare out the front window. "Talking to myself."

Shrugging, Cindy went back to fanning her face. "Well, you know what they say about talking to yourself," she said grinning.

Kevin sharply turned his head and gave her a fowl look.

Cindy rolled her eyes.

Kevin gripped the steering wheel tightly, his knuckles going white. He wondered if his brother and his sisters had noticed the missing chickens and trampled corn yet. He snickered at the thought.

"Oh, how I wish I could have been there to see their shocked faces!"

"You're talking to yourself again," said Cindy, smirking as she glanced sideways at Kevin.

Kevin ignored her as he pushed down on the accelerator pedal a little harder, urging the old Holden to go faster. He couldn't wait to wreak a bit more damage on the farm.

Growing up, Kevin had always hated living on the home-stead. He hated the smells of the animals, he hated having to get up early to do the never-ending chores, and he hated the manual labour that went with them. Driving the tractor, ploughing the fields, stacking the hay, feeding the animals. It went on and on. Kevin couldn't understand what Zac Lilly and Katie loved about it. The very thought of living back on the farm made Kevin's skin crawl with anxiety. When Broc had given him the chance to leave his *agricultural prison*, Kevin had jumped at the opportunity. He was more than happy to leave his family behind. If the whole farm had burnt to the ground that night, Kevin would not have been troubled in the slightest. He would have rejoiced.

Unfortunately, it wasn't meant to be, and now Kevin was going to have to finish what Broc and his gang had started. He gripped the steering wheel harder in anticipation as he peered out along the endless highway stretching eastward. The road looked just like a long, straight strip of black liquorice, taking him closer and closer to his destination.

Kevin wanted revenge. Revenge for all the nagging and bossing his older brother and sister had subjected him to when he was growing up. Revenge for having to live in a small backward country town and revenge for the death of his mate Broc. The stealing of the chickens and the trampling of the corn had only been the start. Now he had the help of two extra *soldiers* he wanted to create more trouble. He just wasn't sure what that was going to be yet.

Glancing back at the two gullible younger kids from Gracetown sitting in the back seat, the corners of Kevin's mouth turned up in a smile. By the time they reached Jasper's Bay, those two would have no choice but to help him. They would be a long way from home, and if they didn't agree, he would leave them stranded. Kevin laughed to himself, *Broc would have been proud.*

* *
*

Once again, Cindy glanced sideways at Kevin and wondered what he was smirking about. He was a strange guy, and she didn't particularly like him all that much, but he did have a few good ideas. Plus, he knew how to drive a car, something she had never learnt herself. She supposed all that didn't matter anymore. It wouldn't be long before the petrol they were using ran out or deteriorated and then nobody would be driving anyway. Small towns like Jasper's Bay and Gracetown would become even more isolated. Where you choose to live now was more than likely where you would have to stay. A place where you would remain until you grew old. It would be just like it was in the past before the development of transport like trains, cars and ships.

Cindy continued to fan herself with her book as she thought about her future. *She would have to make sure she chose wisely who she was going to live with and where.* After all the trouble she, Broc and the others had caused in Jasper's Bay, there was no way she would be welcomed there. Cindy ran her fingers through her pink hair, the colour now faded and dull. *Maybe this new town of Gracetown would be alright? The kids there were all very young. Could they be convinced to let her stay?* She gazed out the window deep in thought, wondering how her old school friends in Perth were. The city had become a cesspit of gangs, mangy stray dogs, death and disease when she had fled the area with Broc, Braydon and her friend Debbie only a few months before.

The thought of Debbie brought tears to her eyes, and she quickly brushed them away, not wanting Kally and Jake to see. *If she ever saw that girl Elisha again, the one who had plunged the knife into Debbie's belly, she would make her pay.* Turning her head, Cindy glared with steely eyes out toward their destination. Like Kevin, she too wanted revenge.

* * *

It was almost nightfall when the group reached the outskirts of Jasper's Bay. Kevin could virtually smell it, and his fingers tightened once more around the car's steering wheel. He spotted the tall pine trees lining the farm's driveway long before the others even realised they were there.

Making a sharp right turn, Kevin drove the car down his family's long dirt driveway, toward the farmhouse. He could see the cows in their paddock to the left of him and his lip curled up into a snarl at the sight of the beasts.

"Ooo look, there are cows," squealed Kally with excitement. She squinted through the dusty car window. The cows looked as though they were grazing happily. Kally frowned. "Who owns this farm anyway?"

"No one important," sneered Kevin, his eyes firmly fixed on the dirt road ahead. Cindy gave him a sideways glance but didn't say a word.

Kally and Jake looked at each other uncertainly. The farm didn't look as run-down and poorly kept as Kevin had described. The way he explained it, the place was practically abandoned, and the animals left to fend for themselves. These animals looked healthy and cared for and from what they could see, the fences were all in good condition.

"I hope we've made the *right* decision in agreeing to come here," Jake whispered, taking Kally's hand in his and squeezing gently. She gave him a look that mirrored his own feelings exactly. He silently prayed things weren't going to turn nasty.

Not far away, Lexi and Zac were sitting outside the farmhouse. Each had a warm blanket, a thermos of hot tea and a pack of cards between them. A loaded shotgun rested on the back of Zac's chair, hidden from view. After all the trouble they had a few months ago when Broc and the gang had terrorised the farm, he wasn't taking any chances.

They were in the middle of a fierce game of 'Cheat' in which Zac had already beaten Lexi three times when Lexi suddenly glanced up from her cards. A now unfamiliar sound reached her ears. It was the sound of a car approaching!

Both children hurriedly dropped their cards and rose to their feet. Zac glanced nervously at the gun, deciding to leave it where it sat for the moment, at least until they knew who it was speeding towards them. They didn't want to raise hostilities unless necessary. He did, however, take a step closer to the weapon, keeping it within arm's reach.

Lexi could now see a small blue car hurtling down the dirt road, a stream of dust billowing out behind it like a tornado. She looked over at Zac. "Do you think these are the same people who were here yesterday?" she asked, twisting a strand of her hair around her finger.

"Uh, huh, probably. I didn't really think they would be back so soon." Zac looked towards the house where his two younger sisters and Hadley were playing. "Maybe we should have asked Jason and Ethan to stay too?"

Lexi nodded her head in agreement. "I wish we still had mobile phones. It used to be so much easier with them."

Zac gave her a wry smile. "*Everything* used to be much easier, Lexi. Let's just try talking to them first, and if that doesn't work then I'm going to have to use a little extra persuasion," he said tapping the muzzle of the shotgun with his finger. Lexi hoped that it wasn't going to escalate to that state, however; she knew realistically it probably would.

As the car came closer to the farmhouse, it suddenly fishtailed sideways sending dirt and debris all over Zac and Lexi, before skidding to a halt. Lexi rolled her eyes in annoyance. "If these guys are trying to piss me off, it's already working," she muttered to Zac.

"What are you trying to prove?!" Lexi yelled, standing with her arms folded across her chest. "You can drive a car. Big deal! No one cares anymore!"

Zac laughed. Lexi was right. It didn't make you any more superior just because you could drive a soon to be relic from the past!

Peering towards the car, Zac tried to see who was inside. Even in the fading light of dusk, as soon as the car's first three passengers emerged from the metal cocoon, Zac recognised them straight away. He breathed in sharply. It was his traitorous brother Kevin, Aaron and that bitch Cindy, the one who had tried to humiliate Lilly. *What were they doing here?* The last time Zac had seen Kevin was the night of the bonfire. The night Kevin had betrayed Jasper's Bay and disowned his family. Zac remembered that Kevin had told him he never wanted anything to do with his family again and that he was heading to Perth and wouldn't be returning. *Apparently, Kevin had changed his mind.* Zac's face screwed up in confusion, and he took a tentative step towards his younger brother. He could see three other people exiting the car, however; his eyes were focused firmly on Kevin.

"Brother! I thought you went to Perth. What are you doing here?" Zac asked, frowning. "Have you decided to come home?"

Kevin stood and smirked at Zac, a big grin spreading across his face. "Yeah. Sure, Zac. I've come home."

Zac smiled back. *Maybe Kevin was regretting his decision to betray the town and was sorry for what he had done?*

Opening his arms, Zac continued walking towards Kevin as though to embrace him. He hadn't seen his brother for quite a few months.

Kevin, however, didn't move. He remained as stiff as a rod of steel. "I've come home to take some more of *my* chickens," he said, his voice dripping hostility. "I think I'll take one of the goats too!" Kevin glared at Zac in defiance. His whole body was rigid, and his arms remained folded tightly in front of his chest like a barrier.

Zac immediately stopped in his tracks; his arms dropping to his sides in defeat. He stared at his brother in dismay. *Kevin wasn't here to come home. Kevin was the thief!* Zac couldn't believe it.

Kevin placed his hands on his hips and smirked. He saw the look of disappointment on Zac's face and began laughing loudly. Big rolling laughter that started deep in his belly. "You're such a loser, Zac!" he said snidely, grinning with happiness. "What? Did you think we were going to play happy families again?" Kevin rolled his eyes. "You thought you could be the big man of the house running the farm, while we all bent to your wishes!"

The expression on Zac's face turned from shock to anger. "I'm not trying to be the big man! I'm just trying to help our family and the town survive." His hands shook as though he wanted to shake Kevin in frustration. *Why was he such a wanker!* "The town needs our farm. You *could* stay and help too."

Kevin glared at Zac in disgust. He turned and spat on the ground. "I couldn't give a shit if this town survives. In fact, nothing would make me happier than to see the lot of you starve. I'm helping *these* kids now," he said gesturing to Jake and Kally with his thumb. "And I'll be taking those chickens and anything else I want. It's *my* farm too."

Everyone turned to look towards Jake and Kally. The two youngsters were standing awkwardly to one side of the group, obviously unsure what to make of the situation.

"Did that boy just call Kevin his brother?" whispered Jake, glancing a Kally who was standing by his side. "Is this Kevin's family farm?"

Kally shrugged. Her face was a mask of confusion. "So, why isn't he living here?" She looked angrily at Kevin.

"And, why is he trying to steal from his own family? What the heck is going on?" She took a small step closer to Jake, and he moved a little in front of her protectively.

"Who are you?" asked Lexi, glaring at the two strangers suspiciously. She knew that Cindy and Kevin were dicks, but where had these two younger kids come from? *Were they going to be a problem too?*

Jake's face turned bright crimson. "I um. We're not here for any trouble. We're from Gracetown," said Jake as if reading her mind.

"Gracetown?" questioned Lexi.

"Um, yeah. It's on the coast a couple of hours drive from here."

Zac turned to look at the boy. "Yeah, I know it. What are you doing here with my brother?"

Kally spoke boldly, trying to defend Jake. "Look, we only came because Kevin promised us food. He said you were giving it away." She wiped her hands on her jeans, nervously. "We don't want any trouble, but there are a bunch of us kids in our town, and we're all starving. We're all on our own. There are no adults around to help us!"

Zac looked sympathetically at the young girl. She looked about ten-years-old and was obviously upset. Her clothes were dirty, and she had bruises and scrapes on her legs.

"Look, I understand. There are no adults here either." Zac peered angrily at Kevin. "I'm not sure what my brother has said to you, but the problem is Kevin doesn't live on this farm any longer. He doesn't even live in this town, and he doesn't do any work around here, so he doesn't have any rights to the food. He might think he does, but he doesn't. We've very little food ourselves, so only kids who help out in our town are entitled to it."

The girl dropped her eyes to the ground realising Kevin had been lying.

"I know it sounds harsh, but it's the way it's got to be," added Lexi, taking a step closer to the two strangers. Her right hand was outstretched towards them.

Although Zac and Lexi felt sorry for the younger children, they had to protect their own dwindling food supply. They couldn't just give it away to strangers. At least, not until Jasper's Bay came up with a more regular source of food themselves.

Kevin started whistling. "Well, that was a lovely speech Zac, but it's all horseshit. I want the chickens, and the simple fact is, I'm going to take them."

"No, you're not Kevin!" Zac was fuming.

Kevin continued to grin like a crazed clown at a fair. "Oh yes, I am," he stated firmly, as he made his way to the back of the car and opened the boot. Reaching inside, he pulled out a long, heavy metal shovel and dragged it back to stand beside Cindy. Cindy merely watched him without saying a word. She had been very quiet this whole time. The main two objects of her wrath, Braydon and Elisha weren't here, so she didn't really care what Kevin did on his family farm. She was just here for the thrill, biding her time until she could wreak her own revenge.

"So, big brother," taunted Kevin as he held the heavy shovel out in front of him. "What you gonna do to stop me? I'm not leaving here until I take what's rightfully mine!"

Zac looked over at Lexi, who nodded her head slightly. Kevin had evidently come to the farm for trouble. They were going to have to take this *conversation* to the next level.

"You sure you want to do this, Kevin?" asked Zac, giving his brother one last chance.

Kevin didn't even blink. "Yup."

Zac shook his head sadly before turning his back on Kevin to retrieve his shotgun. He was going to have to threaten him to make him leave.

As soon as Zac turned his back, Kevin took a couple of swift steps forward, quickly lifting the heavy shovel in a wide arc and swinging it forcefully onto the back of his brother's head. Lexi and Kally both screamed in shock at the violence of the act. The unsuspecting Zac grunted in pain before crumpling to his knees and falling forward onto his front, his face lying in the dirt.

For a moment, there was complete silence as the gravity of what Kevin had just done filled the air. Kally and Jake both stood utterly still, their mouths hung open in shock at the violence they had just witnessed. *Who was this guy? Who would do that to their own brother?*

Lexi stared at Zac lying face down on the ground as if she were watching a horror movie, and Zac was the latest victim. *What the hell had just happened?* She could see blood seeping from the back of Zac's head, and she quickly rushed to his side, pulling her jumper from her body as she ran.

As Lexi reached his still form, she sank down beside him and carefully turned him on his side. Rolling her jumper into a ball, she pressed its woollen fibres to the back of Zac's head trying to stem the crimson flow of blood. She checked his breathing and tenderly wiped dirt from his eyes and face with the corner of her shirt. His breath sounded ragged, and he moaned fitfully. Zac probably had a concussion, and he was going to need stitches in the back of his head.

As Lexi continued to apply pressure to the back of Zac's skull, she suddenly became aware of another presence by her side. Her pulse quickened, and her breath caught in her throat. Looking up, Lexi saw Kevin looming over her like a malevolent presence. He had a nasty grin on his face, and his eyes were bright with excitement.

"Wasn't expecting that, was he?" chortled Kevin.

Lexi was suddenly reminded of Broc and the way he had taunted Hadley. Anger rose in her belly and without hesitating, she abruptly stood to her feet and slapped Kevin hard across the face, her hand stinging from the force.

Kevin's expression instantly changed from one of glee to one of shock. He hadn't expected her to retaliate. Kevin had assumed she would start crying and bleating like a lamb. He scrutinised Lexi as she stood staring at him defiantly. When she bent back down to help Zac, he pushed her forcefully to the ground. Being off-balance, Lexi fell to the dirt with a heavy thump.

"You're that girl from the city, aren't you?" Kevin uttered in annoyance. "The one that's been helping organise the town." He looked at her with disdain. "Why would you want to waste your time helping the kids in this pathetic place?" He pointed the shovel towards the direction of the town. As far as Kevin was concerned, it should be everyone for themselves. You looked after yourself, and to hell with anyone else. The way he saw it if you couldn't fend for yourself, you suffered the consequences.

Thinking about Lexi and her position as a leader in the town, suddenly gave Kevin an idea. He motioned with his hand for Cindy and Aaron to join him. "Change of plan," he yelled to them as they moved forward. "Grab her and put her in the car! My sister Lilly is good friends with her. She'll hate it."

Kevin watched in delight as Lexi turned in confusion, unsure of what was happening. "Plus, this town relies on her," he stated, raising his eyebrows. "So, we can use her as leverage to get what we want."

"Good idea," agreed Cindy, eagerly. "Isn't she Braydon's friend too?" *This could be a way for her to get back at Braydon for what he did to Broc.* She yanked Lexi by the hair while Kevin and Aaron grabbed her arms and tried to forcefully march her to the car.

"Let go of me Kevin!" yelled Lexi furiously, twisting her body trying to break his hold. "You'd better get your hands off me!"

"Or what?" Cindy cackled, enjoying every minute. "There's three of us against you. Just shut up and get in the car!"

Lexi aimed a kick backwards at Cindy's leg connecting with the other girl's thigh. "I see your leg's mended."

Cindy let out a grunt and retaliated by pulling Lexi's hair once more as they forced her closer to the car. Lexi grimaced in pain.

"What are you doing?!" yelled Kally. "Why do we need her for leverage? Can't we just take some food from here like you promised?" She shuffled her feet. *This was not how this night was supposed to turn out!*

"Listen," called Jake, feeling increasingly alarmed. He tried to speak reasonably. "We did not agree to any kidnapping. I don't know what's going on here, but we only want some food." He angrily pointed towards the struggling Lexi who was writhing and thrashing in the other's arms as they tried to force her into the boot of the car. "I don't think we should be doing this!" He glanced between Lexi and the boy lying on the ground. *What the hell was going on?*

"I don't care what you think, Jake!" argued Kevin. He was now breathing heavily as he struggled with the uncooperative Lexi. "You owe us for the chickens we brought you," he reminded Jake, pointing his finger at him nastily. "You can either get in the car, or we will leave you here, and you can be stranded. You can find your own way back to those precious little kids in your stupid town." Kevin grinned. His eyes were cold and his lips thin. "Let's see how they fend without you!"

Jake glanced sideways at Kally. "This is fucked up" he muttered under his breath.

Kally gave him an awkward shrug and shook her head. "What choice do we have? It's a long walk back to Gracetown, and I don't even know how to get there." She looked as though she were going to cry.

Jake took Kally's hand and pulled her to the car, trying not to look at the struggling girl. He sighed heavily as he clambered inside. "Maybe we can help her once we get back to town," he whispered to Kally, feeling decidedly unhappy about the whole situation. He peered at the farmland and cows. "I reckon Kevin's entire talk of food has been a bloody lie!" Jake's face was scowling. "They were never going to give us any food. Why would they? Like they said they haven't got much themselves." He looked as though he wanted to scream.

Kally had tears in her eyes. She covered her ears with her hands and tried to block out the sound of Lexi shrieking. Her small body shook.

Lexi continued to kick and scream like a wild thing, trying desperately to break free. However, with three against one, she didn't really have a chance.

By the time Kevin and his group forced Lexi into the boot of the car, the sky had darkened, and night had enveloped the children. A small smattering of stars lit up the sky, and a full moon gave some relief to the darkness. The sounds of screaming had brought Hadley and Katie stampeding through the front door of the farmhouse and into the front yard.

Katie swung a torch around, trying to illuminate the area. As the light made a wide arc along the ground, the first thing she saw was Zac lying on his side in the dirt. He was utterly still, and at first glance, she assumed he was dead. Letting out an anguished scream, Katie ran to her brother's side. Her knees folded as she crumpled to the ground beside him.

"Zac, nooo! What happened? Zac!" her terrified voice rang out in the night.

At the same time, Hadley, who was standing on the porch, took a few tentative steps forward towards Katie and Zac, unsure of what was happening. She could barely see what was going on in the yard in front of her.

As she reached Katie, she could hear people fighting and could see the outlines of a car not far from where she stood. *Was that Lexi? It sounded like Lexi.*

"Lexi?" Hadley shone her torch upwards towards the disturbance, her insides turning cold with fear. The beam of light lit up her sister's white, frightened face as Kevin closed the boot of the car and locked her inside its dark interior as if it were her tomb. Hadley froze. Her eyes widened in shock.

Turning to face Hadley, Kevin bent over breathing heavily. "If you want her back," he yelled, wiping his nose with the side of his hand. "We'll trade her for food and batteries!" Glaring at Hadley, Kevin took one more look towards Zac who was still motionless on the ground before jumping into the car and slamming the door.

Not hesitating for a moment, Hadley immediately propelled herself forward. Her heart was pounding in her chest, and her arms were stretched outward, trying to reach her sister. But she was too late. Just as Hadley reached the car, her fingertips brushing the cold metal, the tyres spun on the gravel road sending sand and grit into her face before speeding away.

Not wanting to give up, Hadley chased after the fleeing car for as long as she could, until she was no longer able to see its evil red tail-lights speeding away in the distance. Eventually, she ran out of steam and stopped running, staring bleakly into the darkness. *What the frick had just happened?* She knew someone had stolen some of the chickens and trampled their corn, but why had Kevin taken Lexi? Hadley chewed her nails anxiously. *Sure, Lexi had been a complete pain lately, but Hadley didn't want anything bad to happen to her!*

Out of breath and feeling afraid, Hadley stared into the darkness. *What could she do? She had to help Lexi!* She brought her hands up and covered her face. Hadley could feel the panic rising inside her. Her breath was coming in quick rapid gasps, her feet frozen to the spot. *You can't just stand here; you must do something!* "Come on," she yelled to herself. "You have to move! Lexi needs you."

Swallowing her panic, Hadley forced herself to turn and start moving. Her feet felt heavy as though she were walking through thick, cloying mud, and each step was an effort. As she slowly gained control of her fear, Hadley picked up her speed and started to run. She knew she needed to get back to the farm to see what had happened to Zac, then she was determined to rally the other kids and find Lexi. Hadley knew Lexi must be feeling terrified locked inside that car boot, not knowing where she was being taken. Hadley increased her pace. She had to hurry, and her feet thumped loudly along the bitumen road in the quiet of the night.

Suddenly realising she was all alone out in the darkness; she looked from side to side as she ran, swinging the small beam of light from her torch into the bushland beside her.

"I hope you're not out there Elisha," she muttered, swallowing fearfully. Even with the full moon, it was so dark without street or house lights. An encounter with Elisha out here in the darkness on her own was the last thing Hadley needed right now. She gripped her torch tightly and kept moving.

"I hope I don't get lost." Suddenly feeling unsure of her surroundings, Hadley stopped. She peered through the darkness, trying to spot a familiar landmark with her torchlight. Once again, she could feel herself starting to panic.

"Oh, come on," she berated herself. "Stop being a baby, you can do this. You know you can." Taking a slow, steadying breath, Hadley once again looked around her. Peering to her left, she noticed tall shapes stretching out in a line. That wasn't natural, that was man-made. "It's the farm's row of pine trees! Oh, thank god. I'm not lost!"

Hadley gripped her torch tightly, not wanting to drop it and began to run. She needed to hustle, both Zac and Lexi were relying on her and time was paramount.

CHAPTER TEN

Gracetown

When Lexi was forced into the boot of Kevin's car, she heard Hadley frantically calling her name. Even though the two sisters had been fighting an awful lot lately, it reminded Lexi that Hadley still cared for her and it gave her some needed courage. She knew Hadley would find help.

As the roof of the boot slammed shut, and Lexi was engulfed in darkness, she could feel the terror rising in her throat, and she tried not to freak-out. *You must find a way out!* She told herself as she unclenched her fists and tried to calm down. Lying on her back with her legs bent, Lexi brought her hands up by her head and tried to push the boot open. She groaned and strained with all her strength against the hard surface, her hands aching with the exertion. However, no matter how hard she pushed, it wouldn't budge. The boot was firmly closed.

Lexi tried to think of something else. *What else could she do? It was so cramped.* She now knew what it felt like to be an animal being smuggled in a tiny box through an airport quarantine. Her heart started to race at the idea, and she soon found herself thinking about the nightmare she had the other night. The one where she had been trapped in a small room, unable to breathe. Lexi started to panic. *If only this were a nightmare she could wake up from!*

Thumping her hands against the solid roof, Lexi screamed for help until her throat ached. She pummelled her fists and arms against the roof of the boot until there were bruises from her wrists to her elbows. The space inside the car boot was extremely claustrophobic, making her feel as though she were suffocating. The air was stale, and she could smell her own sour sweat. It was also terribly hot in the enclosed space and to make it worse, she desperately needed to pee.

Trying to manoeuvre herself into a more comfortable position, Lexi felt something poking into her leg making her feel even more irritated. As she tried to wiggle away from the hard object, Lexi found herself hitting the back wall of the boot. She placed both arms on either side of her and pushed. It was so tight a space that she couldn't unbend her arms. She couldn't straighten her legs either, and her head was jammed uncomfortably against the back wall. There was no room to move. It was if she were entombed! Clenching her fists, tears of frustration formed in the corners of her eyes and she began screaming again.

After a while, Lexi wiped her eyes and shook her head trying to clear her mind. "Get a hold of yourself," she muttered through gritted teeth. If she wanted to escape, she had to keep her wits about her. It wasn't doing any good her breaking down. If her nose became blocked from crying, it would only make it more difficult to breathe, and besides, she didn't want to let Kevin or Cindy have the satisfaction of seeing her distressed.

However, no matter how hard Lexi willed herself to stay calm, she found herself becoming upset. Whenever the car went over a bump in the road, her body was thrown upwards before landing with a jarring thump against the hard floor. She could practically feel the bruises forming under her tender skin every time she landed. The thin carpet covering the surface did little to protect her. The battering she was receiving soon turned her frustration and fear into anger. *How dare they do this to her. They were treating her like an animal!*

The pressure on her bladder was now unbearable. As the car sped around a sharp bend in the road, Lexi was once again flung into the hard metal. "I'm going to make you pay for this!" she screamed in a fury. "You're all wankers!" her voice was sharp and bitter.

Turning onto her side, Lexi once again began to feel around the compartment as best she could in the tight space. *She had to do something.* The boot was empty apart from the hard object by her right thigh. With her hand stretched downwards, Lexi used the tips of her fingers to gradually coax the long object into a position where she could grab hold of it. It felt cool to her touch, and although she wasn't sure what the item was, she was sure anything hard could be useful. *She could always hit that bastard Kevin with it if he tried to touch her again!*

Bringing the object up close to her face, Lexi peered at it trying to work out what it was. In the darkness, it was difficult to know, however to her fingers, it felt thin, hard and cold as though it were metal. *Maybe it was the car tyre lever? Well, whatever it was, it could be useful,* she thought. *It would make an excellent weapon.*

Feeling along the edge of the boot interior, Lexi wondered if she could use the tyre lever to prise it open. It would be difficult in the darkness and limited space; however, she had to give it a try. It might be her only chance to escape!

Using her fingers to trace along the ridge of metal, Lexi carefully placed the sharp end of the tyre lever into the groove. Then, gripping the bar with two hands, she pulled downward as best she could.

Just as she felt a tiny bit of give in the metal, the car sped over another bump in the road, and the lever was jerked from her hands hitting her on the side as her body was flung upwards.

"Ow, slow down, you idiots! I'm getting pummelled in here!" she yelled, hoping the others in the car might hear her.

Either they didn't, or they ignored her because the car did not slow at all.

Lexi tried over and over to prize open the boot; however, each time the lever would slip from the small groove or be flung from her hands. She started to gasp as her exertion and frustration made her breathe heavily. The air inside the car boot was becoming stale as the oxygen became thin. Sweat covered her face and hands in a thin layer making her grip on the metal slippery.

"I need air," she panted, holding her hand to her throat. She began to feel dizzy.

Twisting her head from side to side, Lexi looked about her for a solution. Even though her eyes had adjusted somewhat to the darkness, Lexi couldn't see much in the closed space. She stretched her fingers out in front of her and once again felt about. She could feel hard, cold metal, carpet and plastic.

Plastic! *Maybe that was one of the car's taillights. Could she smash it with the tyre lever?*

Gripping the lever close to the pointy end with both her hands, Lexi reached above her head and began chipping away at the hard plastic.

Nothing happened.

"Oh, come on!"

Gritting her teeth, she tensed all her muscles and rammed the lever into the inside of the taillight as hard as she could. "Yaaa."

A small hole appeared in the plastic!

Lexi hit the light again and this time the plastic covering shattered sending bits of orange and red debris onto the road below.

Quickly bringing her hands to her side, Lexi tilted her head backwards and craned her neck, moving her face closer to the opening. Wonderful fresh air! Opening her mouth, Lexi breathed deeply. She wasn't going to suffocate!

After taking in a few big gulps of fresh air, Lexi turned onto her back and once again felt for the tyre lever. Feeling the cold metal on her fingertips, she brought the weapon up to her chest and tightened her grip around the hard piece of metal. She wanted to be ready to use it in case she got the chance.

"If those bastards think they can just kidnap me without a fight they've got it wrong," she muttered with a snarl. Lexi knew her captors probably wouldn't be expecting her to fight back and she was more than happy to surprise them. She wiped the perspiration from her eyes and smiled. "I'll be more than happy to give them a fight."

* * *

As Kevin's car sped along the highway back to Gracetown, the children in the back seat could hear Lexi yelling and screaming from within the boot.

"Don't you think we should stop and let her out?" said Jake, his eyes wide. "It must be damn hot in there."

"No," replied Kevin. "We haven't got time to stop."

Jake glanced at Kally; his eyebrows knitted together in concern. "What the fuck is wrong with this guy?" he muttered.

Kally bit her jagged fingernails. "But how do you know she can breathe in there!" she asked Kevin in a shaky voice. "We don't want her to die!" she leaned forward in the car seat until her face was close to Kevin's.

"Listen!" exclaimed Kevin loudly. His voice sounded hard, and his nostrils flared at the sides. "She'll be fine, and unless you want to join her, I suggest you shut up and sit back until we get home!"

"Home!" said Kally, squinting her eyes at Kevin. "It's not *your* home!" She crossed her arms firmly across her chest and slumped back in her seat. She really hated Kevin.

Kevin laughed. *These young kids were so sensitive!*

*
  *
*
  *

After an hour, Kevin drove into the main street of Gracetown. It was now completely dark, and the road was deserted. Without any electricity, no one wandered the streets at night. The noises of dingos and other night animals could often be heard in the darkness, and many of the children were afraid of the dark. All the town's children were in their houses.

Parking the car in front of an unused set of office buildings, Kevin got out of the car and walked towards the rear. He could hear Lexi banging and thumping from inside the boot.

"Grab the rope from the gym bag on the floor of the front seat," he whispered to Cindy not wanting the others to hear.

Cindy smiled in delight and ran to retrieve the rope.

"What are you doing?" asked Jake in alarm. He had no idea how far Kevin was willing to go with this kidnapping.

Kevin suddenly ran at Jake and shoved him to the ground. He promptly sat on Jake's chest, Kevin's substantial body pushing painfully into the skinny boy's bones. "Look, mate. I'm getting sick of your whining! We need somewhere to keep this girl and unless you want her getting hurt you had better help us!" Kevin leant forward until his face was right up close to Jake's.

Jake turned his head to the side away from Kevin's hot breath. "What are you going to do to her?" He asked, defiantly.

Kevin sat up. "Oh, don't panic, mate. I'm not going to do anything *to* her. I'm not an animal." Kevin laughed. "I was only joking! We just need somewhere to keep her until my brother gives us what I'm entitled to." He looked at Jake's worried face. "It's harmless fun. Don't worry so much!" He stood with his hands on his hips, and his chin jutted forward.

Jake didn't think Lexi would think it was all *harmless fun*. "Why does she have to be in Gracetown? Can't you take her someplace else?"

Kevin grinned. "No, mate. You're our friends," he said, winking at Cindy who had brought him the rope. "We like this town and besides," continued Kevin, getting up and taking the rope from Cindy. "You said you would help us. And you're either *with* us, or you're against us. You don't want to be our enemy like her, do you? Kevin nodded meaningfully towards the boot of the car.

"No. I don't want to be your enemy," agreed Jake. "I just don't think what you're doing is right. We should let her go."

Standing, Jake began walking toward the car. "We don't want to be involved with this," he started to say.

Cindy, who had been watching him intently, suddenly grabbed the rope from Kevin and swiftly whipped it towards him. The rope flung forwards missing Jake and striking Kally sharply across the face.

"What the hell?!" yelled Jake as Kally cried out in pain. "Stop! What do you think you're doing!"

"Show us a room we can use then," Cindy threatened as she pulled the rope back towards her and started curling it around her arm. She glared at Kally meaningfully. Her earlier pretence of friendliness had disappeared.

Jake glanced towards Kevin and Aaron. They were both standing with their feet spread apart, arms folded across their chests, and mouths set in a thin hard line. They weren't pretending to be friendly anymore, either. Hostility was radiating from them.

"Jeezus, alright!" yelled Jake as he stepped away from the car. He swiftly turned and began running towards Kally, who was holding the side of her face with her palm. Her eyes were wide. "I'll show you a room!"

Cindy stopped coiling the rope and nodded. Her eyes lit up with satisfaction.

Jake glared at her before pointing to an office block across the road from where they were standing. "There's an old cellar in that building," he said, placing his arm tenderly around Kally's shoulders and turning her away from the others. "It's down the stairs at the back," he added before starting to lead Kally away.

"Hey! Where do you think you're going?" yelled Cindy as she shoved the end of a hessian bag into her back pocket.

Jake glared at her; his eyebrows drawn together. "I'm taking Kally home and then I'm getting some water and blankets for that girl." His voice was steady and calm. No one was going to stop him. "We've had enough of your violence!"

Cindy laughed. "Geeze, I hardly touched her."

Kevin turned to stare after Jake and Kally for a moment before deciding he couldn't be bothered arguing.

"Time to get this chick out of the car!" Kevin crowed happily. "Come on, Aaron. Don't just stand there. Come and help."

Aaron, who had been standing silently to one side, walked towards Kevin. His face held a touch of eagerness to please just like an obedient dog. He wasn't someone who liked confrontation, so he usually did whatever Cindy or Kevin wanted.

"Cindy, open the boot," ordered Kevin, as he handed her the car keys. In the darkness, he hadn't noticed the broken taillight.

Cindy laughed as she placed the key into the lock on the car. "I can't wait to see the state she's in. Probably covered in dirt, sweat and piss!" Still grinning, Cindy lifted the boot of the car.

As soon as the boot was opened, Lexi sat up and swung the tire lever outwards in a wide arc. She squinted in the moonlight, unable to see properly for a few moments.

Unfortunately, Lexi missed, and Cindy jumped out of the way. "Whoa, watch out!" yelled Cindy. Her face was a picture of surprise. "The bitch has a weapon!"

"Let me out of here!" screamed Lexi as spit flew from her mouth. Her hair was plastered to her face with sweat, and her cheeks were pink from the heat.

The others watched her suspiciously as she climbed from the car. Her posture was bent forward as she forced her stiff body and legs to move. "Give me the keys to the car! I'm driving myself back to Jasper's Bay!" Lexi swung the tyre lever about in a fury. Her eyes looked crazy. All she felt was pure rage.

"Ahh. No, you're not!" laughed Kevin. "You are staying right here until I get what I want. *My* share of the farm's food."

Kevin's comment infuriated Lexi even more. She turned to face Kevin's car and began to smash the remaining tail-light with the tyre lever. "I said, give me the car keys!"

Kevin rolled his eyes. He didn't care if she smashed the car. It wasn't even his, he had stolen it a few weeks ago. He uncoiled some of the rope and made it into a makeshift lasso. *Something he learned on the farm might actually be handy,* he thought to himself in amazement.

Lexi continued to loudly smash the windows of the car.

Kevin nodded to Cindy and Aaron to get ready. He then stepped forward and expertly lassoed Lexi around the waist. Tugging hard on the rope, he upset Lexi's balance and sent her crashing heavily to the ground. She grunted as she hit the dirt, the tyre lever flung from her hand.

Feeling winded, Lexi slowly got to her knees and began to crawl towards the tyre lever trying to retrieve it. Watching Lexi, Cindy had anticipated her move and ran forward, reaching the weapon first. She picked up the metal bar and waved it tauntingly in front of Lexi's face.

Lexi lunged forward and bit Cindy's hand. Hard.

"You bitch!" shrieked Cindy, as she looked at the bite mark on her hand.

Lexi grinned at her. She knew she had drawn blood. Lexi could taste it. She sat back on her haunches and considered Cindy. *Should I try and fight her for the tyre lever?* Her hands curled into tight fists, and her heart was racing. Lexi could feel her pulse pounding in her temples as though her head was about to explode. What was going on with her body? She needed to calm down.

Uncurling her fists and bringing her hands to her cheeks, Lexi closed her eyes for a moment, trying to steady herself. Her breath was becoming erratic, and her face felt like a furnace it was so hot.

When Cindy saw Lexi close her eyes, she lifted the tyre lever high in the air, intending to swing it at Lexi's face. As the metal bar reached its top arc and began to come down towards Lexi, Kevin stepped forward.

"Cindy! Stop. I want her undamaged." Kevin grabbed Cindy's shoulder. "They won't barter for her if she's damaged."

Cindy frowned, obviously unhappy. She stopped and looked at the metal bar, then she glanced at Lexi who was now, glaring at her. Cindy smiled and gripped the metal bar harder.

"Cindy! Hand it over," ordered Kevin when he saw Cindy smile.

Cindy groaned in frustration with her lip turned up in a sneer. She looked at the tyre lever once more before throwing it away. The discarded metal bar skidded along the dirt sending up a plume of red dust. Not waiting for instruction from Kevin, Cindy reached into her back pocket and pulled out the hessian bag.

"Stop looking at me bitch!" she snarled as she roughly yanked the bag over Lexi's head. The course material scratched Lexi's face.

At the same time, Kevin and Aaron tied Lexi's hands tightly behind her back and dragged her across the dirt towards the office buildings. Once they reached the building, Aaron ran ahead to find the old cellar Jake had informed them about.

Even with her head covered and hands bound, Lexi continued to thrash about and kick out with her feet. Kevin kept his distance from her as he waited for Aaron to find the room.

Once Aaron returned, Cindy and the two boys hurriedly dragged the uncooperative Lexi down the stairs and into a dark, damp room at the back of the building. Shoving her into the room, they quickly slammed the only door and bolted it shut. As the trio of captors walked away, they could hear Lexi begin to scream.

Cindy winked at Kevin. "We've caught a *big fish* this time!"

Kevin smiled. "Now let's see what my stupid brother thinks of that."

CHAPTER ELEVEN

As Lexi was dragged down a flight of steps and thrown into a small room, the dread she felt rose inside her. Sweat was running from the back of her neck down her spine and into her jeans. Her t-shirt stuck to her, and she could smell her own stench. It was disgusting. All she wanted to do was cry and scream, but she knew if she was going to find a way out, she had to keep control. Her breath was now coming in short rapid gasps.

Dropping her head to her chest, Lexi tried to calm down. She had felt herself lose control and go into a rage when Kevin let her out of the car, and it frightened her. Lexi began to breathe heavily. Every part of her felt hot. Her cheeks were flaming and raw. Her bloodshot eyes burned, and so did her throat. All in all, she felt terrible, as though she had the flu.

"Nooooo!" she yelled suddenly as realisation swept upon her. Her face twisted in dismay. *The virus must be fully formed within her. She was going to have to tell the others. That's if she ever saw them again.*

Lexi ran her tongue over her parched lips. She wanted to cry in frustration. *I have to get this bloody bag off my head!* It was scratching her skin and it was difficult to breathe. Plus, she wanted to know where the hell she was!

With her hands tied behind her back, there wasn't any way Lexi could reach the bag with her fingers. Bending forward and lowering her head, Lexi proceeded to shake her head from side to side, trying to dislodge the bag. Slowly, with the help of gravity and motion, the bag slipped downwards and onto the floor. Standing upright, Lexi arched her back and took a huge gulp of air.

Feeling a little better with the bag removed from her head, she started peering around the room trying to get a sense of where her captors had put her. Wherever she was, it was very dark. The room didn't have any apparent windows, and the only light was coming from the slit underneath the single wooden door. As far as Lexi could see, the door was the only way in or out of the room. She rested her back against the thick, limestone walls and took a breath through her nose. The air in the room smelled musty with a strange hint of alcohol as if she were in an old wine cellar.

Lexi wriggled her fingers. Her hands were secured tightly behind her back with a course scratchy rope that cut into her skin. When she tried to pull against the rope to test how tightly it was tied, pain shot up her arm, making her gasp.

Sliding her body down the wall until she was in a squatting position, Lexi tried to pull her hands under her feet and towards the front of her body. "Ahhh, I can't do it!" she moaned when pain flared in her wrists. "Either my butt's too big or my arms are too short!" She let her body now saturated with perspiration, sit with a thump onto the hard floor. Thankfully her legs were unbound, and she pulled her knees towards her chest. Lexi scanned the room as best she could in the darkness. As her eyes adjusted to the light, she spotted several small moving shapes in the corner of the room.

"What the heck is that?" she wondered, leaning forward to get a better look at the objects.

Suddenly, Lexi leapt to her feet in alarm, almost falling over as she tried to regain her balance. Rats! She could make out their long thin tails as they scurried about.

"Oh, no, no, no," she cried. "Let me out of here!" She ran awkwardly towards the door, trying not to fall. Running with her hands bound tightly behind her back was not easy, and without the use of her hands to break her fall, Lexi was frightened of losing her balance.

When she reached the door, she turned her body and felt for the doorknob with her hands. As her fingers gripped the metal, Lexi pressed down on the handle. It was locked.

"Shit!" Pressing her ear to the wood listening for any noise, Lexi strained her ears trying to hear anything that could tell her where she might be. It was silent.

She kicked against the door with the back of her heel. "Hey. Let me out of here! You can't keep me locked down here!" her voice sounded shrill.

Silence. Either they were ignoring her, which was a distinct possibility, or no one was out there. "Come on!" Frustrated, Lexi rigorously pulled back and forth on the handle. However, it remained locked.

Giving up, Lexi let her body slide down the door to the floor. Once again, she brought her legs up to her chest and lay her hot forehead on her knees. She felt terrible. Her skin itched, her arms ached, plus, she needed a drink and a shower.

"The night is dark and full of terrors," she whispered to herself quoting her favourite TV show. What did Kevin and Cindy want with her? What did they plan to do to her? She felt helpless. As she peered into the darkness feeling defeated, large hot tears rolled down Lexi's burning cheeks.

*　*　*

Sometime in the night, Jake came down into the old cellar and brought Lexi a plastic bottle of water, two blankets, a metal bucket for a toilet, and two small candle stubs. "I'm sorry about this," he said, carefully lighting the candles with matches he kept in his pocket. He looked as though he wanted to say more; however, Cindy and Aaron were both standing right behind him, their bodies were so close they were almost touching. They had followed him down into the cellar making sure he didn't attempt to free Lexi.

After dripping some melted wax onto the floor, Jake positioned the candles into the hot wax and pressed them down hard so they wouldn't fall over. Giving Lexi a sorrowful smile, he turned and walked out of the room.

As soon as he left, Aaron shoved Lexi onto the floor and sat on her legs, making it difficult for her to move.

"What the hell!" yelled Lexi, wondering what they were going to do to her now. She twisted her head around trying to see.

"Just be quiet!" snapped Cindy, putting her knee into Lexi's back and leaning into her with all her body weight. She then pulled an old cloth from her pocket and tied it tightly on Lexi's mouth gagging her. The smelly rag pulled uncomfortably on the sides of Lexi's mouth, and she found it difficult to breathe properly as her nose was blocked from the fine dust in the room.

Slowly taking her time to get up, Cindy removed her knee from between Lexi's shoulder blades. "I'd love to stay and chat," smirked Cindy as she walked towards the door. "But we have some tasty BBQ chicken that needs eating. Byeee."

Aaron stood and walked out with Cindy. He didn't say a word to Lexi. He barely even looked at her.

Lexi turned onto her side and watched the two of them leave. Her eyes had become small slits as she glared at their retreating backs. As soon as Cindy slammed the door firmly shut, Lexi pulled her legs into her chest, rolled onto her knees and sat. Without her hands to help her balance, it was difficult to stand.

Lexi turned her head to glance at the items Jake had left her wondering why he had done so. With her hands tied tightly behind her back and her mouth gagged, using any of these items was going to be extremely difficult. She couldn't unscrew the cap on the bottle of water and using the bucket for a toilet when she couldn't undo her pants was going to be impossible. She sighed and stared at the candles. Several small moths were flitting around the naked flame.

"At least I'm not in the darkness anymore," Lexi murmured as she scooted backwards on her bottom towards the wall. Pushing her back against the wall, Lexi was able to use her legs to stand.

Walking over to the pile of items, she nudged the water bottle with her foot. "Christ," muttered Lexi, staring at the container lying on its side on the floor. After the long journey in the boot of the car, her throat and mouth were dry and raspy, and her cracked lips were stinging. *How am I going to be able to open this bloody thing with my hands tied?*

Having an idea, Lexi manoeuvred her body close to the bottle, then squatted so the water bottle was directly behind her. Using her bound hands, she felt for the container with her fingers and managed to grasp hold of the plastic cap. Feeling encouraged, Lexi gripped the lid and twisted it open.

Unfortunately, as the bottle was on its side, water started flowing from the open top onto the ground.

"Shit!" mumbled Lexi, twisting around. The contents were now half empty! Quickly kneeling in front of the bottle, she bent down to try to slurp some of the water, however, with her mouth obstructed by the gag, it was impossible. Lexi wanted to cry. She was so thirsty!

As she bent forward and lay her face on the ground, some of the water seeped into the cloth covering her mouth. Lexi began sucking at the material eagerly trying to obtain any moisture she could. It was better than nothing, and at least it made her mouth less parched.

Suddenly, Lexi heard a squeaking sound and looked up to see two mangy brown rats running towards her. Their long thin tails were stretched out behind them as they ran. Being afraid of rats, Lexi quickly moved from kneeling to standing and jumped to one side. In her haste, she almost lost her balance and fell over. *Why were the rats running at her? She didn't have any food!*

As the rats came closer. Lexi's breath turned to small gasps, and her heart thumped rapidly. She quickly scurried over to the wall. However, the rats didn't pursue her. Instead, they went directly to the water. *Her* water! Her *only* water!

The plastic bottle was laying on its side, and by nudging the bottle with their mouths, the rats were able to release more water. They drank thirstily. Lexi stared at them for a moment before forgetting her fear and running towards them. With her mouth gagged and her hands tied, she could do little to scare them away. She tried stamping her feet to no avail, the rats simply ignored her.

She watched as the rats pushed the bottle once more and even more of the precious water spilled onto the ground. There would be very little left if she didn't do something soon. Feeling a little remorseful, Lexi kicked out her foot and sent one of the rats flying into the corner with a squeal.

"I'm sorry but I can't have you biting me!"

The other rat paused still for a moment, watching Lexi before it too ran away and disappeared into a small hole at the base of the wall.

Moving her body, she quickly felt for the water bottle with her fingers and turned it so that it was once again standing upright. Watching the hole for a while, when the rats didn't return, Lexi finally let herself relax and kneel on the ground. She let out a small sob. Lexi hated harming animals, but what else could she do. She needed that water.

Not long after, Lexi's fingers started to tingle as the ropes tying her hands began to constrict the blood flow. She tried to manoeuvre her arms from the back of her body to the front. But it was hopeless, and Lexi almost dislocated her shoulder attempting it. Unfortunately, she had never been flexible, and the task proved to be impossible for her.

After a while, Lexi gave up and lay down on her side amongst the jumble of blankets. She stared at the flickering candles and wondered if Zac was alright. There had been a lot of blood seeping into her jacket when she had held it to his head, and he hadn't looked at all well when she had been forcefully whisked away from him. *At least Katie and Hadley were at the farm. They would find him and find help.*

But whose going to help me? She knew Hadley would want to, but how on earth would she find her. Hadley couldn't drive, and they didn't even have any fuel for a car if she could. Besides, where would her sister know where to look for her. *Had Kevin told Hadley where he was going?* Lexi couldn't remember. *Perhaps Hadley would never find her! Maybe she would never see daylight again! Was she going to die down here?* Lexi's mind raced with questions and doubts.

She closed her eyes for a moment and took a calming breath determined not to become upset.

Her friends would come looking for her. She would just have to be patient and wait for them to arrive. If not, she would just have to kick Kevin in the balls as soon as he ventured down here to gloat and make a run for it herself! The thought brought Lexi a glimmer of happiness in her dire circumstances. She'd love to see the look on Kevin's face when she escaped!

The next morning, directly across the road from the building Lexi was in, a fierce argument was ensuing between Kevin and the younger Gracetown kids.

"You can't use *our* town like this!" yelled Jake, his face flushed. "Just because you're older doesn't mean you have the right to order us around. You're not our parents!" argued Jake, his hands were placed firmly on his hips in defiance.

Kevin just stared at the younger, skinny boy with pure disinterest. "Like I said before, I don't care what any of you think, or want." He shook his head. "It doesn't interest me in the slightest."

Twelve-year-old Jake dropped his arms loosely by his side. He stared at Kevin with his mouth hanging open.

Kally stood by Jake's side, and several of the younger town kids had come out to see what the commotion was all about. Little four-year-old Daisy pulled at Kally's sleeve and wanted to know if they were going to have any breakfast. She had dark rings under her eyes, and her ribs were protruding. Kally looked down at the little girl and tried to quietly explain that they hadn't had time to go fishing so she would just have to wait.

"Yes. There's nothing for *you*," snarled Kevin. "Go away and play, little girl. You're annoying me!"

Daisy took a step away from Kevin and hid behind Kally. Her dirty face was screwed up as though she were going to cry.

A trickle of sweat ran down Jake's cheek, and he stared at Daisy's frightened face in horror. "I have to do something," he whispered to himself. "He doesn't care about our town or any of us."

"Look," said Jake, pointing his finger angrily at Kevin. "You have to let that girl go and then you have to leave. You agreed to help us find more food, and you didn't!" His face was red with anger. "We didn't agree to be a jail. It's not right to keep her down there."

Kevin laughed. "Well, look who's grown some big ones!" He regarded Jake for a moment. "The thing is, Jake. Either Lexi stays down there, or..." Kevin took one step towards little Daisy and roughly pulled her towards him. "We can let Lexi out, and this little girl can take her place. How does that sound to you?"

Cindy quickly positioned herself next to Kevin and pinned Daisy's arms to her side, making it difficult for the little girl to move. Daisy began to cry.

"No!" wailed Kally. "You can't do that! Let her go, she's only four!" Kally took a tentative step towards Cindy, her voice pleading. "She'd be terrified down there in the dark."

Kevin smiled evilly at Jake, enjoying the power he had over the younger boy. "Well then, Jake. What's it to be? Lexi, who you don't even know. Or poor little Daisy here!"

Jake dropped his head in defeat. He didn't like the idea of Lexi being locked in that old, cold cellar, but he couldn't let them imprison Daisy or any of the other kids from Gracetown either. They would never forgive him, and he would never forgive himself either.

Jake looked at Kevin and nodded. "Let Daisy go."

Kevin smiled, a big grin spreading across his face.

Sighing, Jake took a long sideways glance at Kally before slowly turning and walking away. "I'd better go and catch some fish for the younger kids to eat, or they will have another night going hungry."

Cindy released Daisy who promptly ran into Kally's arms and started sobbing, her little face turning red and splotchy. Kally turned to glare at Kevin and Cindy before leading the little girl away from the others.

Watching them leave, Cindy and Kevin started laughing in glee. Kevin rocked back and forth on his heels in merriment. "Yeah, that's what I thought! Bunch of losers."

Jake could hear Kevin and Cindy laughing as he walked down the street. He clenched his fists tightly by his sides. *Who did these jerks think they were?*

"I can't believe we're in this situation!" he muttered, looking up to the sky. "Yes, we've been going hungry, but we've been alright. I should never have trusted them!" He looked down at his feet and angrily kicked at an old soft drink can lying on the side of the road. He glanced back towards Kevin and the other children. "I would rather go hungry than be bullied into this shit!"

"I need to get rid of Kevin," he said to himself. His mouth had become a thin line, and his eyes were full of determination.

Deciding to pay another visit to Lexi before he went fishing, Jake crossed the road towards the building where she was being held captive. He wanted to make sure she was okay. Jake had tried to speak to her last night when he had brought her the blankets, but Cindy and Aaron had been there too, and he hadn't had the chance. Lexi obviously knew Kevin. *Maybe she had some ideas on how to make him leave Gracetown.*

As the others continued to argue, Jake sneakily made his way to the back of the building where Lexi was being held. He quietly let himself inside and crept towards her *prison*. The cellar was in the basement of the building at the bottom of a flight of stairs. Just as he made his way to the top of the stairs, he noticed someone standing at the bottom. It was Aaron.

"What are you doing here?" Jake asked, peering down towards him.

"I'm on guard obviously. And just as well by the look of it," Aaron replied haughtily. "What are *you* doing here?"

"I want to talk to Lexi," Jake stated with his arms folded against his chest.

"Nope."

'What?"

"No one is allowed in to see her except Kevin." Aaron nodded his head towards the closed door.

Jake chortled in disbelief. "What? Does he think he's the king or something! What do you mean no one can speak to her except Kevin?"

Aaron shrugged. "That's what he said."

Jake stared at him for a moment before taking a step downwards onto the first step. "And what. You just do everything he says, do you?"

Aaron folded his arms defensively across his chest and took a couple of steps upwards, blocking Jake's way. He shrugged again.

Jake shook his head in annoyance. "Oh, for Frigg's sake! This is ridiculous." He made his way back out of the building and walked to his house to retrieve his fishing gear. For once, he couldn't wait to get out onto the water and away from these people.

Kevin saw him leave the building and called out snidely to him. "Enjoy your visit?!"

Jake gave him the bird without turning to look at him and kept walking. He'd had enough of that idiot for one day.

* * *

Jasper's Bay

By the time Hadley reached the farmstead, her heart was thumping in her chest, and her lungs felt as though they were going to explode. She placed her hands on her knees and breathed deeply.

As she waved the little plastic torch in front of her, the first thing she saw was Katie kneeling on the ground, cradling Zac's head in her lap. She had a towel pressed to his head, and her face was bent towards him.

As Hadley ran to her friend, she could hear Katie talking to the unconscious Zac. "Come on, Zac. Wake Up! Come on, Zac!"

"How is he?" asked Hadley, squatting beside Katie. "He doesn't look good."

Katie glanced up at Hadley and shook her head. "He won't wake up." She tenderly brushed the hair from Zac's face with her fingers. "Who did this. Who was in the car?" her voice had turned angry.

Hadley placed her hand on Katie's arm trying to ready her for the shock of what she was about to say. "It was Kevin!" she exclaimed frowning. "I couldn't catch up to him. And he's taken Lexi in the boot of his car!"

Katie's mouth dropped open. "What! Kevin? My brother, Kevin?!"

"Yes, I don't know what the hell he's up to," said Hadley as her face screwed up in anger. She twisted her hands in her lap.

Katie continued to stare at Hadley with her mouth hanging open. She blinked rapidly as if unsure what to say.

"He said he was going to Gracetown or something." Hadley looked at Katie's shocked face. "I don't know why he's taken Lexi. She looked terrified, and I couldn't help her!" Hadley bit her lower lip as she turned to look over her shoulder into the darkness.

Katie grabbed Hadley's hand in hers, finally speaking. "I'm so sorry, Hadley. I don't know why Kevin is doing this. He's always been annoying, but he's never been this bad!" Tears started forming in the corners of her eyes as she looked pleadingly at Hadley.

Leaning forward, Hadley hugged her friend. "It's not your fault, Katie. You can't control what your brother does!" Katie nodded solemnly.

The movement of the two friends knocked Zac's head as he lay between them, and he gave a small moan. The girls immediately returned their attention to him.

Hadley leaned in closer to peer at Zac's face. It was ashen white. "He looks bad, Katie," she murmured, adjusting the towel pressed to Zac's head. "I think we should try and get him inside and off the ground. Do you think you can carry him?"

Katie looked at Hadley and nodded. She had blood on her hands and face where she had wiped her forehead, and the corners of her mouth drooped downwards; however, her eyes were focused. "Uh, huh," she agreed determinedly.

"Come on, then," said Hadley, quickly standing. "I'll help you carry Zac inside, then I'm going to run into town to find Jason and the other older kids. We need their help."

"Okay," murmured Katie as she placed her hands under Zac's shoulders, ready to lift him. Hadley took his feet.

Both girls heaved and grunted trying to lift Zac from the ground; however, they only managed to move him a short distance. Every time they lifted his body, Zac's head would drop backwards, and he would groan in discomfort.

"Let's swap sides" suggested Hadley as she placed Zac's feet on the ground. "His shoulders are the heaviest part."

Katie agreed. Perspiration had broken out in beads across her forehead and her cheeks had turned bright pink; however, she continued to look resolute in helping her brother.

"Okay. One, two, three!" encouraged Hadley grunting as she lifted Zac's bulky shoulders.

This time the two girls managed to move him a little farther towards the house, but they could not lift him up the stairs. He was just too heavy.

"I don't like the way Zac's groaning whenever we lift him, and we're wasting time," said Hadley, shaking her head. "I'm sorry, Katie, but he's going to have to stay here. I don't think we should risk moving him anymore."

Hadley could hear Katie sniffing in the darkness. "I don't know what to do," she murmured quietly.

"I know, Katie. It's going to be alright." The girls laid Zac on the ground, and Hadley went to stand by her friend. "Listen, I'll stay here with Zac for a moment. I want you to go inside the house and fetch a blanket and clean towel, plus a bucket of water."

Katie glanced fretfully at Zac. "Okay," she said nodding vigorously, before bounding up the stairs and into the farmhouse. "A towel, some water and a blanket," she repeated to herself as she ran.

While she waited for Katie to return, Hadley carefully rolled Zac onto his side, bent his knee and stretched out his arm to prevent him from rolling forward. She then reached out and tentatively felt the back of Zac's head with her hand. Zac moaned when Hadley touched his scalp, causing her to quickly pull her hand away. It felt sticky and wet. "Damn it, I think his head is still bleeding," she muttered to herself, unable to know for certain in the darkness.

Quickly making her way back to where she had laid the torch on the ground, Hadley switched it on and ran back to Zac. Thankfully the torch continued to work, and Hadley shone the light towards the back of Zac's head. There was a lot of dried blood and sand matted in his hair, and the wound looked bloody and weeping. It was a nasty cut. Hadley screwed up her nose. "Eek, he's going to need stitches," she said in concern as Katie returned with the items she had asked for. Polo came bounding out from the house beside her.

Katie gently lay the blanket over her brother before rubbing his arm as she knelt beside him. She had deep creases between her eyebrows and her eyes widened in horror as she looked at his wound. Her hand froze on his arm, and she stared at him.

"Katie," said Hadley as she placed her hand on Katie's shoulder and gently shook her. "I have to leave. I'm sorry to leave you on your own, but I need to go and get help."

Katie glanced at Hadley with a glazed look on her face. Her eyes remained wide and frightened.

Trying to rouse Katie, Hadley shook her shoulder again. "Katie, listen. While I'm gone, I want you to bath Zac's head, okay? You need to gently clean all the dirt and dried blood away. Understand?" She handed Katie the clean towel and pointed to the bucket of water sitting beside them.

Katie stared at her, rubbing her eyes. "What if it won't stop bleeding?" she pointed at the wound, grimacing.

Hadley looked at Zac. "Just make the area as clean as you can, then fold up the towel and hold it firmly against his head. I'm going to find Logan so he can stitch the cut."

Katie glanced at the towel and nodded. Her eyes had lost their frightened appearance, and she now looked determined. "Okay. I can do that."

Both girls leaned forward and hugged again. Their arms gripped each other tightly. Neither wanted to be alone, but they both knew they each had a job to do.

As Hadley rose to leave, Katie pulled at her arm. "Aren't you scared of running into town in the dark?"

Hadley looked from Katie out into the darkness of the bushland. She swallowed.

"What if you see a dingo or step on a snake?" asked Katie as she held onto Hadley's arm.

Hadley peered down at her torch, hoping the batteries would last. "I'm more worried about running into Elisha," she said, her voice shaking a little betraying her nervousness.

"Oh, cripes, Elisha!" said Katie as she let go of Hadley's arm and dipped the corner of the towel into the clean water. "You should take Polo with you. He can warn you of any danger."

Katie began dabbing the wet towel onto Zac's scalp causing him to stir restlessly and mumble incoherently. Hearing him moan, she quickly pulled the towel away, her eyes widening again.

Hadley frowned. "I'd better go. I'll be as quick as I can," she promised as she called Polo to her side. "Will you be alright?" Hadley called over her shoulder as she began running down the farm's long driveway.

"Yes. No worries," replied Katie, waving her away. "Just hurry."

As Hadley reached the junction between the limestone driveway and the bitumen road that led into Jasper's Bay, she paused and peered behind her, back towards Katie and the farmhouse. It was both pitch black behind her and pitch black in front of her.

Taking a deep, steadying breath, Hadley tightened her hand around the torch and shone the feeble light out in front of her feet. "Let's do this, Polo." She looked nervously at the bush lining the road and began running with Polo trotting happily beside her. The light wavered as Hadley swung the torch from side to side, trying to see if anything or anyone were hiding in the bushes ready to jump out at her as she ran past.

Hadley was just about to comment on *how it wasn't so bad to be out there* when she heard a loud rustling sound to her right! She froze and immediately turned the torch towards the thick bushes. Her hand shook, and her knuckles turned white as her fingers gripped the torch. The dim light barely lit up the scrub and only served to cast eerie shadows on the road. She shivered. Leaning forward she peered intently into the foliage. *Was that a crouching form she saw?* Hadley suddenly had the intense urge to pee! *What should she do? Run!*

Just as Hadley was about to sprint down the road, Polo began growling loudly, the fur on his back standing up in spikes. She quickly bent down, trying to grab his collar and calm him. However, before she could get a hold of the thin leather band, Polo suddenly lunged forward, running towards the rustling bushes! Hadley frantically tried to grab him. "No Polo!" she yelled in alarm, her voice shaking. Her arm was stretched out in front of her desperately reaching for the dog.

Taking a couple of cautious steps towards the bushes, Hadley called out in alarm. "Come back! It might be a dingo! He'll rip you to shreds." Hadley's voice had become a shriek.

As if hearing the fear in her voice, Polo stopped and turned his head to face Hadley.

Taking advantage of Polo's distraction, Hadley called to him. "Come on, boy," she yelled as she tapped her thigh with her hand. "Come here!" her voice was urgent.

Polo immediately stopped growling and came running back to her, his little tail wagging vigorously as if it were a game. Hadley quickly bent forward and grabbed his collar. "Good boy," she said in a playful tone, even though her heart was hammering wildly in her chest. She once again glanced towards the now still bushes wondering what was hiding there. She wasn't going to wait to find out.

Dragging Polo after her, Hadley began sprinting along the road. She wanted to make as much distance between themselves, and whatever was in those bushes as she could. The light from her torch was gradually growing dimmer as the batteries were draining and she did not want to get stuck out here in the darkness even with Polo by her side.

Her feet made slapping noises along the bitumen as she ran as though she were a sprinter. However, after a few minutes, Hadley had to slow down. Her feet hurt, her legs ached, and her lungs were burning. She couldn't keep up the pace. She slowed to a walk, looking back over her shoulder at the darkness behind her. Hadley couldn't shake the feeling that someone or something was following them.

Swinging the torch from side to side, her eyes darted around. She couldn't hear anything except the cicadas and frogs hiding in the scrub. As she looked down at Polo, Hadley's torch suddenly began to flicker and fade. The already feeble light quickly dwindled to a dim glow barely lighting the bulb.

"Oh No, you don't!" she muttered through gritted teeth, slapping the side of the torch with her palm. "Oh, please don't do this!" Hadley could feel fear creeping into her insides as she now stood in complete darkness. Her legs started to tremble, and her hands shook. "Oh no, no no!" she cried as she bent down, trying to feel for Polo.

The little dog thrust his head into her face and began licking her cheek. Hadley hugged him tightly, burying her face into his fur. She took a deep calming breath, refusing to succumb to the fear she felt.

Trying to give herself courage, Hadley began to sing. Quietly at first and then more loudly. "Shake it off, shake it off. Ooo ooo. Shake it off." Her voice wobbled as she sang.

Gradually feeling a little more confident, Hadley slowly made herself stand and once again began walking towards town. One foot after the other. She shoved the useless torch in her jacket pocket and rubbed her hands together. "You can do this, just keep walking."

Just as Hadley was beginning to feel a little calmer, Polo abruptly dashed ahead of her into the darkness. Hadley's mouth dropped open. "Wait, Polo. Don't leave me!" Hadley once again began running, trying to keep up with the dog.

A few meters ahead, Polo stopped and waited for Hadley, before darting to the left. Raising her eyes from the road, Hadley tried to peer after him. Her eyes had now adjusted to the darkness, and she could make out several large, dark shapes looming to the left of her. She realised with relief; they were houses. She stopped and placed her hands on her knees, letting her head droop down. "We made it."

Hadley breathed out in a long slow breath. *Polo had brought her to the edge of town.* 36 Rosewood Avenue, her old house would be just up ahead. "Oh, thank God!" she cried out, her bottom lip trembling.

Finding an extra burst of energy, Hadley sprinted toward the houses. She needed to find Jason. As she reached number 36, she realised that the house was very dark. Frowning, Hadley wiped her sweaty forehead with the back of her hand and licked her dry lips. *Something wasn't right.* Even without electricity, the children would burn one or two candles or even a small gas lamp if they had one. Hadley couldn't see any light at all through the windows. *Maybe Jason was at the rear of the house?*

Walking up the stone pathway that led to the front of the house, Hadley made her way to the porch and carefully felt for the steps with her foot, before making her way to the front door. "Hey, Jason!" she yelled as she opened the unlocked door. "Jason! You here?"

No one answered. The house was silent.

"Shit. Now what?" Hadley puffed out her cheeks as she used her hands to feel along the wall until she reached the kitchen. Dropping the spent torch onto the kitchen bench, she opened the top-drawer hoping Jason hadn't taken the spare torch they usually kept there.

Feeling around the drawer, her fingers bumped the hard plastic of the torch. "Oh, yes. Thank you!" she exclaimed as she retrieved the torch and switched it on. "We have light!" Hadley breathed out not realising she had been holding her breath. Hadley hated the way complete darkness made her feel so vulnerable.

Looking around the small, familiar kitchen, Hadley spotted a full bucket of water. She smiled. "Hello bucket, nice to see you!" Quickly scooping a cup full of the clean water for herself and a bowlful for Polo, they both drank deeply.

When she had finished drinking, Hadley bent to scratch Polo behind the ears. She looked around. "Well, my friend. Jason is obviously not here like he's supposed to be." Polo lay down in front of her, and she began rubbing his belly. "I bet he's at Logan's house. Looks like we can't stop yet. Sorry boy."

Hadley smiled at Polo before walking into the bathroom to collect a few supplies. Taking a canvas satchel hanging from the doorknob, Hadley opened the bathroom cabinet and loaded the bag with two white crepe bandages, a bottle of antiseptic wash and a pack of paracetamol. *At least the trip to the house wouldn't be a total waste of time.*

Walking back out the front door with Polo at her side, Hadley slung the satchel over her shoulder and started making her way to Logan's house. As much as she wanted to flump down into one of the comfortable chairs in the loungeroom and rest, her journey wasn't over yet. Zac and Lexi still needed her. She still needed to find help and quickly.

CHAPTER TWELVE

H adley was right about Jason being at Logan's house. In fact, Ethan was there too. All three of them had been half-way through a serious game of Risk when Hadley had come bursting through the front door with the news of what had happened to Zac and Lexi.

As Hadley told her story, the three boys stared at her in disbelief.

"I can't bloody believe it!" yelled the normally quiet Jason. He stood quickly and began pacing the room. "We have to get back there right now!"

Logan grabbed Jason's arm, trying to calm him. "Yes, we do, but first we need medical supplies. We have to think clearly about this."

Jason nodded his head. "Right."

Hadley unslung the satchel from her shoulders and plonked it down on the table, knocking over a few of the game pieces. "I grabbed a few things from Rosewood Ave," she said, opening the bag to show the boys.

Logan peered inside to see what Hadley had found. "That's great, Hadley. I just need to go next door to my dad's clinic to collect a couple of extra items." He looked at Jason. "We're going to need a strong needle and thread, butterfly closures and gauze pads."

As Logan and Ethan went to collect the extra supplies, Jason took hold of Hadley's hand and squeezed. "You did a great job getting here so quickly, Hadley. Are you going to be able to run back again? You must be tired."

Hadley smiled weakly at him. "I am, but I'll be alright." She looked towards the back door of the house. "I just need to pee before we go!" she said as she ran towards the door. "I've been holding it all the way here! I was too scared to go in the bushes!"

Jason laughed. "Fair enough I'll just go and help Logan get ready. Then we had better go. The sooner we get to the farm, the sooner we can help Zac, and work out what to do about Lexi." He looked around for Hadley, but she had already run outside.

Once the small group had made their way back to the farm, everyone had pitched in to help carry Zac into the house. Katie had been beside herself with fear for her brother and was so relieved at the sight of them that she couldn't speak for a full 10 minutes. Hadley wrapped a blanket around her small trembling shoulders and helped Katie inside while Logan attempted to stitch the back of Zac's head.

About an hour later, Jason, Ethan and Logan all stood around Zac's bed with Hadley and Katie peering down at the resting Zac. The heavy shovel Kevin had used to king-hit his brother had opened a nasty gash on the back of Zac's head, and he had lost a lot of blood. His face was a pasty white colour, and his lips were blue. Jason and Ethan rubbed Zac's hands between theirs, trying to increase his circulation.

Being the one with the most *medical experience*, Logan had volunteered to stitch Zac's head and made sure he didn't have a concussion. It hadn't been easy, and Logan had needed to shave the back of his friend's head to see the cut properly. Logan had made sure to douse Zac's head with the antiseptic wash Hadley had brought and tried to keep everything as clean as possible, hoping Zac wouldn't develop an infection. He used the flame of a candle to sterilize the needle and scissors and washed his own hands in liquid Dettol, hoping that would be enough to kill any bacteria. The only antibiotics they had left in town were two boxes at his dad's old vet clinic. They were meant for animals; however, animal antibiotics could be used for humans if needed. Logan had also given Zac a couple of painkillers he had locked away in the clinic in case of injuries and emergencies like this one. They soon calmed him down.

Zac had been in a real state when he gained consciousness and wanted to run after his brother then and there. That was before the pain kicked in. Now he lay quietly in his bed, listening to the others talk, his eyes half-closed.

The group of friends stood looking down at Zac with worried expressions on their young faces. Now that he was stitched up and the bleeding stopped, they needed to work out how to help Lexi.

Listening to the others talk, Hadley was striding back and forth across the room, anxious to go after Lexi and Kevin as soon as possible.

Zac suddenly opened his eyes and pulled at Jason's shirt sleeve. His voice was slurred as he spoke. "Those k-kids said they were from Gracetown on the c-coast. That's about 40km w-west from here."

Jason looked at Logan and sighed. "Jeez, that's a long way. It's too far to walk. I suppose we could try and syphon petrol from the old cars in town?"

"I doubt we would find a car that's working, responded Logan, shaking his head in dismay. "No one has driven them for at least six months; the batteries will be flat."

Gingerly raising his head, Zac mumbled something to the group, his voice heavy with the effects of the painkillers.

Katie bent close to him to hear what her brother had to say. She tenderly brushed his sweaty hair from his forehead.

"Use the h-horses," Zac muttered close to her ear. "Just rest them h-halfway, and they'll be fine."

Katie smiled and nodded her head in agreement. *The horses!* That was a great idea. They were going to have to get used to other means of travel now that cars were no longer an option. The farm had four horses, and each one could carry two people.

"Great thinking, mate!" said Ethan, patting his friend on the shoulder. "I'll go and make sure they're watered and fed so we can leave when the sun is up. We should leave early in the morning before it gets too hot."

"I'll help you," offered Jason even though he knew nothing about saddling horses. "The rest of you might want to get a couple of hours of sleep before we go. It won't be long before sunrise," he said, as he started to follow Ethan to the stables.

Before they left the room, Zac groggily tried to sit. "I'm coming too!" he stated emphatically peering determinedly at the others.

Jason cleared his throat and frowned. He walked back over to Zac's bedside. "Err, listen, mate. I don't think that's a good idea," he said, trying to encourage Zac to lay back on the bed. "You don't sound too good, and besides, without an x-ray and stuff, we don't really know your condition."

Grabbing Jason's hand, Zac argued the point. "I'm f-fine. Besides, Kevin is my brother, and I n-need to talk to him." He looked unwaveringly at Jason. "I'm going w-with you!"

"You think you're managing alright now," stated Logan looking at Zac as he waved the box of painkillers in the air. "But that's just because of these. You wait until they wear off." He smiled at his friend. "You're gonna have a nasty headache then, mate."

Listening to Logan, Zac reached behind and touched his fingertips to the back of his head. The wound was incredibly tender, and his fingers could feel the coarse stitches and dried blood on his shaved scalp. *What could have made Kevin do such a thing? He was too young to have the virus so it couldn't be that.* Zac looked back at the others, his voice grave. "I'll deal with that when it h-happens. Just give me some more p-painkillers before we leave, and I'll be alright."

Logan looked at him dubiously. "Hmm. Well, as your *doctor*, I suggest you get some sleep, and we shall see how you are in the morning." He smiled at Zac indulgently before plonking himself in the big comfortable chair by Zac's bed. "I'll stay here in case you need anything."

Zac looked trustingly at Logan and smiled nodding in agreement. He made an excellent *makeshift doctor* for a vet's son! The others slowly made their way out to feed the horses and get some sleep themselves.

"Just make sure you don't l-leave while I'm asleep!" yelled Zac as they wandered out. "I'll n-never forgive you if you do!"

Jason and Ethan glanced at each other awkwardly for a moment before turning to look at Zac. They promised they wouldn't leave without him, even though that was precisely what they meant to do.

CHAPTER THIRTEEN

It was five am, and Hadley was wide awake. She hadn't been able to sleep. She was too worried about Lexi and what had happened to her. It wasn't every day you saw your sister being forcefully shoved into the boot of a car and sped off to an unknown destination.

Peering dismally out into the darkness, Hadley willed the sun to rise so the others could start their long journey in search of her sister. Tapping lightly on the glass of the window with her finger, she dislodged the red dust that had settled there and wondered how long she would have to wait. Hadley wasn't usually a morning person, much preferring to sleep in. However, this morning, she couldn't wait for the sun to rise. Although she desperately wanted to find Lexi, Hadley had agreed to stay with Katie on the farm and look after baby Sarah and the animals while the older kids went searching for her. Besides, she didn't have any idea how to ride a horse. None of the city kids did, which meant they were going to need to share horses with the country kids.

Jason spotted Hadley staring glumly out the window as the first tell-tale orange glow masked the sky signalling the start of the new day. He tapped her lightly on the shoulder. "Do you want a cup of tea? I was going to light the fire and boil some water." The farmhouse had a lovely stone fireplace the children were using to cook and boil water for bathing. This was quite civilised compared to what they were using in town.

Hadley hadn't noticed Jason walk up behind her and nearly jumped out of her skin in fright. She gave a squeal. "Jeeze, Jason! You scared the life out of me. I thought everyone was still asleep?"

Jason perched on the arm of the couch. "Yeah, they are. I couldn't sleep. I suppose it's the adrenaline. Can't you sleep either?"

Hadley shook her head. "Listen, Jason. Do you think you guys could delay leaving for an hour?" She peered out the window, willing the sun to rise faster. "I'd really like to go and see Braydon and Lilly before you leave."

"Why?"

"Well, I think they would want to know what happened to Lexi. Plus, Lilly should know about Zac, he is her brother after all."

Jason thought about what Hadley had said and agreed. He had momentarily forgotten that Lilly was Zac's twin.

Moving away from the dirty window, Hadley cleared her throat before starting to say something else. She had a plan and needed Jason's help. "There's one more thing. I want you to ask Braydon and Lilly to go with you to Gracetown."

Jason, who had just lit the fire and was blowing gently on the smouldering embers, stopped and stared at her. "I'm not sure that's a good idea, Hadley." His expression had turned to one of concern. "I know you are worried about Lexi but taking Braydon and Lilly with us might make things worse."

Hadley threw a twig on the infant fire and shook her head adamantly. "How much worse can it get? My sister's been kidnapped, and Zac is lying in bed with a probable concussion!" She glared at Jason in frustration. "You need more numbers. You're not going to be very threatening with only the three of you, are you?!" Her voice rose emotionally.

Hearing raised voices, Katie had ventured into the living room to see what the commotion was. She had baby Sarah perched expertly on her hip while feeding her a bottle of powdered milk. Katie had overheard what Hadley had said and was already looking for her gumboots and hat. "I'll come with you, Hadley." Her eyes shone brightly with determination. "I want to see Lilly."

Placing her younger sister on the floor, Katie started to look under the couches for her missing boot. She hadn't seen Lilly for weeks, and there was no way she was going to miss the opportunity to see her now. She had heard the older kids saying Lilly was camped nearby, she just had to find out where. Her eyes settled on Jason. *Maybe he could take them to her sister?*

Jason could feel someone staring at him and swiftly turned around. He immediately saw Katie standing behind him with a pleading look on her face. Looking from Katie to Hadley, he held up his hands in defence. "Oh, no. I don't think it's a good idea. What if they go feral?"

"They won't."

"They might."

"They won't. They've got the bush tonic, haven't they?" Katie argued determinedly. She stood with her hands placed firmly on her hips. "Besides, I'm going to go and look for her no matter what. Wouldn't it be better if you just took us there with you? It would be safer than me, Sarah and Hadley wandering around the bush until we find them. We might get lost!" She smiled cheekily knowing from the look on Jason's face, she had already won the argument.

Reaching forward and placing a billy can full of water on the fire ready to make tea, Jason sighed heavily, his shoulders slumped in defeat. "Alright. I'll take you. We can't stay too long though. I think that too much social interaction irritates them."

"Agreed," stated Hadley. "Besides, you have a long ride ahead of you on the horses."

Jason grimaced at the thought. "Well, I hope Logan knows how to ride a horse because I sure don't!" He started laughing loudly before putting his hand over his mouth, trying not to wake the others. "I don't even know how to put the saddle on!" It was one of the new skills all the city kids would have to learn.

"Come on then," Jason sighed as he stood. His tea would have to wait. "I can hear the others stirring. I'll just let them know where we're going. I don't expect they'll be pleased about it though."

Not far from the farmhouse was the little area where Braydon and Lilly were staying. The improvised camp consisted of two tents with sleeping bags and foam mats, a small camp stove, two solar lamps and a ten-litre plastic container for water. The flies were terrible and the mosquitos persistent, however, compared to where they had been sleeping previously without any protection at all, it was a luxury. Braydon was in the process of hanging a makeshift washing line when he froze at the sight of others approaching. He called for Lilly, who immediately scurried out from her tent and stood stiffly as if she was on roll call.

"Who's there?" Lilly called out anxiously, reaching for her flask of bush tonic attached to the belt of her scruffy jeans. In the dim morning light, she could see three bodies approaching.

Braydon dragged a large branch from beside his tent and held it over his shoulder like a baseball bat. His heart hammered in his chest, and he could feel the heat flaming in his cheeks. He breathed in deeply and slowly through his nostrils, trying to control the impending rage.

Suddenly a white form flashed past him running toward Lilly. Alarmed, Braydon raised the branch ready to swing.

"Lilly!" yelled the white form, enthusiastically. "I've missed you!" she held forth a yellow and white daisy chain weaved into a crown.

Braydon blinked his eyes rapidly. *It was only a little girl wearing a long white nightdress. A small toddler was clinging to her like a monkey.* Quickly dropping the stick by his side, Braydon dived into his tent, trying to reign in his emotions. It wasn't easy, as the fire raged in his belly like a hot phall curry, heating him from the inside. Bringing his bottle of bush brew to his lips, he drank deeply. All the time, breathing slowly and rhythmically as if he were a yoga instructor.

At last, Braydon calmed the wave of emotions and poked his head from the tent to see who the visitors were. The young girl who had run past him was now hugging Lilly tightly around her neck and whispering in her ear. He could tell that Lilly was finding the closeness difficult, but she was persevering. Although he had never met them, Braydon figured they must be Lilly's two younger sisters.

Glancing sideways he saw that Jason was also here, as was Hadley. Pulling the tent flaps aside and stepping out, Braydon happily looked around for Lexi. He was unable to see her and wondered where she was. He hoped she had managed to brew some more of the bush tonic as they only had a few bottles left.

"You alright, Braydon?" asked Jason, warily holding onto Hadley's arm.

Braydon gave him a lopsided smile, raising the bottle of tonic to show him. "I'm okay thanks. Where's Lexi?" he asked cheerfully looking forward to seeing her again. He hadn't been able to stop thinking about her ever since they met up yesterday.

Jason cleared his throat uncertainly and looked down at Hadley. She nodded her head. They had to tell them what had happened at the farm last night. They both had a right to know, especially Lilly.

"Katie. You and Sarah come and sit by Hadley," suggested Jason pointing to a fallen log. Even though Katie wanted to sit with Lilly, Jason thought it best they leave a gap between them. He wasn't sure how Lilly and Braydon would accept the bad news they were about to tell them. He had been shocked and extremely angry himself when Hadley had come running into town to tell them the story only a few hours before. Heaven knew how these two would handle the news, as volatile as they were, even with the tonic in their systems.

Jason cleared his throat once more and began to describe the events of the last few hours. Katie and Hadley spoke up whenever he missed something out.

Lilly stared at Jason in disbelief as he described what Kevin had done. "Are you really talking about Kevin? I can't understand how he could do that to Zac!" She closed her eyes for a moment and breathed in deeply. "They have never really got along, but to do something so vicious is unbelievable." She stood and ran her fingers through the short stubble on her head. Her long hair had not yet grown back from where Broc and the gang had shorn her head only a few weeks before. She looked so sad.

Walking over to where her two sisters sat still and watchful. Lilly reached forward and took baby Sarah's face in her hands. She kissed her tenderly on the top of her head, breathing in her clean baby smell. Sarah gurgled and reached for Lilly's finger, trying to thrust it into her mouth with her chubby pink fingers. Lilly smiled. Something she hadn't done much of lately.

Positioning herself to sit next to Katie, Lilly grabbed her sister's small hand. It had been a long time since they had the chance to talk or play. "You weren't there when Kevin hit Zac, were you?" Lilly asked with concern leaning in closer to Katie.

"No. I was inside with Hadley, and Sarah was asleep," said Katie, turning to smile at Hadley.

Lilly breathed a sigh of relief. She squeezed Katie's hand. "I really miss being on the farm with you guys," Lilly whispered, her chin quivering. "I'm so glad I'm not out here on my own," she said, glancing sideways at Braydon who gave her a small smile. "But I wish I could come home. I hate being out here."

Katie put Sarah on the ground and moved closer to Lilly. She wrapped her arms around her neck and hugged her tightly. "I wish you could come home too," she whispered in her ear.

Lilly pulled back from Katie, she had tears in her eyes, and her cheeks were flushed with emotion. "I'm coming back to the farm with you," she said, her voice trembling. "I need to be with my family, and I need to see how Zac is."

Jason started to speak in protest, but Lilly held up her hand. "Don't worry. I won't stay long. I can keep myself under control for a short while. I really need to see my brother." Being twins, both Zac and Lilly had a special bond, and now they were apart, she felt isolated.

Lilly continued. "Plus, I want to help rescue Lexi. After all, it's because of Kevin that she's in trouble. I think I owe her that." Lilly stood and pulled Katie to her feet, ready to walk to the farm.

Jason looked as though he wanted to protest, but what could he say? What right did he have to tell Lilly she couldn't see her injured twin or help rescue her friend? Instead, Jason turned to stare at the early morning sky now lit with beautiful pinks and purples. Another day was beginning. "Come on then. We'd better make our way back. The others will be waiting."

In a nearby Marri gum tree, a Kookaburra and his mate looked down on them and let out their laughing cry. Jason placed his hands on his hips and peered at the birds. "I hope you're not laughing at us!" he said smirking. "Just because we plan to ride over 40km on horseback to a town we've never been to before, with an unstable girl who could blow at any moment riding beside us. There's no need to laugh. We know exactly what we're doing." Jason shook his head and scratched his chin. It did seem like a completely crazy idea, but what choice did the group have. They couldn't just abandon Lexi to an uncertain fate.

* * *

Hadley, who had been quietly watching Lilly and Braydon, hoping they would agree to help, breathed a sigh of relief. Standing in front of Lilly, who now wore Katie's daisy crown on her head, Hadley gave her a huge smile. "Thank you for agreeing to help Lexi," she said.

"It's the least I can do," replied Lilly, looking at Katie and Sarah. "I know how horrible it is not having your sister around."

Hadley nodded and turned to face Braydon. He was standing quietly to the side, watching the group. His hands were shoved deep into his pockets. "And you're coming too. Right, Braydon?" asked Hadley hopefully. "We need you to help rescue Lexi."

Braydon looked down at his dirty, scuffed shoes. There was a small hole forming in the right sneaker just where his big toe was. He examined that hole as if it were the most fascinating thing in the world. Anything to not have to look up at their expectant faces.

"I know what you want, Hadley," Braydon said quietly. "You want me to ride in and rescue Lexi like a knight in shining armour, but I just can't do it!"

It wasn't that Braydon was a coward or that he didn't care enough for Lexi. In fact, he cared deeply for her. It was just that he was afraid of losing control and killing someone again. The fight with his cousin Broc on the night of the bonfire and his unexpected death at his own hands had shocked Braydon to his inner core. To lose complete control like that had been alarming.

He wasn't ready to put himself in that situation. He never wanted to kill anyone ever again.

Without looking up, Braydon shook his head, before swiftly turning around and striding into the bush. "I need to be alone," he called out to the others as he left.

Hadley yelled after him, her eyes wide, and her voice thick with emotion. "Wait, Braydon! Don't you want to help Lexi?!" she sounded shocked.

Braydon kept walking; his face grim. *They didn't understand, he just didn't trust himself yet, even with the bush tonic calming his nerves.*

Hadley stared after him, uncertain of what to say. She had been so sure that he would want to help.

"Come on," said Jason pulling on Hadley's arm. "We had better get back to the farm. The others will want to be leaving soon."

"Yes, and I want to see Zac before we go," Lilly reminded him as she looked back over her shoulder at Braydon. She hoped he wasn't beating himself up too much about his decision not to join them. Lilly knew it can't have been easy for him.

As the group made their way back to the farm, Katie asked Lilly if she wanted to carry baby Sarah. Lilly quickly declined, preferring to keep her distance from the others a little as they walked. Even though she was managing to control her rages to some extent, the proximity of other people increased the difficulty. Lilly didn't want to risk any outbursts in front of her little sisters. The last thing Lilly wanted to do was give Katie and Sarah nightmares about her.

Once they reached the farm, Lilly ran straight to Zac's bedroom. The window was open, and the sound of the early morning cicadas could be heard throughout the room. As soon as Lilly entered, she gasped in horror. Her usually robust brother looked pale and drawn and obviously in pain. The sight of Zac propped up in bed with a large white bandage wound around his head brought tears to her eyes.

"Oh Zac, what has Kevin done! You look a mess."

Zac laughed. "Thanks, sis. Nice to see you too! Y you look like you could do with a hot shower yourself." They laughed together. It was nice to be bantering again, and it brought a smile to Lilly's face.

"I suppose I probably do stink a bit." Lilly sniffed her armpit in distaste. "Braydon and I have been doing it tough out in the bush. The tents you guys set up will make things a lot easier, though."

Lilly went over to stand by Zac's bed. "Let's have a look at what he's done to you," she said carefully lifting the bandage from the back of his head and peeking underneath. She could see a nasty red wound with course black stitches in a jagged line. The injury looked clean though, and she thought Logan had done an excellent job of stitching him up.

"How are you feeling?" Lilly asked as she carefully replaced the bandages.

"I...I. I've got a sh... shocking headache, and I feel a bit dizzy," replied Zac stuttering. "But I'm all...all right."

Lilly leaned forward and peered at Zac's face. He had dark rings under his eyes and there was a smudge of dried blood on the side of his cheek.

Leaning back once more, Lilly place her hands on her hips and asked, "what's with the stammer? Maybe you've got brain damage."

Zac frown at her. "Gee, t thanks, sis. That makes me feel so m much better!"

Lilly shrugged. "I wasn't trying to be mean. I've just never heard you stutter before, that's all."

Just at that moment, Logan came into the room to check on Zac. He stopped when he noticed Lilly standing beside Zac's bed.

"Oh. Hi, Lilly," he said, a little surprised at seeing her. He ran his fingers through his hair and glanced at her nervously. "How are you, feeling?"

"I'm fine, Logan," she replied, patting her flask of remedy attached to her belt. "I just wanted to see Zac. He seems to be stuttering an awful lot."

"I'm ok," interrupted Zac as he straightened himself in his bed. "It's only a stutter. I'm sure it will go away eventually."

Logan frowned as he walked up to Zac's bed. He leaned in close to Zac and peered into his eyes. His pupils *looked* normal. And he didn't seem to have a temperature. "I'm not sure what to make of it, Zac. Maybe you're still in shock?" he said, hoping the stuttering wasn't a permanent thing for Zac's sake.

Lilly handed Zac a glass of water before taking a drink herself from the flask hanging at her hip. She now carried some of the bush tonic with her wherever she went. It really helped her stay relaxed and calm. Screwing the cap back on the bottle, she looked at her brother in concern. "Why did Kevin do it Zac?"

Smoothing the bedsheets in front of him, Zac explained that Kevin had previously been stealing chickens from the farm and ruining the corn. Last night he had returned with Aaron and Cindy the two old gang members, plus a couple of younger kids and demanded the rest of the chickens. When Zac had refused, Kevin had hit him over the head with a shovel when his back was turned and kidnapped Lexi!

Even though Lilly had heard the same story from Jason and Katie only an hour before, she still couldn't quite believe it. No one could work out why he had resorted to such violence? Lilly stared out the window looking for some answers.

Soon after, Ethan knocked on the bedroom door. "Sorry to interrupt," he said quietly. "The horses are saddled and ready to go. We had better make a start, it's a long way, and we have to ride back again too after we find Lexi."

Lilly quickly stood. "Yes, let's make a start. I've got a few things I'd like to say to Kevin!" she strode briskly out of the room.

Zac pulled the bedsheets back from the bed and swung his legs onto the cold floor. He was fully clothed and ready to join the others.

Hearing movement, Lilly twisted around to look at her brother. "Zac! What do you think you're doing?" said Lilly, her voice anxious. "Get back in bed and rest. *I'll* go and sort out Kevin."

Ignoring his sister, Zac bent over to put on his boots. He felt a wave of nausea and dizziness pass over him as he leaned over; however, he kept that to himself. If he mentioned the slightest feeling of being unwell, the others would try and force him to stay in bed.

"No way, Lilly," argued Zac as he pulled on his boots. "I'm coming too. I'm the reason Lexi is in this mess." He sounded annoyed. "I asked her to come over and help keep a watch on the farm. She would be at home with Hadley if our brother weren't such a wanker!"

Lilly placed her hand on Zac's shoulder. "I know he *is* a wanker, but that's hardly your fault. You need to rest."

Zac, however, was adamant that he was going with them and no amount of reasoning could persuade him otherwise. Eventually, the others gave up and agreed to let him join them. They didn't particularly think riding a horse was a good idea with his recent injury, however, apart from tying Zac to the bed, *which they did briefly consider*, there wasn't much else they could do.

* *
*

Soon after, the group set off to Gracetown. Loaded with water, food and a map, the little company hoped they would be able to rescue Lexi. Hadley and Katie stood at the main gate and waved them off, wishing them good luck. Hadley was especially teary and thanked them all for going such a long way to find her sister. She knew she would never have been able to do it without their help.

Just as the children were about to turn from the farm driveway onto the main road, a lone figure came sprinting after them. It was Braydon. He said he had changed his mind and wanted to help.

Hadley watching from the farmhouse grinned and clapped her hands when she saw him. "I knew Braydon wouldn't be able to resist helping Lexi," she nudged Katie in the side.

Katie nodded and smiled. She too waved good-bye as she watched the departing group leave.

Lilly and Zac were on one horse, Logan and Jason on another and Ethan on the last. Braydon quickly scrambled up behind Ethan as Lilly looked at him questioningly. Braydon gave her a slight nod as if to say, *I'll be alright*. He lifted the flap on his backpack to show her two extra bottles of remedy tucked inside. She smiled thankfully, having only remembered to bring one bottle herself.

With everyone now ready to leave, the group of rescuers rode away in search of Lexi and her captors in Gracetown, each of them wondering what they would find when they reached their destination.

"You have taken some of the remedy, haven't you?" Ethan asked Braydon, his voice nervous.

"Yeah, mate. I have," smiled Braydon as he gripped tightly to the saddle. He looked down at the full flask of bush brew attached to his belt, hoping it and the extra he had brought would be enough to sustain him on the journey. They had a long way to ride and sitting this close to another person was already making him feel uncomfortable.

Trying to calm his thoughts, Braydon looked to the sky and prayed that he would make it.

Chapter Fourteen

Gracetown

The ride to Gracetown was long and monotonous. To stay on track, the group used Zac's compass and an old road map of the south-west of Australia. They had decided to stick to the main highway leading south out of Jasper's Bay.

As they made their way out of town, the group passed the local rubbish tip. The children of Jasper's Bay had continued to dump their rubbish there and without any bulldozers to push the refuse into the dirt the place stank. Long before they reach the tip, they could smell it. Remnants of rotten food, discarded plastic packaging, and cardboard cereal boxes littered the ground. Large brown rats scurried along the piles of garbage and flies swarmed the area. It was disgusting.

The children stopped to look at the rubbish tip.

"Oh my God!" exclaimed Lilly, as she pinched her nose, trying to quell the smell. "That stench is getting worse!" She turned her head away and tried not to dry heave.

Zac pulled a face. "Geeze, it does reek," he agreed. "I haven't been out here for a while. Been too busy on the farm."

"We're going to have to do something about it soon, or some kid is going to get typhoid or something," said Jason, squinting his eyes and peering distastefully at the stinking heap. "Oh, lord. There are rats everywhere!" he shivered in disgust.

"Add it to the long list of things we need to do," sighed Zac. "Come on, we'd better keep going." He squeezed his thighs into the side of his horse to get her moving again. They had a long way to travel and had only just begun.

The long stretch of road out of town was hardly any better than the rubbish tip. The highway was littered with abandoned cars and other junk. Used aluminium drink cans, plastic bags and old discarded newspapers tarnished the landscape. They were the futile signs of the people who had tried to outrun the KV17 virus and failed.

After a couple of hours of riding, the children stopped for a much-needed rest. Zac had spotted a little creek not far from the road, and they decided it was the perfect place to take a break and refill their water bottles. Everyone's bums and thighs were sore from riding, and the horses needed a drink. There was a cluster of tall eucalypt trees under which they could sit, and the creek water looked clean. Ethan had a pack of purification tablets in his backpack, so they added those to their water bottles just for extra safety. No one wanted to get dysentery from contaminated water, and they didn't know what was upstream from them.

While Zac and the others led their horses down to the creek bed, Jason decided to look in one of the abandoned cars on the highway.

Wandering a short distance from the others, Jason made his way to a red Holden Commodore parked on the side of the road. The vehicle looked as though it had been sitting for a long while as it was covered in dust and grime. Walking up to the car, Jason used the sleeve of his shirt to rub a clean area on one of the side windows and peeked inside. His curiosity was making him nosy.

"Oh Jeezus!" he exclaimed, immediately reeling away from the car. Jason's face had turned a shade of green, and his mouth stretched downwards in a grim line. He covered his mouth with his hand.

In the front seat of the car were the decomposing remains of two adults and in the back, an infant's tiny body sat strapped into its baby carrier. Without the parents, the baby didn't have any chance of surviving.

Perspiration formed on the top of Jason's lip and his stomach reeled. Quickly turning his head, he vomited on the ground, barely missing his shoes.

"What's wrong?" called Lilly, seeing Jason puke. "Are you alright?" she ran up to where Jason stood bent over with his hands on his knees.

Jason turned his head and peered up at her, his face still looked peaky. He pointed back towards the car.

Lilly cautiously wandered closer to the vehicle. She hesitated for a moment before peeking inside just as Jason had done. "Oh. That's so horrible!" cried Lilly, quickly stepping backwards. Her eyes were full of hot tears. "Why didn't anyone help it?" She stared at the remains of the baby.

"Look around Lilly," said Jason with his arms stretched wide. "There's no one else here. We're in the middle of nowhere."

Lilly wiped the tears from her eyes with the back of her hand and nodded. "I guess you're right. It just seems so brutal."

"Yeah, it is brutal," said Jason as he put his arm around Lilly's shoulders and led her back towards where the others were resting. Everyone was enjoying being in the shade and out of the burning sun.

"Come on," Jason said to the group. "We'd better keep going." He glanced sadly back towards the abandoned car. "We don't want to end up stuck out here like them."

The group slowly got back onto their horses, still feeling saddle sore and tired. They continued their journey onto Gracetown in silence. After Jason and Lilly described the awful scene of the family in the car, nobody felt like talking. It was a horrible reminder of the loss of their own families. Jason didn't stop to look in any more vehicles, and neither did anyone else.

Eventually, after five hours of solid riding, the small group finally made it to the outskirts of Gracetown. The horses had done a supreme job of carrying them all the way through the inhospitable terrane of dust, flies and boredom! Zac, Lilly and Braydon all looked a little worse for wear, with Zac looking particularly pale. However, now they had finally made it to Gracetown, all three were determined to see the journey to its end.

The small company decided to stop on the edge of the town and get their bearings. Having never been to Gracetown before, none of them were sure of the layout and didn't want to *run* into anyone before they were ready.

Lilly's skin was pink from sunburn, and she looked exceedingly uncomfortable. Gripping onto the saddle, she carefully dismounted from her horse. "Yikes, my thighs hurt. I'm going to be walking bow legged for a few days," she said grimacing.

"Me too," agreed Jason, who was not used to riding a horse.

Lilly smiled at him and began looking around. The first thing she noticed was a little graveyard just ahead of them. There were tall clumps of grass and weeds on the edges of the cemetery, and it looked like a good place for the horses to rest and graze. Now they had found the town, which hadn't been easy without GPS or Google maps, they needed to agree on their next course of action.

"Zac and I need to find Kevin and have a *family chat* with him," suggested Lilly as she stroked the neck of her horse.

"Yes, you two do that. Jason, Ethan and I will look for Lexi," agreed Braydon, standing with his arms folded across his chest. His face was covered in perspiration.

Jason glanced warily at Braydon, taking a step away from him. "Are you okay, mate?"

Braydon pulled the bottom of his shirt up and wiped his sweaty face. "Yeah. I'll be alright. Let's just get this done as quickly as possible. Don't forget. If any of you get into trouble, blow on your whistle," he said, pulling a plastic whistle from his pocket and placing the string around his neck. His hands were shaking.

The others did the same.

Jason turned away from Braydon and faced Ethan. "Is he going to be okay?" he whispered, raising his eyebrows.

"God, I hope so. We won't be able to get him home if he freaks out." Ethan shook his head. "It probably wasn't the wisest choice to bring him along," he murmured behind his hand.

Jason rubbed his chin and took a long drink from his water bottle. "Hmm. Well, it's too late now. Isn't it?"

Hearing the boys talking, Braydon looked at his half-empty bottle of tonic, swirling the contents around in the container. He took a small sip, trying to make it last. Overhead, a flock of bright red and green Rosellas squawked noisily as they flew over the group. Braydon tilted his head upwards and distractedly watched the birds fly over. They gave him an idea.

Tapping Zac on the shoulder, Braydon asked, "if you and Lilly can distract Kevin and his pals for long enough, it might give the rest of us a good chance of finding Lexi. Don't mention that we are here with you. Hopefully, he will think it's only you two come to see him." He shrugged.

"Y..y..yes," agreed Zac, his stutter continuing to affect him. "That's a g.g.good idea. Better if he doesn't know you're h.h.here."

Zac used his finger to scratch underneath the irritating bandage on his head.

Braydon patted him on the shoulder and went to stand by Lilly who had wandered over to the little graveyard. "You alright?" Braydon asked Lilly as he offered her his drink flask.

Lilly nodded. "That's ok. I have my own," she said, showing him her flask. "Better keep yours for yourself. It might be a long, difficult day. I hope we can keep it together."

Braydon sighed and gave her a lopsided smile. Both of them were going to find it a challenge to remain calm. Especially if things got heated with Kevin.

Lilly pointed to one of the graves "Look. Some of these are obviously homemade." The grave Lilly was gesturing to consisted of two pieces of timber tied together with the deceased's name written in marker pen. Three of the tiny *homemade* graves stood side by side as a stark reminder of how fragile life was. One of the graves had two small metal match-box cars tenderly positioned on the gravesite. Another had a faded coloured pin-wheel and a pink toy rabbit that was missing a glass eye.

"They look new," said Braydon sadly. "The ground isn't covered by weeds like the other plots." Picking up the pink rabbit, Braydon turned it over in his hands, before returning it to the child's grave.

"Yeah, I think you're right," agreed Lilly, as she wrapped her arms around herself and squatted to take a closer look at the children's graves. Her eyes filled with tears. "The kids in this town have obviously been doing it tough just like us," she whispered, breaking off a dandelion flower from a nearby plant, and placing it on one of the graves.

Clearing the dust from the cross with her fingers, Lilly suddenly stood and wiped her hands on her pants. She blinked away her tears. "My bloody brother is taking advantage of these kids! Come on. We should get going," suggested Lilly with a fierce look on her face. "I want to talk to Kevin."

"Yes, and we need to find Lexi. Shall we leave the horses tied up here?" asked Braydon, pointing to a clump of Eucalyptus trees. "They'd probably be safer than in the main part of town." The last thing they needed was someone stealing their horses. There would be no way of making the journey back to Jasper's Bay without them.

Jason agreed, adding that the group's arrival would be less noticeable if they didn't take the horses with them. Plus, if Kevin thought Lilly and Zac were on their own, it would give the others a chance to find Lexi and free her before Kevin realised what was actually going on.

The group considered leaving someone behind to guard the horses, but in the end, they decided to risk leaving them on their own. After the long ride to Gracetown, no one wanted to stay behind and miss out on all the action. It was agreed to leave the horses to rest in the shade of the tall eucalypt trees, while the children walked the rest of the way into town on foot.

"G..good luck," Zac said to Ethan, waving his hand. "I hope sh.. she's okay."

Ethan peered at his friend, sadly. Zac's face was a pasty white colour. He could see Zac was suffering after the long ride. "You should have stayed home Zac. You don't look so good."

Zac looked up and nodded. "I f f feel bloody lousy, but I'll manage." He smiled weakly. "I just w…want to speak to Kevin again. I w..want to know why he's doing this," he said, as he slung his black backpack onto his broad shoulders.

"Yeah, I know," said Ethan in sympathy. "Just try and stay out of the sun when you can. We don't want you getting heatstroke." It was now the middle of the day, and the temperature was sweltering.

Logan walked over to the two boys and handed Zac his thermos of water. "Take this with you, Zac. You're going to need it."

"What about you?"

Logan waved a water bottle at Zac. "I've got another one," he said, smiling.

"Thanks," said Zac, nodding. "Well, let's go," he suggested, walking towards Lilly. The group would need to find Lexi soon if they were going to make the long trek back to Jasper's Bay before it became too dark.

As the children made their way on foot into Gracetown, they noticed just how run-down the place was. Many of the houses on the outskirts of town, looked abandoned. Tall, waist-high weeds covered the front yards. Broken timber slats hung loosely from the walls, and most of the windowpanes were smashed, leaving the interiors open to the elements.

Several mangy dogs growled at them as they walked past the overgrown yards. Left without anyone to care for them, they had become skinny and hostile. Ready to bare their teeth at anyone who ventured too near. The children gave them a wide berth as they walked past.

There were broken glass bottles, rusty soft-drink cans and spindly weeds covering the little-used sidewalks. Everywhere they looked, there were signs of hardship and neglect. It was difficult not to feel some sorrow for the children of this town, who were obviously suffering.

As Lilly and Zac separated from the others, it wasn't long before the rest of the group reached the central part of town. Once thriving businesses and shops lined the small street. Like the abandoned houses, the shopfronts were covered in black graffiti. Obscene words marked the walls in tall jagged letters, and crude pictures defaced the bricks.

Looking further down the street, Braydon noticed a couple of young children squatting in the dusty road playing with faded toy cars. The children seemed to be around three or four years-of-age and were extremely dirty. Their clothing was torn and hanging from their shoulders, and their hair stood out in matted clumps. A thin red Kelpie dog sat by the youngsters as if keeping guard.

Braydon nodded his head towards a side street. "Let's go down there," he whispered, not wanting to be seen.

Ethan and Jason agreed, and the trio snuck down the side street on their search for Lexi. Unsure of the layout of the town, they had no idea where to begin looking and hoped for some kind of sign to point them in the right direction.

As Braydon peered at the row of buildings facing them, he scratched his head in dismay. "This is going to take all day. We can't just go from building to building looking for her," he complained. "Why don't we just ask one of those younger kids if they know anything? Most little kids are honest."

Ethan looked at Braydon doubtfully. "Hmm, I'm not so sure," he replied. "Why don't we start looking in this group of buildings and if we come across anyone, we can ask them?" He shrugged. "I doubt they'll tell us, though."

Braydon grinned at him, feeling much happier since he had been consuming Lexi's tonic. "Have some faith mate. Not everyone is all bad. Look at me, I came good."

Ethan laughed and nodded. "Yeah, okay. You're right. I guess *not everyone* is bad. Come on then," he said, walking towards a small brick building. "Let's start in this one."

Carefully pushing open the door to the nearest building, Ethan cautiously peeped inside, not sure what he would see. It looked to be an old convenience store. Most of the shelves inside were picked clean of food and other useful items leaving only packets of hair dye, shaving cream and arthritis lotions. *How quickly these toiletries and medications had become unimportant and disregarded in a world inhabited by children.*

Ethan squinted his eyes in the dimness and scoured the room, looking for signs of Lexi.

Piles of old magazines and newspapers littered the floor, and the unmistakable smell of mildew and decay filled the air. As Jason stood holding the door open, a giant brown rat scurried across the floor. The light streaming into the dim room from the open doorway had disturbed its slumber.

Leaning forward, Jason reached to pick up an old computer magazine only to find it covered in animal urine and droppings. He hastily dropped it to the floor in disappointment. "She's not here," he muttered. Jason's shoulders drooped. "Let's move on," he called out wanting to leave. "This shop reeks, and it's depressing." He picked up a squashed box of cornflakes before throwing the empty packet away in disappointment.

Leaving the store, the trio turned towards the next building, an old real estate office. "Next one," said Jason pushing the door open with his shoulder. He wrinkled his nose as a strong smell of mould, and rotten food wafted from the doorway. Just as he was about to step inside the building, a voice called out from across the street.

"Hey!" yelled the voice. "Who are you! What do you think you're doing?"

Jason paused and came back into the street. He raised his hand to his face shielding his eyes from the glare of the sun while trying to see who was calling to them.

It was a young boy of about eleven or twelve, and he looked as though he were carrying something. The boy watched them for a moment before crossing the road towards them. He took small cautious steps as he walked, continually looking over his shoulder.

"What do you want?" said the boy once he reached them. His face held a deep scowl, and his lips were pursed together. The young boy held a fishing rod in one hand and two large silver fish in the other. They looked freshly caught.

Braydon, with his arms folded tightly across his chest, returned the boy's glare before taking a large step towards him.

Not wanting the situation to escalate, Jason quickly moved in front of Braydon, holding him back with his palm on Braydon's chest. "Let's keep this friendly," Jason said quietly. "Maybe this kid can tell us where Lexi is?"

Braydon took a step back.

Jason held up his hand in a friendly manner. "Hey, how's it going? Nice fish," he said, pointing to the boy's catch.

The boy looked down at the fish before quickly hiding them behind his back.

Jason laughed. "Don't worry. We're just here to find our friend, and then we will be gone." He gave the boy a big toothy grin trying to look friendly. "You haven't seen a teenage girl with long brown hair around, have you? She might be with another boy and girl."

The young boy's face turned red, and he looked embarrassed. He rested the handle of his fishing rod on the ground and peered a little anxiously at the three older boys. "Um, hi. I'm Jake," he said, nodding his head slightly.

"Hi, Jake. Do you know where our friend is?" asked Jason, raising his eyebrows. "Her name is Lexi, and it's important we find her."

"Yes," replied Jake quietly, glancing behind him. "I know where she is."

"Where?!" demanded Braydon pushing past Jason to roughly grab Jake by his shirt. He glared at Jake, his eyes bulging as he loomed over the younger skinny boy. Braydon's mouth had become a twisted snarl.

"I can take you to her!" Jake cried out, trying to break away from the older boy. His fishing gear falling to the ground with a clatter. "I just want you to know that us kids here in Gracetown, didn't want any part of this!" His voice was now high-pitched and frantic.

Jake went on to tell them about the bullying and threats made by Kevin and Cindy, and the dire conditions they were living in. He explained how they had been desperate for food and so reluctantly agreed to go to Jasper's Bay with Kevin who had promised them provisions. Jake held up the two fish he had caught. "I'm the only one providing any food," he sighed heavily. "If I don't catch any fish, we don't eat."

Braydon slowly let go of Jake's now crumpled shirt and backed away. He unclenched his fist and quickly took several swigs of the tonic in his hip flask, trying to regain control of himself. The contents were bitter the back of his throat burned as he swallowed. Standing with his hands on his hips, facing away from the others, Braydon tried to take long, slow breaths. Gradually, he began to calm down.

Looking back at the young kid, Braydon sighed and rubbed his top lip. "Look, mate. I can see you're doing it tough and I'm sorry, but right now we're here for our friend, Lexi. Can you show us where she is?" Braydon asked with his voice now calm.

Looking relieved, Jake nodded to Braydon and pointed to a two-story office building down the road. The buildings used to belong to the town council but now stood abandoned and useless.

"I'll take you the back way, so you won't be seen," suggested Jake as he bent to pick up his fallen fishing rod. "Kevin won't be happy if he knows you're here."

Braydon laughed and started walking towards the direction the young boy had pointed. "I couldn't care less what Kevin thinks," he said saltily. "And neither should you."

Jake straightened his shoulders and smoothed out his crumpled shirt. He quickly walked to catch up with the taller boy with the mass of red curly hair. "You're right," he agreed, looking up at Braydon. "It doesn't matter what Kevin thinks. He's a stranger here."

Braydon stopped for a moment to look at Jake. "That's right mate. This isn't his town, it's yours," he said winking. "Just remember that."

Jason and Ethan watched Jake run after Braydon. "How old do you think he is?" asked Jason.

Ethan peered after the boy and shrugged. He was obviously malnourished as his ribs were clearly showing through his thin white dirty t-shirt. "He looks young. He clearly knows how to fish, though, so I don't know why he's so skinny." Ethan started to trot after the boy and Braydon. "Maybe he's looking after a lot of other kids."

Jason wiped the sweat from his forehead with the back of his hand and peered up at the endless blue sky. "Yeah, probably. I feel sorry for them. It must be difficult for these young kids without any adults around. It's bloody difficult for *me*," he muttered, before running to catch up with the others. As harsh as it was, right now, their job was to rescue Lexi, not solve everyone else's problems. They could give the young boy some advice, but ultimately, the kid would have to work out how to survive on his own. They all had to.

Jake took the other boys to a building not far from where they had been standing.

"At least we were in the right vicinity," said Jason, a wide grin spreading across his face. He began walking towards the building with a bounce in his step.

The building looked like an old warehouse and once again, all the windows at ground level, and a few of those higher up had been smashed. The white paint had faded and was peeling from the tin walls, and like everything else in this town, it was looking run down.

As Jason reached the building, he peered up at the metal walls. He frowned. All his good humour now vanished.

"So, where is she?" Jason asked heatedly, his voice gruff with emotion. He touched his hand to the metal wall and pulled it away quickly. The metal was hot to touch. "We have to get her out now! Lexi will be roasting in there in this heat!"

"Yes, I know. And I'm trying to help," explained Jake as he looked at Jason pleadingly. "She's in a room at the far end, down the bottom of a flight of stairs. You can't miss it. It's the only room down there," he said, backing away. "It used to be a wine cellar."

"Hey! Where are you going?" growled Braydon glaring at Jake.

"I have to prepare these fish before they turn bad. I've got mouths to feed," Jake explained, calling over his shoulder as he jogged away. "I've helped you as much as I can."

The youngsters in town hadn't eaten since Jake and Kally had returned from Jasper's Bay. If the group had been able to bring food back with them, it would be different. As it was, Jake was again going to have to try and feed the ten of them with two fish.

As Jake turned the corner and jogged towards his home, he looked down at the two fish dangling loosely in his hand. "I hope there will be enough to go around," he murmured.

Looking up from the fish, Jake slowed his jog to a walk and peered down the street towards the centre of town. He couldn't see anyone about apart from a couple of the younger kids playing in the street.

"I'd better keep this catch a secret from Kevin and that lot. There is no way I'm going to share it with them, not after the trick they pulled on us!" he muttered angrily, gripping the fish tightly.

He stopped and glanced back over his shoulder at Braydon and the other two boys he left at the warehouse. His face was conflicted with his eyebrows drawn together. "I hope Lexi's alright," he said quietly, before running towards his home once more.

Braydon watched Jake run away. "Come on," he said, his eyebrow twitching. "We know where Lexi is, we don't need him anymore." He leaned against the heavy door with his forearm, pushing it open as quietly as he could. He held his finger to his lips. "We don't know if Lexi is being guarded," he whispered, wanting to use the element of surprise in their favour.

The other two boys followed close behind Braydon, ready for whatever they had to face. Both boys were armed with knives, which they held tightly in their fists. As they crept into the building and down the passageway, Jason had to stifle a giggle.

Hearing Jason snicker, Braydon turned and gave the other boy an uncomfortable stare. Braydon's eyes narrowed in annoyance as he glared at him, quickly stopping any giggles Jason felt.

"Sorry, it's just nervous energy," Jason whispered, before taking a deep breath. "It just feels like we're in a video game."

Braydon didn't look impressed. His eyes were narrowed, and his lips were pursed. Just as he was about to say something, Jason held up his hand.

"It's okay," Jason said quickly. "I'm in control. Let's keep going." Jason didn't want to get on Braydon's bad side, especially not in this close environment

The boys continued forward and soon found the landing and flight of stairs leading down to the room Jake had described. Braydon lent his body flat against the wall at the top of the stairs and cautiously peered down below. The stairs were not that steep, and he could see someone asleep at the bottom. The person was resting up against the door with their head drooping at an uncomfortable angle. Their mouth hung open, and their eyes were closed. They were either asleep or very good at pretending to be.

Braydon took a few cautious steps down the stairs, peering nervously at the guard below. About half-way down, he abruptly stopped and cocked his head to one side, examining the sleeping form. "You bastard!" He suddenly yelled out while thrusting his body down the stairs towards the unsuspecting person. "I know him! It's bloody Aaron!" Braydon yelled back at Jason and Ethan, who by now had run down the stairs after Braydon.

Aaron awoke startled to see the three boys descending on him like a group of crazed shoppers at the Myers end of the year sale. Their eyes were wide open, and they looked determined. He quickly rose to his feet and scampered out of the way.

"Braydon, mate," he said hurriedly. "I'm only here because Kevin asked me to be." He held up his hands in defence, a smile on his face as if kidnapping someone and keeping them against their will was a completely natural thing to do.

Braydon glared at Aaron in outrage, and roughly shoved him out of the way. "Well, it's about time you started bloody thinking for yourself then, isn't it, Aaron?!"

Aaron moved to leap up the stairs, in a feeble attempt to escape and inform Kevin of what was happening. Ethan, who had been watching him, quickly stepped in front of Aaron, blocking his path.

"You're not going anywhere," said Ethan as he slowly shook his head and wiggled his finger in front of Aaron's face.

"Sit!" snarled Braydon, pointing to the floor.

Aaron sat.

"Ethan, make sure he doesn't leave," ordered Braydon as he turned the knob on the door to where Lexi was being held. Quickly going inside, his hands shook slightly as he tried to keep his rising emotions under control. As he pushed open the door, Braydon peered into the ominous darkness assessing the situation. The small room was stiflingly hot, and the air inside was stale and musty. He couldn't see anything for a moment as his eyes tried to adjust to the dimness of the room, then finally he saw her. Lexi was lying on a tumble of blankets, her hands bound behind her back and a gag covering her mouth. She didn't look to be in a good way.

Hurriedly running to Lexi, Braydon helped her sit up. From what he could see in the gloom, Lexi was covered in sweat, her hair plastered to her forehead and her top soaked. Jason used his knife to cut the rope binding her hands, while Braydon carefully removed the thick gag from Lexi's mouth. Two small candle stubs flickered weakly giving a feeble glow of light in the dank surroundings.

Lexi leaned forward and enthusiastically hugged both boys. "It is sooo good to see you," she smiled thankfully. "You don't have anything to drink, do you?" Her lips were badly cracked from dehydration.

Jason pulled a flask of water from the satchel slung over his shoulder and handed it to Lexi. After the long ride to Gracetown, the water was warm, but at least it was wet. She took a long drink.

Braydon helped Lexi to her feet, holding her tightly as she wobbled on her stiff legs. She rubbed at her wrists, trying to get some circulation back into her hands.

"Oww," she cried, shaking her hands. "I've got pins and needles all up my arms!" Her wrists were raw from the rope, and her fingers tingled.

"God! How dare Kevin do this!" fumed Braydon, looking at the state Lexi was in. "Who the hell does he think he is!" Braydon reached for his flask, fumbling with the lid as he tried to take a drink, obviously attempting to control his temper. His jaw was clenched, and the veins were throbbing in his neck. His face looked murderous. It didn't look as though it would take much more to push him over the edge.

"Here, Braydon. Let me help you," whispered Lexi taking Braydon's flask in her bruised hands and opening the lid for him.

Braydon quickly took the flask from her and took a swig. "Come on," he said, staring at her. "Let's get you out of this bloody room!" he muttered, in an outraged voice. His lips were pressed together as though he were trying not to yell. Grabbing her hand, Braydon led her out of the claustrophobic room and into the hallway.

As the trio left the room, Braydon took one look at Aaron who was now cowering by the wall and stomped over to him, his hands reaching for the other boy's neck. "How could you keep her in there!" he yelled through clenched teeth.

"Wait, Braydon!" Lexi called after him not wanting trouble. "It's not worth it."

Braydon looked back at Lexi. "Yes, it is!" he muttered grabbing Aaron's shirt and dragging him along the ground. He reached the open doorway and roughly threw the simpering Aaron into the tiny, dim room.

"See how *you* like it in there, Aaron!" he exclaimed angrily, slamming the door shut and locking him inside. *He was lucky that was his only punishment!*

As the boys helped Lexi up the stairs and outside, she brought her hand up to shield her eyes from the bright sunlight. She breathed in the fresh air, thankful to be out of that dark room with its mildew, dust and rats!

"Did Hadley tell you where I was?" Lexi asked, resting her hands on her knees as she bent forward.

"Are you okay?" asked Braydon in concern. Lexi's face was pink and sweaty.

"Yeah. Just a little shaky and I've got a splitting headache."

"Here. Have some more water," suggested Jason offering his canteen. "Hadley was amazing," said Jason, smiling. "She ran all the way from the farm in the darkness to tell us what had happened. She wouldn't let up until we organised a search party to find you!"

Lexi smiled gratefully. She knew her sister wouldn't let her down. ""Well, I'm sure glad you came." She leaned against Braydon for a moment. "It was getting seriously hot in that room. I felt as though I was going to pass out!" Lexi took another drink of water. "I don't know what plans Kevin had for me, but I'm happy not to be around to find out!"

Lexi squatted on the ground, placing her hand on the dirt to steady herself. "How did you get here anyway? Did you find a car?" Lexi asked, cocking her head to one side.

"No. We rode horses," said Ethan, with a big grin on his face.

"Horses!" Lexi laughed.

"Yeah. They were Zac's idea," replied Ethan. "Pretty clever, eh. We should have thought of them before. Guess were just used to only getting around in cars!" he laughed.

"Omg! Zac," exclaimed Lexi as her face fell. "Is he alright? Kevin walloped him with that shovel." Lexi stood quickly, swallowing hard. She was waiting for the bad news.

"He's not in great shape," said Jason, shaking his head. "He's developed a stutter, so I'm not sure what that means. We tried to stop him, but he was determined to come with us."

"Here?!"

"Yeah. He's with Lilly looking for Kevin."

Suddenly, Lexi felt her head start to spin, and her knees buckle under her as though she were going to faint.

Braydon, who was standing next to her, felt her begin to crumble and caught her before she hit the ground. "Jesus," he exclaimed, his eyebrows drawn together. "Let's get her into the shade.

"She's probably dehydrated or got heatstroke," suggested Jason as he helped lift Lexi's feet. "There's a tree over there," he said, pointing to a small Karri tree. Its white trunk was obvious against the green bushes around it.

The Karri tree provided a little shade from the hot sun. The boys gently placed Lexi at the base of the tree with her feet raised under Jason's small rucksack. Ethan fanned her face with his hand and poured a trickle of water over her brow.

The water helped to rouse Lexi, and she sat up feeling alarmed. "What happened?!"

Braydon took her hand in his, a concerned expression on his face. "It's alright, Lexi. You passed out."

"Wow. That's a first. I've never passed out before."

"Well, you probably haven't eaten or drank much since yesterday," remarked Jason, leaning forward and peering closely at Lexi's face.

Lexi nodded squinting. She had a fierce headache forming behind her eyes.

"It's dehydration. You just need to drink water and keep cool for a while," suggested Jason. He undid a bandana he had tied loosely around his neck and wet it with water from his flask. "Here. Put this on the back of your neck. It will help cool you."

As Lexi reached for the bandana, she noticed the red, raw skin around her wrists and the black bruises on her arms and hands. The evidence of her harsh treatment inside the hot, unpleasant room. The rash from the virus was also obvious on her bare arms. She breathed in sharply at the shocking sight.

Swallowing deeply, Lexi glanced up to see Braydon staring at the bruises on her arms. His mouth was tight and angry, and his eyes dark.

"It's okay, Braydon," whispered Lexi urgently. "I'm out of there now. Let's just go and find the others. I want to go home."

Braydon's hands were clenched in fists at his sides. The veins sticking out on the back of them, his knuckles white.

All of a sudden, Braydon slammed his fist against the trunk of the tree, dislodging pieces of white bark onto Lexi. "That Bastard!" he yelled. "How dare he do that to you!" Braydon began pummelling the tree, his fists slamming into the tree in a fury.

"Braydon, stop!" yelled Lexi, standing up quickly. "Drink some of the tonic!" she said in alarm, her voice high and strained.

Jason's eyes whipped between Braydon and Lexi. Her grabbed at Lexi's arm.

Lexi brushed Jason away and stepped forward. Unafraid, she reached towards Braydon and pulled the flask from his belt. Quickly unscrewing the lid, Lexi brought the drink to Braydon's mouth hoping he would take some. "Drink." She ordered.

Braydon's eyes flicked to Lexi. He snatched the flask from her and stumbled back away from the group.

"I'll be alright," Braydon muttered through clenched teeth. "I just need some space for a minute." Braydon took a long drink from the flask and walked around the corner of the building trying to get a little space between himself and the others while he regained control. His knuckles were bloody and torn.

"That was close," murmured Jason, his eyes wide.

"Too close," agreed Lexi glancing from the bloody marks on the trunk of the tree to the rash on her arms. She swallowed hard.

"Are you alright?" asked Jason in concern, following her gaze towards her arms.

"Actually, I desperately need to pee!" Lexi replied, changing the subject. "I'll be back in a minute. Don't leave without me!" she called, running towards a clump of tall bushes.

"As if," he called back, frowning deeply. "I hope we can get Braydon and Lexi back to Jasper's Bay in one piece," Jason murmured rubbing forehead.

"Me too," agreed Ethan as he peered after Lexi. "Me too."

CHAPTER FIFTEEN

Meanwhile, only a short distance from where Lexi had been rescued, another drama was unfolding. Zac and Lilly had found their brother Kevin, and unlike most family reunions, he wasn't pleased to see them.

"Why do you despise us so much, Kevin?" asked Lilly, her brow furrowed in confusion.

"Because you exist," Kevin replied snidely. He stood with his arms folded tightly across his chest, and his eyes shone with an almost evangelistic fever.

Zac and Lilly looked at each other in dismay. *How were they supposed to respond to that?*

A small group of the Gracetown children had gathered close by to watch the disturbance They stood in a small tight cluster, alarmed by the raised voices and wanted to know what was going on. One of the older ones raced to find Jake and Kally and inform them about the trouble, while the others stood nervously holding hands and clutching frayed stuffed toys.

"Did you bring the stuff we asked for?" piped up Cindy, who was standing next to Kevin. Her hands were placed firmly on her hips in a defiant stance.

"We're not here to talk about that," replied Lilly, turning her back on the annoying girl.

"*We're not here to talk about that,*" mimicked Cindy in a high-pitched mocking voice. She pouted and rolled her eyes. Cindy hated it when she wasn't the centre of attention. "I see your hair hasn't grown back," she laughed, pointing rudely at Lilly. "You're as ugly as ever."

Lilly self-consciously went to touch her head with her hand before clenching her fist and thrusting it in her pocket. She refused to let Cindy's taunts rile her. Trying to ignore the girl, Lilly once again addressed her brother. "Kevin, why don't you come back to Jasper's Bay with us? You don't have to live on the farm, you could live in one of the abandoned houses," she suggested.

Kevin stared dully at her without saying a word. He yawned and tapped his foot.

Looking at Kevin's uninterested expression, Zac sighed loudly. He placed his fingers on either side of his head and massaged his temples. Both Zac and Lilly had been trying to reason with Kevin for at least half an hour with no success.

"Listen, Kevin," said Zac, rubbing his eyes. "It's been a l long, uncomfortable ride to this town, the heat is w w withering, and my head feels like a rock is being slammed into my skull. I d d don't want to do this anymore." Sweat was forming under Zac's bandage, making his head itch and he really wanted to get out of the burning sun.

Kevin raised one eyebrow but didn't say a word. His arms remained firmed crossed.

"Okay, Kevin," Zac stated in irritation. "Whatever. I... I just want to sh-show you one last thing and then w we'll go."

Kevin burst out laughing at his brother's stammer. "Well, h-h hurry up then!" he sneered. "I'm sick of talking to you two l.. l..losers. Where's that traitor Braydon? I thought he'd be here to try and rescue his girlfriend. What a coward!"

Zac's shoulders slumped, and he looked away. His face was flushed with embarrassment. The stutter he had developed was not going away. He slowly turned to pick up his backpack. Zac had thrown the heavy bag to the dirt earlier and now wanted to retrieve a precious memory from inside. Undoing the buckle,

Zac reached into the front pouch to locate an old photograph of Kevin, Zac and Lilly taken a long time ago when they were mere toddlers. It was a time before their younger sisters, Katie and Sarah were born. The photo showed three smiling faces looking up at the camera, their hands full of mud as they sat together in the sandpit, making mud pies and sandcastles. Their eyes shone brightly, and they looked as though they were having the best time of their lives. In a last-ditch effort to reach out to his brother, Zac and Lilly wanted to show the old photograph to Kevin to remind him they did have some fun times together as a family.

Although Kevin had been acting bored, he was in fact, watching his brother intently. As soon as Zac's back was turned, Kevin pulled a gleaming blade from the pocket of his jeans. He took several large steps towards Zac and thrust the knife towards his brother, cowardly aiming to stab him in the back!

Lilly saw the shine of the metal and instantly knew what her younger brother meant to do. She stood closest to him and reacted quickly, throwing herself towards Kevin. Lilly meant to grab the knife from him before he could inflict any damage.

As she propelled herself forward, trying to reach the knife, Lilly suddenly gasped in pain. The cold hard steel had slashed her hand then continued forward, penetrating the soft folds of her belly. The pain was immediate and intense, and she crumbled to the ground in shock.

Just as Lilly fell to the dirt, Brayden, Lexi and the others walked around the corner of the street to see Kevin looming over Lilly with the bloody blade gripped in his fist.

Lexi screamed in horror. Her voice sounded raspy and strained after many hours without water.

Hearing the scream, Zac abruptly turned around in confusion. "What just happened?" he yelled as he stumbled towards Lilly. He looked towards Kevin and noticed the bloody knife gripped firmly in his hand. Zac's eyes grew wide and incredulous. He opened his hand and let the family photograph flutter to the earth. There would be no reconciliation now. No uniting and no forgiveness.

"What have you done, Kevin!?" bellowed Zac. His voice broke with emotion. He stood in shock for a few moments glaring at Kevin, before racing to where Lilly lay in the dirt.

Lilly looked up at Zac as he came towards her. Her eyes were glassy, and her face had become chalky white. Moaning quietly, Lilly gripped her stomach with her hands. Her yellow shirt had turned crimson with the spread of blood from her wound. She closed her eyes. Lilly was losing a lot of blood.

Desperately placing his own hands on top of hers, Zac tried to stem the flow of blood seeping from her body. *Why wouldn't it stop?* No matter what he did, it would not cease. Zac looked around him frantically as he began to panic.

"What do I do?"

Lexi and the others rushed forward to see if they could help. Jason placed his folded jacket under Lilly's head, and Ethan placed his water bottle to her lips.

Lexi fell to her knees beside Lilly and took her hand. She squeezed it gently, watching helplessly as Zac struggled to save Lilly's life. As Lexi watched the drama unfolding before her in complete horror, her hand shot to her mouth, and her heart dropped to her stomach. The sight of Lilly lying on the ground as the life drained from her young body made Lexi feel sick. She let out a cry of anguish, her voice straining with emotion. *Had Kevin really just brutally stabbed his own sister?*

Rage flooded through Lexi's body. Without thinking of her own danger, she leapt to her feet and ran toward Kevin, determined to take the knife from him. She would not let him cause any more damage. Feeling an immense heat rising inside her body as if her blood were on fire, Lexi quickly covered the ground between herself and Kevin before lunging to grab the knife.

Kevin, who by now had realised what he had done, surrendered the knife willingly. It wasn't the revenge he had planned, and he was a little shocked at what had happened.

"Kevin, you bastard! What have you done! All the trouble you've caused, I should use this on you!" Lexi brandished the bloody knife in front of Kevin's startled face. Her insides burned in a fury, and all she could think about was using the blade on Kevin to rip him to shreds. *How dare he do this! What right did he have? He ought to be punished!*

"Did you think you could kidnap me and stab Lilly and get away with it!" she screamed, spit flying from her mouth. Lexi's fingers tightened around the handle of the knife, and the thought of using the blade on Kevin consumed her thoughts. She could think of nothing else. *It would only take one swift lunge and Kevin would get a taste of his own medicine.* Lexi stared at the weapon in her hand. Her fingers turned white as she gripped the handle.

Just as Lexi was about to step forward to inflict her own punishment on Kevin, a settling hand covered her own. "Wait, Lexi!" cried Braydon. "You don't want to do this!"

Braydon's sharp voice brought Lexi back to reality. *What was she doing?* As she turned to see Braydon standing reassuringly by her side, the rage Lexi felt inside started to subside. His hand held her own firmly, preventing her from using the knife.

Feeling a little calmer, Lexi looked down at the bloody weapon in her hand and blinked in surprise. What just happened had felt like a dream. Braydon nodded supportively, and she quickly passed the knife to him happy to be rid of temptation.

Taking the weapon from Lexi, Braydon swiftly handed it to Jason who stood nearby. Braydon's face was covered in perspiration. He was in a heightened state himself, barely keeping his own emotions in check. The last thing he wanted was a knife in his possession.

Kevin eyed Lexi with scorn and spat on the ground. "Stupid female!" he said, laughing dismissively.

Lexi's eyes narrowed. She couldn't believe this kid. *What a wanker!* Letting go of Braydon's hand, Lexi stormed towards Kevin her anger rising once more. Her feet thumped the ground as she walked.

Lexi stood right up close to Kevin. So close that she could smell the sour sweat on his body and her nose twitched. Stepping even closer, Lexi stared hard at Kevin's face, her dark eyes blazing with contempt.

Kevin stood rigid and still. He stared right back at Lexi without uttering a word. His mouth was turned up in a nasty sneer, and his hands were planted firmly on his hips.

Lexi's fingers twitched before closing into a tight fist at her side. Her chest tightened as she pictured her body thrown into the boot of the car like a piece of luggage. Lexi wanted to punch this mongrel square on his smug mouth. It would be easy; she would simply let the anger consume her. She could see from the corner of her eye that everyone was watching, and Lexi knew they would all be more than happy to see her do it. Her breath started to quicken. She felt the rage bubbling deep in her belly, and just as Lexi raised her fist ready to strike, she suddenly thought of Hadley.

The thought of her younger sister made Lexi pause. She blinked hard and took a shaky breath. Lexi didn't want the anger to consume her as she knew once it was released, there might not be any coming back from it. She thought of Elisha. Remembering the rash on her own arms, a sure sign of the virus, Lexi willed herself to drop her fist. It was one of the hardest things she had ever had to do. Every ounce of her body wanted to pummel Kevin, but somewhere deep inside of her, she understood that she would regret it. She didn't want to end up like Elisha, no longer able to control her emotions. If Lexi ended up like that, she would never be able to see Hadley again. She clenched her teeth.

"You're not worth it, you bastard," Lexi scowled finding it difficult to talk. "In the end, karma will be a bigger bitch than I ever need to be!" She leaned in close to him, her nostrils flaring in anger as she struggled to maintain her composure.

"One day soon when you're all alone and have nowhere to go, you're going to regret your actions, Kevin." Lexi poked Kevin in the chest with her finger before swiftly turning on her heels and stomping towards Braydon.

Understanding her struggle, Braydon took Lexi's hand in his and quickly led her away from the others. "Lexi, it's okay," he said soothingly, his voice calm. "I know exactly how you feel, but you did the right thing walking away. Believe me, you don't want to go through the guilt and remorse I feel every day for the death of Broc." He pulled Lexi closer to him. "Drink some of this," Braydon suggested, offering Lexi his flask of bush tonic.

Lexi shook her head adamantly pushing the flask away. "No. You need it." Her hands were trembling, and she was breathing hard.

Braydon took Lexi's face in his palms and looked into her eyes. His expression was serious. "Lexi, right now *you* need it," he said meaningfully. "I think you've just joined the *Dev's* club!"

Lexi looked at Braydon in understanding and nodded sombrely, reaching for the flask. "Fantastic. I've always wanted to be a *Dev!*" she said sarcastically through gritted teeth. *Dev's* was what they called the older kids who had contracted the KV17 virus.

Smiling bleakly at Braydon, Lexi squatted on her haunches. She felt terrible. Her insides were churning, plus her neck and face felt burning hot as if her body had a fever. Lexi didn't need Braydon to tell her she had the virus; she already instinctively knew she was not well.

Taking a long drink before handing the tonic back to Braydon, Lexi suggested they move into the shade of one of the buildings away from everyone else for a moment. The anger and resentment churned in her belly, and she wanted to be away from the crowd in case she lost control. She needed space. Trying to reign in the anger Lexi felt towards Kevin was taking every ounce of will-power she had. Braydon agreed, and together they moved away from the others.

After taking the knife from Braydon, Jason rubbed the blade in the dirt, trying to remove Lilly's blood. He gripped the knife between his thumb and finger, holding it away from his body. Looking at all the blood, his face turned pale, and he placed his hand to his stomach. "God, this is revolting. What am I going to do with this evil thing!"

Glancing up, Jason noticed Lexi stumble from the group. He breathed in sharply. "She is definitely *not* healthy," he whispered. "I'd better get rid of this thing." He quickly pocketed the blade and zipped his pocket, making sure the knife did not fall out. It wouldn't be good if Kevin got hold of it again.

Thinking about Kevin, Jason looked over at him and studied the younger boy. Kevin was hovering nearby Zac and Lilly as if unable to leave. His hands were shoved deep into his jean pockets, and he had a small smile on his face as if enjoying all the drama he had created.

"What a dick," muttered Jason as he stood and strode back to where Lilly lay. He made sure to roughly shove Kevin with his shoulder as he ran past him. Kevin just laughed.

"She's lost so m-much b-blood," stuttered Zac tearfully, as Jason squatted next to him. "I can't stop it. It just keeps oozing out!" He wanted to scream in frustration. Both his hands were pressed firmly upon Lilly's abdomen, his fingers crimson red.

"Let me help, mate," offered Jason replacing Zac's hands with his own.

Jason's face went white, and he tried not to look at all the blood. He swallowed and smiled weakly at Zac. "There's nothing you can do, Zac. The wound is too deep. She needs a doctor." His voice wobbled. "Just hold her hand Zac and talk to her. It's what she would want."

Zac stared at Jason for a moment, trying not to cry as his words sunk in. "Is Lilly going to die? How is this happening?" his voice broke with emotion. "We came here to *talk* to Kevin, not this!"

Lilly slowly opened her eyes as Zac took her hand in his. She smiled weakly with her lips trembling. "It's alright, Zac, I wasn't well anyway. Who knows how long I would have lasted in the bush?"

Zac squeezed her hand. "Yeah, but to have Kevin do this to you!" He looked about to blow. "How could you do this," he bellowed at Kevin, his eyes full of fury.

Lilly put her finger to Zac's lips wanting him to be quiet. "I don't want to talk about Kevin." Her face was a pasty white colour, and she spoke slowly, the energy draining from her body. "I'm glad there's a chance you're immune to the virus brother. If only we could bottle your blood. We could have made a fortune selling it to the big pharmaceutical companies in America! That's if they still existed. We would have been rich!"

Zac smiled a little sadly. Trust Lilly to joke about that.

Lilly watched Zac, her expression turning serious. "Promise me you'll look after yourself Zac," she whispered, lightly touching his bandaged head. "That's a nasty wound you've got there. Promise me you'll take a few days off from the farm work and rest."

Zac stared at her, unable to talk.

"Promise me!" Lilly raised her voice in agitation. Blood flecked spittle flew from her mouth as she spoke.

Resting his hand gently on Lilly's shoulder, Jason spoke quietly. His voice was quivering with emotion. "Don't worry Lilly, we'll make sure Zac rests."

Lilly looked up at Jason and nodded gratefully. She closed her eyes for a moment, before turning once again towards Zac. "Tell the girls I love them, and I'm sorry I didn't get to play tea parties with them one last time." She paused for a while as her voice became choked with emotion. A single tear seeped from the corner of Lilly's eye and rolled down her pale face. Lilly breathed out slowly before beginning again. "And show baby Sarah a photograph of me when she gets older, I want her to remember what I looked like." Lilly closed her eyes again, her face screwed up in pain.

Zac bit his lip hard, struggling not to cry. He put his hand comfortingly on Lilly's shoulder, solemnly watching his once playful, energetic sister slowly fading away.

Lilly took Zac's hand in hers once more and squeezed reassuringly. "I know you'll do a great job on the farm, Zac. I only wish I could have seen the family home one last time." Lilly shifted her body on the hard, rocky ground. "I always wanted to be a nurse and help people, ever since I was little, remember?" she asked Zac looking up at him.

Zac nodded and gave her a small smile. "I remember. You used to practice wrapping Katie and me in bandages."

Lilly laughed, blood trickling from the side of her mouth. "I would have made a good nurse," she said quietly, before slowly closing her eyes.

"Yes, you would," whispered Zac, his shoulders trembling. He gently placed his hand on Lilly's forehead. It felt cold and clammy.

Lilly suddenly moaned and gave a chesty cough. Her face was covered in a thin sheen of sweat, and her lips had turned blue. "I'm so scared Zac," she cried, opening her eyes to look at him.

Zac leaned forward "It's okay, Lilly. I'm here with you."

Lilly closed her eyes once more. Gradually her breathing slowed, and as she breathed her last breath, her young life drained from her body. *Her* pain was now gone, only the others watching continued to suffer.

As Lilly's hand fell to the ground, Zac opened his own to find the little toy spider he had given Lilly, nestled in his palm. It had always been their personal joke and seeing it once more released the flood of anguish and tears he had been holding back. Raising his head to the sky, Zac moaned in torment.

The sound of Zac's grief was heartbreaking. His life would never be the same without his twin. Lexi was watching her friends from a distance. She wanted to be with them but didn't trust her own emotions just yet. She stared at Lilly lying prostrate on the hard ground. Her life had been so short. *Why was life always so hard?* With all that had happened in the past 24 hours, Lexi suddenly felt overwhelmed by sadness, and fat tears rolled unchecked down her cheeks. She gasped big gulps of air and began to wail loudly. Frantically gripping onto Braydon's hand, Lexi held on tightly feeling the warmth in her own.

"Come on," Braydon said, noticing Lexi's increasing discomfort. "Let's get away from here for a moment," he suggested as he pulled Lexi away from the heartbreaking scene.

"Help me gather the horses. We're going to need them to get home." Braydon wanted to distance himself and Lexi from the others until she could regain control of her emotions. Plus, he wasn't exactly feeling all that calm himself just now.

Only a few steps away, Cindy watched Braydon and Lexi leave. "Just scamper away Braydon!" she hollered snidely hating the sight of him. "That's what rats are good for! Running away and playing with filth," her voice was full of loathing. Cindy stood with her arms folded tightly across her chest, and her feet planted firmly on the ground. "You're an ugly crier, Lexi!" she hollered after the retreating pair.

"Be quiet, Cindy," said Jason, getting to his feet.

Snorting in merriment and rolling her eyes, Cindy turned to face Jason. She gawped at Lilly lying amongst the dirt and rubble, and a big grin spread across her face. "I never liked her either," she said snidely. "At least there's one less bitch in the world!"

"Not from where I'm standing," retorted Jason, glaring at Cindy. His eyes were narrowed in anger.

Kevin, who had walked to stand by Lilly and Zac, was also staring at Lilly. He had watched her die without uttering a single sound. It was as if he felt nothing, no sadness, no emotion and no remorse. Her death obviously meant little to him.

Yawning, Kevin kicked his sneakers in the dirt, making shapes in the red dust as if he were now bored with the whole drama.

The flurry of movement caused the crouching Zac to glance sideways at Kevin. He stared open-mouthed at the disrespectful faces of Cindy and his younger brother for a moment in utter disbelief. Cindy had a stupid grin plastered on her face, and Kevin looked utterly uninterested in what he had just done! Watching the two of them, Zac stood in anger, his hands clenched in tight fists, his arms shaking.

Zac had never hated anyone or anything more than right now. His eyes were lit with fire and utter disdain. "Get the fuck away from me, Kevin!" he bellowed. His voice was a ball of fury. "I don't care what you do with your life, Kevin, but from this day forward, I n never want to see you again. Ever!" Zac's face and neck were crimson, and his eyes were bulging. "Don't you d dare take one step into Jasper's Bay, or this town ever again. Because if you do, I won't hold back, I'll k-kill you myself!" Zac's mouth had become a hard-straight line, and his whole body was shaking with rage

Kevin took a step back away from his brother and for the first time, he actually looked a little disconcerted. He had never heard Zac speak so aggressively before. He was usually so calm. Kevin stared at him, open-mouthed.

Ethan and Jason moved to stand beside Zac, shoulder to shoulder, showing their solidarity. "You'd better leave now," suggested Jason forcefully, his voice low and threatening. "Or suffer the consequences." Jason and Ethan pulled their knives from the back pockets of their jeans.

Jake and Kally who by now had joined the other children from Gracetown, crowded around Cindy and Kevin shaking their heads and muttering. There was much discussion on whether they should keep Kevin's car or siphon the remaining petrol from the tank.

"Let's just let them leave with whatever fuel they have left," suggested Jake. "I just want them gone and as far away from here as possible." He scowled at Kevin and Cindy.

The other children agreed to let Kevin and Cindy go, hoping they would never see them again.

"This is a pathetic town anyway!" screamed Cindy flicking her hair and storming away.

As Kevin moved to follow Cindy, Zac turned in Kevin's direction. Zac's face was as dark as thunder, and his eyes were like slits. Refusing to look at his brother, he simply called out loudly and clearly.

"Kevin!" Zac shouted; his voice strained. "I want you to know your time will come." Zac's nostrils flared with emotion as he spoke, and he sounded bitter. "If I ever g get the opportunity to seek revenge on you for what you have done to our sister, I will take it. I'm done with being your b brother!"

Turning his back on Kevin, Zac sank to the ground and cradled Lilly's head in his shaking hands. He never wanted to see Kevin ever again.

Kevin snorted, regarding Zac with disdain for a moment before strutting to his vehicle and climbing inside. His brother's threats had fallen on deaf ears. "I'll go wherever I want to, brother. You can't stop me," he muttered as he started the car's engine.

Kevin smirked as he spun the wheels of his car in defiance and he and Cindy drove away, leaving Aaron still locked in the dark cellar. Kevin didn't care about Aaron, and he didn't care about any of the others. He was utterly bored, and while he felt a little mollified in his revenge on Zac, Braydon was another matter. Kevin didn't care what Zac had said. He would bide his time before seeking revenge on that murderer Braydon. Gripping the steering wheel while smiling to himself, Kevin headed away from Gracetown and onto the open road. He and Cindy would find somewhere to lay low for a while.

Hearing the car leave, Zac refused to give Kevin a single glance as he drove away. When he said he never wanted to see Kevin ever again, he meant it. Instead, he carefully moved to carry Lilly in his arms. Braydon and Lexi had returned with the horses and Braydon helped him raise Lilly onto one of the mares.

"Is it alright if I take this," said Braydon quietly as he took Lilly's bottle of remedy from her belt.

Zac stared at Braydon as if unsure about what he was asking. He was obviously still in shock.

Lexi put her arm around Zac's shoulders. "Are you okay," she asked, knowing there was no way he was alright but asking anyway.

Zac shook his head. His eyes were full of tears. "I hate seeing her like this," he murmured, staring sadly at Lilly draped face-down over the horse. "I know it's the only way to get her home, but it's just so undignified."

Lexi patted Zac on the arm. "Are you sure you don't want to bury Lilly here in Gracetown?" she looked towards the group of Gracetown children huddled together watching from a distance. "I'm sure Jake and the others wouldn't mind."

Zac shook his head and wiped his nose with the back of his hand. "No. I want to take her home." He peered towards the horizon in the direction of Jasper's Bay. "She should be buried on the farm."

"Okay, Zac. Then that's what we'll do," agreed Lexi, before moving away to be with Braydon. She didn't know what she could say to Zac to make it any easier for him. The whole situation sucked. It must be awful to have seen your brother murder your sister.

Once Zac and Lilly were settled on their horse, Braydon turned to Jason. "I'm leaving now with Lexi to ride back to Jasper's Bay." Braydon put his foot in the stirrup and grabbed the saddle, ready to heave himself upon his horse. "I'm running out of tonic, and we're *both* going to need it."

Jason, who had been busily covering the pool of blood left on the ground where Lilly had lain, stood and brushed his hands together. He looked questioningly between Lexi and Braydon. "So, are you certain that Lexi...?" he started to say suspecting the worst.

Lexi nodded at him before he could finish his sentence. They both knew what he was going to say. Lexi's mouth was turned down, her face betraying her emotions. "Don't worry about me," she said with obvious false happiness. "It's going to be alright, Jason. We'll work something out." Climbing up onto the horse behind Braydon, Lexi bit her bottom lip. *Was everything going to be alright?* Sitting closely behind Braydon, Lexi waved to Jason as they started the long journey back home. *If she could make it back to Jasper's Bay without either herself or Braydon having a meltdown, maybe things would be okay.* Lexi took a deep breath and clung on tightly, hoping Braydon knew how to ride.

As Jason watched the trio depart, his forehead wrinkled, and the crease between his eyebrows deepened. "Is it going to be alright?" Jason sighed. "It's been pretty far from alright this whole day!" He shook his head slowly before brushing the dirt from his knees and walking over to where Ethan stood, waiting with the remaining horse.

Ethan looked at Jason as he walked towards him. "We had better head back too if we want to make it to Jasper's Bay before it gets dark," Ethan suggested peering up at the late afternoon sky. "There won't be any electric street lights to guide us in, and I don't want to get lost. That would just top this whole bloody day off nicely!" He gathered the reins in his hand and mounted the horse.

Jason agreed, but he had one last thing to do before they could head home. "Just give me one moment," he asked Ethan, before wandering over to where the Gracetown children stood in a tight little bunch.

Jason's sullen face brightened a little. He smiled warmly at Jake and Kally. It must have been a shock for the younger children to see such violence unfolding in their town, and he wanted to do something to reassure them that not everyone was terrible.

Jason unslung his back-pack from his shoulder and handed Jake the bag. "This is for you," he said happily. "Plus, you can keep the chickens you stole. Just don't come looking to steal any others!" *It would be impossible to get the chickens back to Jasper's Bay on horseback anyway.* Jason rubbed his chin. "Remember, we'd be happy to trade with you in the future, but no more stealing, alright?"

Jake and Kally both nodded sheepishly. Jake's cheeks flamed pink, and Kally coughed.

"And another thing," continued Jason. "You'd better build them a proper chicken coop, so the dingoes and foxes don't get them. If you treat the chickens properly, they might lay eggs for you." Jason turned to walk back to Ethan. "You have to start thinking of the future," he called over his shoulder.

Jason suddenly stopped and turned back to face the younger children. "Are you going to be alright on your own?" He considered the two kids before him. They looked so skinny and frail. Plus, quite a few of the other children had cuts that looked infected, and most of them had runny noses and hollow cheeks. "You could come back to Jasper's Bay with us?" suggested Jason walking back to stand beside them. "We have room."

Jake smiled warmly at the older boy. "That's okay. Thanks for the offer but I think we'd all prefer to stay in our own homes. We know this town, and we know this area. Besides, we're fishing people, not farmers." He laughed good-naturedly. "We like the sea!"

Jason chuckled and patted Jake on the back in a friendly manner. "Fair enough," he said, making his way to his horse. "Well. Good luck. I think you should teach the rest of the children to fish too."

Jake nodded, agreeing wholeheartedly. *That was a good idea.*

"Don't forget to plant the seeds," Jason called to Jake as they rode away.

Jake stared after Jason. *What did he mean?* Unzipping the back-pack, Jake reached inside. The heavy bag was full of pears! Jake pulled one out and held the precious fruit in the palm of his hand. Feeling amazed, he slowly raised the pear to his nose and breathed in deeply.

Tears sprung in the young boy's eyes; Jake hadn't seen fresh fruit for so long! Now he knew what Jason meant by *plant the seeds*. They could begin to grow their own food. Maybe they could become farmers after all! Jake laughed and showed Kally the fruit.

"Are they really for us?" she asked, her small face beaming.

Jake put his arm around her shoulders. "Yes, they are, and we're going to do our best to grow some more." He carefully placed the pear back in the bag and zipped it up. "That's after we eat them, of course!" Jake started whistling in merriment. *Maybe something good would come out of this day after all.* He grabbed Kally's hand and pulled her along, swinging his arm as they walked. His face glowed as though a huge weight had been lifted from his shoulders.

Jake held his head high and led his small tribe of youngsters back into the centre of town, back into Gracetown, their home. Finally, they were free of strangers, and it felt so good!

CHAPTER SIXTEEN

Jasper's Bay

The small group eventually made their way back into Jasper's Bay. They were exhausted both mentally and physically after the long ride, and no one spoke much. By the time they reached Zac's farm, it was almost midnight.

As soon as they reached the farmhouse, Jason and Ethan helped Zac to pull Lilly's body from the horse and carry her inside. During the ride, her body had become stiff, and it was awkward trying to move her through the front door. Zac's bottom lip trembled as he held tightly to Lilly, afraid they might drop her.

As the boys lay Lilly's body on her bed, Zac carefully covered her with a sheet, pulling the material over her head. "I'd better go and wake up, Katie," he said quietly, his eyes full of tears. "She'll want to know what happened."

Jason reached over and placed his hand on Zac's shoulders. "We'll attend to the horses," he said, casting a quick glance at Lilly. He shook his head sorrowfully and wandered outside with Ethan following behind him. "We'll be outside if you need us," Jason called back over his shoulder.

"Thanks," nodded Zac solemnly as he went to wake Katie.

As Jason and Ethan came down the house steps, Braydon dismounted from his horse and looked towards them, his face looked grim.

"I'm taking Lexi back to the campsite with me," Braydon suggested as he helped Lexi down from the horse. He handed the reins to Jason. "There's still a few bottles of tonic there. We both need it."

Jason looked towards Lexi, his eyes questioning.

"It's okay, Jason. I think I'm probably better off away from everyone for the moment," she said, nodding her head. Her voice sounded defeated. "I'll come back to the farm in the morning. I want to be here when you bury Lilly," said Lexi as her eyes filled with tears and her voice shook.

She took a small step closer to Jason. "Can you please tell Hadley where I've gone. She'll be worried. I don't want her to see me so messed up." Lexi was stepping from foot to foot as if anxious to leave and was wringing her hands together, looking at Jason pleadingly.

Jason nodded. "Of course, Lexi. I'll tell her where you are." Jason hesitated, obviously uncomfortable. "But what do you want me to tell her about. Er." Jason stopped what he was saying and pointed at Lexi's arms. Her sleeves were pushed up, and the rash from the virus was clearly visible.

Lexi peered down at her arms to see what Jason was looking at. "Oh," she said quietly as she pushed her sleeves down. "Actually, Jason. Can you not mention me flipping out and the virus and all that stuff?" Lexi raised her eyes to look directly at Jason. "I want to tell her myself."

"No problem. Are you going to be okay?" He peered closely at her face.

Lexi's hands had started to shake again, and she suddenly felt immensely tired and drained. "I hope so." Lexi turned her hands over and peered at her wrists. They were inflamed and trembling badly.

"I think I had better go, Jason," she said, her voice quivering. "Please say goodbye to Zac for me and tell him I'll be back tomorrow to help."

"Don't worry about that, Lexi," said Jason, frowning. "Go and rest. And drink some of the bush brew."

Lexi smiled weakly as she turned and ran with Braydon towards the campsite on the outskirts of the farm. Rest sounded good. *Tomorrow was going to be an emotional and challenging day for everyone.*

* *
*

Back inside the farmhouse, Zac was sitting with Katie in her bedroom.

"Katie, I have something to t tell you," he said, his voice shaking. He placed his hand gently on her shoulders.

"What is it?" Katie asked, climbing out from her covers. She rubbed her eyes, wiping the sleep away.

Zac sighed and looked up at the ceiling as if unsure how to tell her what he needed to say "There was a f f fight at Gracetown," he said, unable to look directly at Katie. He paused, swallowing hard. "And well, the thing is, K Kevin killed Lilly." Zac dropped his eyes to meet Katie's and his face immediately crumbled in anguish.

Katie was staring at Zac in disbelief. Her eyes were wide-open, and her chin quivered. She looked as though she had just been slapped hard across the face. "What! Why would he do that! I don't understand," she shrieked in anger, her voice straining.

When Zac didn't say anything, Katie abruptly stood, her small body shaking. Her face had turned a pale white as all the colour drained from her cheeks. "I don't believe you! Where is she? I have to see her! I must go to Gracetown!" Katie tried to push past Zac, who reached out and grabbed her arm.

"No, Katie!" he wept, tightening his grip. "You don't have to go to Gracetown. She's here, but you don't want to see her."

Katie stopped and turned to face Zac. "You brought her back home? All the way from Gracetown."

Zac nodded, dropping Katie's arm.

Katie's angry face suddenly dissolved into tears, and she flung herself at Zac, hugging him tightly. "Oh, thank you for bringing her home. She would have hated being stuck in Gracetown, especially with Kevin there." She wrapped her arms around Zac's neck as big heartfelt sobs wracked her little body.

Zac brushed Katie's hair from her face and looked her in the eyes. "He's not in Gracetown any longer, and he's not coming b back here either. I told him I n never want to see him again."

Katie looked at Zac and nodded. Her cheeks were now flushed and damp from her tears. "Well, good. I don't ever want to see him again, either. I just don't understand why he would kill Lilly." Katie started to cry again, her little chin wobbling.

Picking at his fingernail, Zac tried to explain what had happened. "We were arguing with him, and I think Lilly just got in the w way."

Katie frowned; her eyebrows drawn tightly together. "What do you mean?"

"I think he was trying to kill *me*," clarified Zac as he absently touched the back of his head.

Katie glanced at Zac's bandage, which was now dirty from the dust and grime on the long ride. "Oh," she said quietly as she took Zac's hand. "But I still don't understand why he would want to kill you either, or any of us? We're his family."

Slowly standing, Zac shrugged. "I don't think he wants us as his family any longer." He walked to the window and stared out into the darkness. "And that's fine by me. I don't want him as part of our family anymore either." His face looked sad.

Walking over to Zac, Katie placed her arm around Zac's waist. She looked up at him with tears brimming in her eyes. "Zac, I need to see her."

Zac looked at Katie's tear-stained cheeks. His shoulders slumped, and he nodded slowly. "Alright. B.b but I've covered her in a sh.sheet," he mentioned taking Katie's hand in his. "You can't look under it, alright. Sh-she wouldn't want you to."

Katie looked towards the door, hesitating for a moment. "Alright," she said nodding. "Shall we wake Hadley? She's in the other room."

"No. Let her sleep," suggested Zac, walking towards Lilly's bedroom. "This is *our* time to say goodbye to Lilly."

CHAPTER SEVENTEEN

As Lexi and Braydon walked from the farmhouse to the makeshift campground where they were staying, Braydon reached out in the darkness and grabbed Lexi's hand. It felt small in his own, and to his relief, she didn't pull away. His heart was racing as though he were a racehorse.

"Are you alright?" he asked quietly.

"I think so. I just need some more tonic, and I'd really like to wash!" Lexi pulled her sweat-drenched t-shirt away from her skin. She laughed a little. "I really do stink!"

"I'll start a fire and boil you some warm water," suggested Braydon, tactfully not commenting on how Lexi's smelt. "It won't take me too long to collect some from the creek. It's not too far from the campsite."

Lexi smiled at him gratefully, her whole face lighting up.

Braydon smiled back. "I'm surprised at how well you're taking all this," he commented, scratching his eyebrow. "You're pretty courageous."

"Oh, geeze. No, I'm not," Lexi replied, shaking her head. "I just know how to hide my anxiety." She held her hands out in front of her and showed him her fingernails. They were bitten to the quick. "I might look calm on the outside, but inside my stomach feels like jelly."

"Well, I still think you're brave. The way you stood up to Kevin and Cindy was awesome," Braydon said seriously as he made his way to his tent.

Lexi peered after him. "Yeah. Probably more like stupid," she muttered to herself with a small smile.

Braydon emerged from his tent, holding out two t-shirts. "Do you want to borrow one of these while your own top is drying," he asked as he wiggled the two shirts at Lexi. "The green one is mine, and the yellow one is Lilly's."

"Oh," said Lexi, looking at the shirts. "Um, do you mind if I borrow yours. I'd feel weird wearing Lilly's." Lexi's mouth turned downwards, and her hands were clasped tightly in front of her. "I can't believe she's gone."

"I know," said Braydon, coming over to Lexi and taking her hand. He gave it a squeeze. "I'll go and get that water for you so you can be more comfortable."

Lexi nodded her head slightly. "I'll find some firewood," she suggested as she peered out into the scrub. She was going to have to get used to living in the bush.

After washing her shirt and hanging it by the fire to dry, Lexi sat on an old fallen log, trying to get warm. She could hear the cicadas chirping amongst the bushes, and several black cockatoos were noisily foraging for food in a nearby Banksia tree. Lexi watched them as they used their sharp beaks to break open the seed pods. She wondered if the family were her neighbours or if they were just *passing through*. Lexi smiled. She would never have seen birds like that back in Perth. They didn't seem to be worried about her or Braydon at all.

Turning her gaze towards Braydon as he brought her a bottle of tonic, Lexi exclaimed, "well, that was an intense couple of days!" She ran her fingers through her drying hair. They had both come very close to losing their cool and having a feral episode.

"Yeah, you could say that," agreed Braydon as he peered into his flask, examining the fragrant contents.

Lexi watched him for a while. She was both relieved and comforted to have someone else with her out in the bush, who was also infected. Braydon might think that she was feeling calm about her condition and everything that had happened to her; however, he was wrong. Although she may look calm on the outside, Lexi was in fact, feeling petrified. It was terrifying not knowing how your body and mind was going to react to the virus. *Would she be able to continue to keep it under control, or would she turn feral like Elisha?*

Being out here having to deal with all these new, intense and frightening feelings was difficult. While she was sure her friends in town wanted to help, those who didn't have the virus couldn't fathom what she was going through. Braydon did, and it sure helped that he was easy to talk to, and more than a little cute! It wouldn't have been nearly as agreeable if she had been stuck out here with Cindy or Kevin!

Lexi scooted closer to Braydon and took his hand in hers. It felt rough and calloused from months of living hard in the Australian bush. She squeezed Braydon's hand and looked up into his worried face. "Are you okay?" it was her time to ask.

Braydon smiled and pulled Lexi closer to him. He nodded slowly. "I'm alright. I suppose I'm just worried we won't have enough of this bush tonic to last us much longer." He pointed to the two remaining bottles sitting by the tents. Bending to pick up his own bottle sitting by his feet, he offered Lexi a drink.

Lexi shifted her body slightly. She could feel the heat radiating from Braydon as he sat close to her. Clearing her throat self-consciously, Lexi wondered if he could see her blushing in the dim light. Feeling the heat rising in her own body, she quickly took a drink from his flask.

"Levi and Ollie said they were going to collect some more of the ingredients for us. Well, originally for you and Lilly, but now I suppose for you and me." Lexi swallowed as she thought about never being able to talk to Lilly again. It was such a waste of a young life.

As Lexi fell quiet, Braydon examined her sad expression and draped his arm around her shoulders in comfort. As he touched her body, his heartbeat rose dramatically as every single emotion became heightened by the virus.

Feeling his body tense, Lexi peered up at him. Braydon's cheeks were flushed red, and his pupils were dilated.

"By the way," said Lexi, clearing her throat. "I've made a map of where some of the medicinal plants are, so we can collect the seeds and pods too." She wanted to be encouraging about the future.

"So, I should be able to brew us another batch of the tonic soon. We're not the only ones who will need it." Her eyes shone brightly as she spoke. Lexi knew that Jason was almost seventeen, and it wouldn't be long before a few of the other children in Jasper's Bay, were too. While Zac *might* be immune, having shown no signs of the virus despite turning seventeen, it was highly unlikely that many other children would be. Sourcing the native ingredients and producing the calming tonic was going to be an ongoing process if they were to have any chance of living a somewhat normal life.

Without the use of scientists, computers or the internet, it would be highly unlikely they would ever find a cure. However, if the tonic continued to alleviate the symptoms and control the *rages,* then Lexi was willing to embrace the natural therapy wholeheartedly.

Looking closely at the red, spiky Grevillia flowers, along with the tall, red and green Kangaroo paws and the bright pink Geraldton wax flowers, growing near her. Lexi began to wonder what other plants and flowers could be used as alternative therapies. She decided as soon as she felt more in control of herself, she would pay a visit to Levi and Ollie. Lexi wanted to sit with them and talk about what they knew of the Australian plants their mum had taught them about.

As Lexi sat with her chin resting on her hands, obviously deep in thought, Braydon watched her expression change. She wasn't good at hiding her feelings, and even in the dim light, he could tell that she was just as worried as he was.

"What are you thinking about?" he asked, reaching forward and tucking a stray piece of her hair behind her ear, his fingers brushing her cheek.

"The future."

"A good future?" he asked nervously, wondering if it involved him.

Lexi gave him a warm smile, her eyes crinkling at the sides. "Yes, a good future."

Braydon felt his own face light up at the positivity radiating from her. That was another thing he liked about Lexi. Nothing much got her down, that's why she made such a good leader. They needed positive people in a time when everything looked bleak.

Taking another drink of the tonic, Lexi passed the bottle back to Braydon and noticed him smiling warmly at her. His eyes were happy and relaxed. The brew was clearly working on both of them.

Lexi suddenly knew what she wanted to do. It was something she had desired for a long while. Reaching forward, taking Braydon's face in her hands, Lexi leaned in towards him and kissed him warmly and deeply on the mouth.

The kiss was exquisite, all her emotions heightened by the virus as though she had taken a mind-altering drug. Her body felt as though she were floating, and she could think of nothing else except Braydon's lips on hers. He tasted of the bitter bush tonic, and she moved closer to him. His hands were on her body and hers on his.

Suddenly, Lexi felt as if she couldn't breathe. Her fingers tingled and heat spread through her body like a bush fire out of control. She quickly pulled away from Braydon, creating space between them and stood. Braydon quickly rose too.

Their encounter had been intense, and she wanted to slow things down just a fraction. Lexi wasn't used to the heightened emotions caused by the virus, and she wasn't sure how she would react if they went any further. She had to admit that the surge in feelings she felt at this moment was a lot more enjoyable than the ones she felt when she was upset or angry, and she smiled happily to herself.

As they stood a little awkwardly in front of the fire, Braydon held out his hand to Lexi. He had a sheepish but pleased look on his face. She took his hand and smiled at him.

"Well," he coughed dramatically. "That was nice. Actually, more than nice!"

Lexi looked at him and burst out laughing. He laughed too.

"Yes, it was nice," Lexi agreed as she grinned at him. "But I think I had better sleep in the other tent tonight," she stated, pointing to the second tent a little distance away.

Braydon laughed again. "Yes, good idea. But only for tonight," he winked cheekily at her.

Lexi smiled broadly before planting a quick kiss on his cheek. She handed the bottle back to him and started to walk towards *her* tent. "I'd better get some sleep," she said over her shoulder. "We've got a difficult day ahead of us tomorrow."

Braydon nodded his head solemnly; all joviality was gone for the moment. "You're right, tomorrow is going to be a big day," he agreed, sighing. They had to bury Lilly and Lexi needed to talk to Hadley about her infection. It was going to be an emotional day.

Both Lexi and Braydon retired for the night, each in their own separate tents. For now.

The next morning was hot and humid. A few white fluffy clouds spotted the sky here and there, but there wasn't any sign of rain. There would be no relief from the summer heat.

Every child from Jasper's Bay, whether young or old, had made the long walk from town to the Bailey farm where Lilly's funeral was to be held. They stood in little clusters around a freshly dug grave, all with sad, sombre faces.

Lilly had been well liked around the town, and the shock of her death and how it had happened was fresh in their minds. If Kevin and his two companions tried to take one step into Jasper's Bay, they would soon be run out of town.

Hadley and Katie had spent time finding several small Boronia plants in the bush, digging them up and planting them around Lilly's grave. Their small, bright pink flowers gave a wonderful sweet perfume.

Katie held tightly to Hadley's hand as both girls stared at the mound of earth in dismay. "I'm glad Zac and the others managed to bring Lilly home," murmured Katie as she turned to face Hadley. Her voice was trembling with emotion. "But the farm is never going to be the same. I feel so empty without her." Katie's face crumpled, and hot tears ran down her face.

Dropping Katie's hand, Hadley turned to hug her friend. "At least you can come and visit her whenever you want to," encouraged Hadley.

"Yes," replied Katie wiping her hand across her eyes and giving a small smile. "Yes, I'm grateful for that." She bent to touch one of the tiny bell-shaped Boronia flowers. "Lilly would have liked these." Sarah, who was sitting at Katie's feet, reached for the bright pink flowers, crushing them in her hand. Katie brushed the top of Sarah's head with the tips of her fingers, fresh tears forming in her eyes. "Will you even remember Lilly?" she asked Sarah as the toddler looked up at her with bright eyes.

A few steps away from the girls, Lexi stood quietly on her own. She had yet to talk to Hadley about her infection, not having found the right time. Katie needed Hadley at the moment, and Lexi did not want to drag her away from her friend.

Lexi distractedly played with the bead on her necklace. Watching Hadley with Katie gave her an idea. The two younger girls had become terrific friends in the six months since Lexi and Hadley had moved from Perth to Jasper's Bay. Katie would need a good friend over the next few weeks as she came to terms with Lilly's death; and after Lexi talked to Hadley about her infection, Hadley was going to need a good friend too. *They would be good support for each other. Maybe Hadley could move onto the farm for a while?* Lexi nodded her head slightly. "That could work," she whispered to herself. Lexi was sure Jason wouldn't mind if Hadley moved out of the house on Rosewood Avenue for a bit. "He spends most of his time over at Logan's house or here on the farm anyway."

Looking around for Jason, Lexi noticed him standing close to Logan. The two boys were holding hands. Lexi smiled. "About time." They had finally become a couple. *I don't think Jason will be worried about Hadley moving out at all!*

Lexi brushed the hair from her eyes with her hand and took another drink of the fragrant bush brew. Lexi screwed up her nose. She hadn't become used to the bitter after taste. Continuing to scan the small clusters of children gathered at the farm, she saw Ethan and Zac standing not far from Jason. Zac looked terrible. There were dark, purple smudges under his eyes, and he had obviously not slept well. The cut on the back of his head had reopened, and blood had seeped into the bandages giving him the look of a battle victim. His arms drooped by his sides and his shoulders were slumped. In his fingers Zac held the little toy black spider Lilly had given him, its spindly legs gripped lightly between his thumb and forefinger. The once robust and energetic boy looked utterly defeated.

Lexi rubbed at the small scar on her cheek as she stood looking at Zac. They were all going to have to help him get through his anguish. His stutter hadn't gone away, and on top of grieving for Lilly, Zac probably had a concussion, if not something more serious. Lexi blinked her eyes rapidly. "I hope he's going to be alright," she sighed, suddenly feeling the strong need to find Hadley and talk to her.

A few steps away from Lexi, Zac stood staring at Lilly's grave. His legs began to wobble, and he suddenly dropped to his knees and started to cry. Only a few days ago, Zac had been clowning around and joking with Lilly, and now she lay cold in the dirt. Zac placed his hands onto the bare earth and let forth a wail of anguish. His voice was deep and guttural.

Seeing Zac break down, Katie ran to her brother's side and placed her arms around his shoulders. They sat together for a moment before Zac broke away and wiped his tear-filled eyes with the back of his hand. Reaching forward, Zac carefully placed the little black spider at the base of the wooden cross marking his twin sister's grave.

"I won't forget my promise, Lilly," Zac said quietly, touching the back of his wounded head. I'll take good care of the farm and our sisters, too," he murmured glancing at Katie and baby Sarah. Katie looked drawn and pale, and she leaned into Zac for comfort, her small hand resting on his back.

As Katie huddled by him, Zac put his strong arm around his two younger sisters and hugged them tightly. The siblings stayed that way for a long while, each needing the comfort and companionship of family.

Seeing Hadley standing on her own, Lexi decided now was the time to speak with her. Walking briskly towards Hadley, her fingers opening and closing at her sides, Lexi leant to whisper in her ear. "Hadley. I need to talk to you."

When she didn't move, Lexi grabbed Hadley's arm and began to pull her away from the others.

"Why? What's going on?" Hadley asked as she let Lexi drag her away to a small patch of grass a little way from the others. They both sat facing each other.

Hadley glared at her sister; her eyebrows raised wondering what was going on. They hadn't spoken much to each other since Lexi returned to the farm that morning.

Once they were both sitting, Lexi glanced nervously at Hadley; however, she didn't say a word. She wasn't sure how to start this conversation. What she had to say was going to be difficult, and Lexi bit her lower lip.

Hadley stared back at her before rolling her eyes in frustration and puffing out her cheeks. When Lexi continued to remain silent, Hadley groaned, pushed herself to her feet and started to move away. "Well, I'm not sitting here all-day Lexi! I want to be with Katie. I'm going back to…"

Lexi quickly grabbed Hadley's ankle, wanting her to stay. "Wait!" she said desperately, looking up at Hadley, her green eyes shimmering with emotion. "I'm infected!"

Hadley stopped abruptly and turned to face Lexi. "What?! What do you mean infected? Have you got a stomach bug or something?"

Lexi slowly shook her head. There was no getting around it, she was just going to have to say it. "No, not a stomach bug. I'm infected with the KV17 virus."

Hadley's legs wobbled, and she slumped to the ground with a heavy thump. She stared at Lexi for a moment, before taking hold of Lexi's arm. Hadley wrenched her sister's long sleeve up, exposing the skin underneath. Below the shirt's concealing fabric was the tell-tale signs of the virus. A red raised blotchy rash extending from the back of Lexi's hand right up her arm.

Hadley gulped and peered at the rash in disbelief. Dropping Lexi's arm, she leaned forward and took Lexi's face in her hands. She stared intensely into Lexi's bloodshot eyes. "B but you haven't got a runny nose, or sore throat, have you?" she stammered, her face screwed up in confusion. "Maybe it's measles or a heat rash?" Hadley said, not wanting to believe what she had just seen. "You can't be infected! You've only just turned seventeen, surely it takes longer than that?"

"You know it's not Measles, Hadley," said Lexi with a weak smile. "It's alright, I'll be okay."

Hadley looked frantic. Her eyes were wide, and her hands were shaking. She pulled Lexi's sleeve back down, covering the rash, not wanting to have to see the evidence anymore.

"You can't have the virus. You won't be okay! I don't want you to die like Mum and Dad!" Hadley started looking around frantically. "We have to find you some of the remedy! Where's Braydon? He must have some of the tonic!" Hadley's voice was shrill, and she started to cry in big sobs, her chest heaving.

Trying to calm her sister, Lexi placed a comforting hand on her arm. "Hadley, stop! I'm not going to die. At least, not from the virus. It's mutated, remember?" She looked closely at her sister's tearful face in concern. "It's alright. I've started taking the tonic, and it's been helping me stay calm." Lexi pulled the metal flask from her belt to show Hadley. "I wouldn't be here otherwise." She gestured to the crowd of children milling by Lilly's grave holding hands and singing quietly.

"The problem is…" Lexi paused and took a deep breath knowing this part was going to be difficult. "As far as we can tell, the tonic only *suppresses* the virus. It doesn't cure it. And without scientists to help, there's not going to be a cure. I have to learn to live with it." She paused again, taking Hadley's hand in hers. "The thing is, Hadley; I'm going to have to move out of town for a while."

"What! Why!?" Hadley's voice rose loudly, and she quickly put her hand over her mouth, not wanting the others to hear.

"Do you remember what Elisha was like?" Lexi asked.

Hadley nodded sombrely.

"Well," continued Lexi, her face sad. "I don't really know how the virus is going to affect me, and I don't know how long this tonic will work." She sighed and scratched at her arm. "It's just too risky me being around you, and everyone else. It's the same for Braydon."

Hadley looked as though she were going to begin crying again. Her face had become pink and blotchy, and she began to sniff.

Quickly pulling Hadley towards her, Lexi hugged her tightly. "I know, Hadley. This bloody sucks!" exclaimed Lexi, as fat tears started to roll down her own face.

Both sisters clung to each other as the tears began to flow in earnest. Neither one of them trying to stop them. Even though the sisters had not been getting along particularly well in the last few weeks, they were the only family each had, and it would be extremely tough living apart.

After a while, Lexi pulled away. She wanted to make sure her younger sister was going to be alright before she moved to the bush. "Hadley," she began, once more taking Hadley's hand in hers. "I think you should move out here on the farm with Zac, Katie and Sarah. Katie is going to need a friend right now, and you can help out." Lexi explained her idea of moving into the tents on the outskirts of the farm and how the sisters wouldn't be that far away from each other. They could see each other regularly.

"I supposed I could bring Polo with me too," said Hadley, accepting the idea. "That's if it's alright with Katie and Zac. Plus, I can help look for the bush foods for your tonic," Hadley said more cheerfully, slowly warming to the idea. "Ollie and Levi can show me what to look for."

Lexi nodded. She knew Hadley would want to feel useful, and it would take her mind off all that had happened. Plus, she and Braydon could certainly use all the help they could get. It wasn't going to be easy living out in the bush on their own. She only hoped that she didn't turn feral like poor Elisha. She didn't think the bush tonic would be strong enough to help once you reached that stage. Lexi shivered.

Hadley touched Lexi's arm. "Do the others know you have the virus?" asked Hadley as she nodded her head towards Jason.

"Well, Braydon does obviously, and I think Jason might know. But I'm not certain about the others. I'm sure they have their suspicions." Lexi coughed and dropped her eyes to the ground. "I kinda lost it in Gracetown when Kevin stabbed Lilly." Lexi looked mortified at her loss of control. "I almost stabbed him. I really wanted to!"

"Oh." Hadley cleared her throat. "Well, that's totally understandable!" consoled Hadley, her voice was hoarse from crying. "Don't worry about it. I probably would have wanted to as well!" She grabbed Lexi's hand. "Kevin *is* a bit of a dick."

Lexi gave a little smile. It was nice to know Hadley supported her. She quickly pulled her hair up into a ponytail behind her head and secured it with a hairband. Her neck felt hot and sweaty, and she was beginning to feel uncomfortable. She flapped her shirt with her hand, trying to generate some air. "I'm really going to miss Lilly," she whispered, looking glum. "I only knew her for a short while, but we really got along.

She was so funny." Lexi fiddled with her necklace and glanced at Hadley.

"Yeah, she was," Hadley nodded, pulling at the edge of her shirt. "Zac and Katie are going to find it really tough with her gone."

"That's why I'm sure Katie would love to have you stay with her for a while," smiled Lexi reassuringly. "And I'd feel happier if I knew you were here. We would be living close enough to see each other every day."

Hadley brought her face right up close to Lexi and held her face in her hands. "What about you? Everything is changing so much lately," she muttered sadly. "Are you sure you're going to be alright out there in the bush on your own?"

Lexi shrugged as she chewed on the end of her fingernail. "I hope so," she replied. "Anyway, I won't be on my own. Braydon will be there too. Remember?"

"Oh, yes. Braydon." Hadley rolled her eyes. "I hope you two are going to be careful out there," she smirked poking Lexi in the ribs making her flinch.

"Hey!" she laughed. "What do you mean, *be careful?*"

"Well, you are staying together by yourselves in a tent!" winked Hadley.

Lexi blushed from her neck to her forehead. "Actually, Hadley, there are two tents! And for your information, things haven't progressed that far yet! I'm not looking for a *boyfriend*. I just like him, and we both need a friend right now. That's all."

Hadley giggled. "Well, just be careful!"

Lexi rose to her feet and pulled Hadley up with her. "I will, Mum!" she said good-humouredly. "Now go and see how Katie is. I have to leave soon, and I need to talk to Jason before I go."

Hadley's face became serious again, and she straightened her shoulders. "Alright," she said. "I'll be fine, you don't need to worry about me." She gave Lexi a quick hug. "Just make sure you say goodbye to me before you go!" she said over her shoulder as she jogged towards a group of children who were standing not far off.

Lexi nodded. It was going to be so strange to leave without Hadley. Ever since their parents had died and they had left the city, the girls had been by each other's side practically every day for the past six months. *Hadley was right. Everything was going to be different now, and it would take some getting used to.*

As Lexi watched Hadley run over to Katie and give the younger girl a hug, she smiled. Her sister agreeing to move to the farm for a while would be a massive relief for her. With everything that was going on, it would be one less thing Lexi would have to worry about.

Stretching her back and taking a drink from her flask, Lexi scanned the crowd for Jason. She soon found him standing off to the side on his own and made her way over to talk to him. Lexi wanted to tell him of her plan to stay at the campsite with Braydon, and she could see by the look on his face that he already knew the reason why. When Lexi showed him the rash on her arms, Jason didn't seem surprised; he just looked a little sad at the news. He seemed to be resigned to the fact that she was infected by the virus and Lexi wondered if Jason was thinking of his own future. He would be turning seventeen himself in a few months time.

When Lexi told Jason of Hadley's plan to move out of the house on Rosewood Avenue and onto the farm, Jason agreed to keep an eye on her. "I'll be working at the farm quite often anyway," he said with a smile. "As you know, I'm not exactly the *outdoors, manual labour* type, but Zac's going to need help with the crops and animals."

Jason turned to look back towards the farm paddocks. "I guess there are worse skills to learn than being a farmer," he grinned. "My old gamer buddies in Perth would never believe I was capable if they saw me now!"

Lexi patted Jason's shoulder. "I think you're more than capable, Jason," she said, smiling. "Besides, I'm hoping to help too, whenever I'm able." She scratched distractedly at her forearm. It felt as though a thousand ants were biting into her flesh, plus, the hot sun was beginning to make her feel uncomfortably warm.

Lexi cleared her throat and pulled her shirt away from her skin. "If I can keep this virus under control, I want to do my part." She took yet another sip of the liquid in her flask.

Jason watched Lexi for a long moment. "Are you alright? You don't seem comfortable."

"I don't feel great," Lexi admitted. Her face was flushed and sweaty, and she was continually opening and closing her fists. "But I'll be okay. I have to make it work."

"I'll always be here to help you if you need me, Lexi," said Jason, his voice trembling a little, and his bottom lip quivering.

Lexi smiled at him and nodded. "Thank you, Jason, you're a good friend." She wanted to give him a hug, but she was beginning to feel extremely unsettled and didn't think she could stand touching him. "I had better go, I want to see Hadley before I leave."

Saying goodbye to Jason, Lexi went to find Hadley, not forgetting her promise to say goodbye to her sister before she departed. Just as Lexi spotted Hadley, Ethan strode over to her. He had a sombre look about him, and Lexi knew he wanted to ask her something. She took a big breath in and out and waited patiently for him to join her. She hoped he wasn't going to talk for too long. She tapped her foot on the ground.

"Lexi," started Ethan, who did indeed want to talk. "Can you please try and help Elisha if you see her? I know she is unstable and frightening to be around at the moment," he said, his voice shaky. "But can you try and encourage her to drink some of that bush brew? It seems to be helping Braydon. I know she's really far gone," he paused and swallowed. "But, well, it might still help her." Ethan watched Lexi hopefully, his wavy brown hair falling in front of his eyes. "And please tell her that I've been looking for her. I haven't forgotten her."

Lexi nodded in agreement and promised to try and talk to Elisha if she saw her again. Ethan was happy with that, so she moved away to say goodbye to Zac, Katie and Hadley. Hadley did not want her to go; however, with Lexi's flask of tonic practically empty, Lexi knew she would have to make her departure soon. The tell-tale signs of increased body heat, throbbing pressure behind her eyes and intense itchiness irritating her skin were beginning to appear. *It was time to go!*

Just before Lexi made her departure, young Ollie came running up to her with a knowing look on his face. He held a white calico bag out to her like a gift from Santa. Peeping inside, she was presented with a fragrant aroma wafting from within. The bag contained lemon myrtle and native basil. There were also ripe bush passionfruit, Lilly-Pilly berries, Wattleseeds and the *magical* sticky oyster bush flowers used to make the native bush brew.

Lexi's lip trembled. "Oh, Ollie. Thank you so much!" she exclaimed, thanking the small boy warmly. With her own supplies of brew almost gone, he had no idea how much he had helped her. Or maybe he did? Lexi always thought the young Indigenous boy was wise beyond his years.

"No problem, Lexi. I hope they work," he replied before running back to join the other younger children.

Feeling much happier, Lexi waved goodbye to Hadley and the others and made her way back to the tents where Braydon waited patiently. His bottle of tonic would be long gone by now, and Lexi wondered what state he would be in.

CHAPTER EIGHTEEN

B raydon was covered in sweat. He lay prostrate with his hands clenched into tight fists, and his body rocked side to side as he lay on top of his sleeping bag. Lexi could see he was suffering and immediately rushed to him, offering Braydon the last few mouthfuls of her bush brew. His eyes had that wild look about them as though he were about to start screaming.

Sitting up, Braydon grabbed the flask from Lexi. He fervently gulped the last remnants of tonic from the flask before falling back on his sleeping bag. He placed his hands over his eyes and moaned.

"I'll brew some more tonic," she said quickly. "Just hold on." Lexi's voice was shaky, and her hands were trembling.

Braydon nodded. His eyes were squeezed tightly shut.

Quickly backing out of the tent, Lexi went outside to start brewing some of the tonic. Braydon needed some more, and she was going to need some herself before too long.

First, Lexi had to make a fire, as the one they had made earlier had now gone out. Deftly gathering pieces of paperbark, dry twigs and little branches, she built a small pyramid structure amongst a circle of large river rocks and carefully started a fire using some matches. Her fingers shook as she lit the match.

As she blew on the smouldering embers, they soon caught, and she was able to carefully add small sticks and bark until she had a good-sized fire. Sitting back on her heels and examining her handywork, Lexi smiled. As a young girl who had grown up in the city and only been camping a couple of times before, she was doing alright out here in the bush.

Once the flames reached a good height, Lexi balanced a large cooking pot filled with river water, over the fire. She crumpled the Lemon Myrtle, Oyster Bush flowers and seeds, and native basil into the water to stew. Several bottles and containers sat ready to be filled with the tonic once it had simmered for an hour.

While Lexi waited for the tonic to be ready, she made her way down to Bryer's creek to fetch a bucket of freshwater. She needed a drink, and she wanted to wet a cloth for Braydon's hot head. Lexi hoped it would give him some relief from the raging heat his body was producing.

As she neared the creek, the flowing water looked so tempting. Lexi's own body was sweltering, and she couldn't resist the cold water. Her throat felt so parched, and her cheeks were flaming hot. Not bothering to remove her clothing, Lexi dove straight in.

As Lexi swam under the water, she felt instant sweet relief as the clear, cold water washed over her bare face and neck. Turning onto her back, Lexi closed her eyes and floated blissfully. It was amazing how soothing the water was.

Oh, how she wished she could stay here all day. However, Lexi remembered why she had ventured down to the creek and reluctantly waded to the bank. Filling the bucket with freshwater, she gazed upward to see a bunch of brightly coloured Rainbow Lorikeets resting on a branch of a Eucalyptus tree. Some of the beautiful birds were preening their red, green and purple feathers, while others were picking at the pink blossoms from the tree.

Watching the birds made Lexi think of Elisha, who used to be an avid bird watcher. Wondering whether she was anywhere near, Lexi decided to call out.

"Elisha!" she called out as she put the bucket of water on the ground and cupped her hands around her mouth. "Cooee! Elisha are you here? It's Lexi." She remembered her promise to Ethan and wanted to tell Elisha about the bush tonic.

Lexi cocked her head to the side for a moment and tried to listen for any signs that Elisha may be near. All she could hear were the sounds of the water flowing in the creek and the chirps of the birds above her. *No Elisha.*

Turning to look to her side, Lexi peered into the bush. She squinted her eyes in concentration. *Did she just see something?* It looked like a flash of colour, obvious in the browns and greens of the Australian bush. *Was it Elisha?*

Lexi froze, ready to run if she had to. *Maybe it hadn't been such a wise idea to call Elisha, after all.* "Bloody stupid," she muttered. "What were you thinking?"

Slowly bending down, Lexi reached to pick up a large fallen branch not far from where she stood. Stretching with her fingers, Lexi pulled the tree branch towards her and stood. She positioned her feet one in front of the other and opened her stance with the branch slung over her shoulder. The tree branch was heavy and awkward, but at least she now had a weapon and was ready to use it if she had to. Lexi hoped Elisha was feeling friendly, and she wouldn't need it.

Hearing movement coming towards her, Lexi thought it sounded exactly like someone walking through the dry leaf litter on the bush floor. As the noise came closer and Lexi could see flashes of colour from someone's red shirt through the thick foliage, her heart began to hammer wildly in her chest. She had an intense desire to turn around and flee, and it took all her courage to remain standing still.

Should she call out? No, better to remain silent.

As the noise drew close, Lexi's fingers tightened around the branch, her toes wiggled in her wet shoes, and she crouched a little, ready to swing. Her breath was coming rapidly as though she were panting, and her face felt ablaze with heat.

Lexi saw a flash of red as the person stepped out from the trees. Not waiting to see who it was, she slung the branch around as though it were a sword and she was a knight. "Yaaa,", she screamed.

Her weapon landed hard and fast on the shoulder of Braydon, and he stumbled sideways, losing grip on the flask of freshly brewed bush tonic. "Jesus!" he yelled, trying to retrieve the fallen bottle before too much of the liquid was lost.

"Arrr," bellowed Lexi, coming after Braydon again.

"Wait!" yelled Braydon as he brought his arms up to protect his head. "It's me, Lexi. It's Braydon!"

Lexi paused for a moment; the branch raised above her head in mid-swing. She was panting heavily, and her eyes looked crazy.

Braydon pushed the bottle of remedy safely into the dirt and looked at Lexi. She was in a rage. "Lexi, it's alright. It's just me." Braydon took a tentative step towards Lexi with his hands raised in front of him in peace. "I've brought you some of the remedy you were brewing, see," he pointed towards the small metal flask. "I've just had some myself. It's a little hot, but you'll feel better when you drink it." Braydon smiled encouragingly. His face was flushed, and his red curly hair was plastered to his head, but he looked a lot healthier than he had earlier that afternoon.

Lexi didn't want any drink. She wanted to yell and stomp about, just like a toddler having a tantrum. "Nooo!" she shrieked running at Braydon once more.

This time Braydon was ready for her. Just as Lexi reached him, he grabbed hold of the branch and wrenched it away from her, the wood leaving long splinters in her palms. This made Lexi scream in anger, and she lunged at Braydon, knocking him off his feet.

250

As they both fell to the ground, Braydon managed to maneuver his arms around Lexi's body, trapping her arms beneath his. "It's alright, Lexi," he whispered. "I'm here to help you. Please calm down." His voice cracked with emotion.

Lexi thrashed against Braydon, kicking him in the shins with her heels and hitting him with her forehead, making his lip bleed. Still, Braydon held on.

Eventually, Braydon felt Lexi slump in his arms, and she grew still. "Let me go, Braydon," Lexi whispered, her voice hoarse from screaming. "I'm alright, now." The anger had left her body as quickly as it had started.

Turning his head to examine Lexi's face, Braydon could see the rage had left her eyes, and her face looked drained. He released his hold on her and moved to retrieve the bottle of tonic he had left nestled by the base of a tree. Still feeling wary, Braydon tentatively held out the metal container to Lexi.

Not looking directly at Braydon, Lexi stood and took the bush brew from him. "Thanks," she said, taking a long drink of the liquid. The mixture felt wonderful on her parched throat.

Placing the metal container carefully on the ground, Lexi rubbed her tender eyes before running to the creek and wading in. She swam out to the middle and dove under the surface, the water cooling her hot face. She floated face down in the water for a while, enjoying the sensation of being suspended.

After a few moments, unable to hold her breath any longer, Lexi raised her head and looked back towards the bank. Braydon was there, squatting by the water's edge, washing his face. "You, okay?" he asked, glancing up at Lexi.

"Yes, I think so," she murmured, not looking directly at him.

Braydon waded into the water and swam towards Lexi. He tenderly took her hand in his. "Lexi, it's alright. Lilly and I have both succumbed to the rages," he smiled a little. "You get to recognise the signs, and the tonic is definitely helping to keep them at bay."

Lexi looked at Braydon's face and saw his top lip was split and swollen. His red shirt was also torn from where she had hit him with the tree branch! Her face flamed red, but this time from embarrassment.

Lexi dropped her eyes and coughed. "Ahem, I'm sorry about your shoulder." She peered up at Braydon's face. "And your lip," she said, pointing at Braydon's swollen mouth.

"That's okay, Lexi," Braydon said supportively. "You weren't yourself." He leaned towards her and tried to kiss Lexi on the mouth. "Oww," he cried, pulling backwards and touching his top lip. "Guess I won't be kissing you for a while!" he laughed.

Lexi laughed too and tried not to look disappointed. She really did like Braydon and was looking forward to kissing him again. *If only she hadn't split his lip!*

"We had better get back to the camp," suggested Braydon cheerfully. "I left the fire burning when I came to find you."

"How did you know I was here?" asked Lexi as she climbed from the water.

"Well, I fell asleep for a while, then after I came out of my tent, I saw that you were brewing some more of the tonic," replied Braydon Picking up the bottle of bush brew. "It smelled like it was ready, so I took the pot off the flames and poured some into this flask." He started shaking his head and flicking water from his hair. "I called out for you, but you obviously weren't around, and that's when I noticed our bucket was gone," he shrugged. "I figured you must have walked down to Bryer's creek to fetch us some freshwater."

Lexi walked closer to Braydon and put her arm around his waist. "By the way," she said, smiling at Braydon, her eyes crinkling at the sides. "Thanks, so much for giving me the last of *your* remedy earlier today. I would never have made it through Lilly's funeral without it."

Braydon put his arm around Lexi's shoulders as they made their way back to their campsite. "That's okay, Lexi. There wasn't enough for both of us." Braydon lightly squeezed Lexi's shoulder. "Plus, Lilly was more your friend, than mine. It was important for you to go. Besides, you needed to talk to Hadley. How did that go?"

Lexi went on to describe her talk with Hadley, the tears and her eventual acceptance of Lexi's condition. "She's agreed to move onto the farm, and Jason is going to watch out for her, which takes a load off my mind." Lexi looked a little sad, her eyes dropping to the ground. "Jason knows too, and I'm sure the others will know as well by now if they hadn't guessed already." Lexi absently wound a piece of her wet hair around her finger.

Braydon hated seeing Lexi downcast and pulled her closer to him. He could smell the lemon myrtle in her hair and on her skin. It reminded him of lemon sherbet.

As Braydon moved closer to her, Lexi could feel his body heat coming through Braydon's thin t-shirt, and she snuggled closer to him. Now they were out of the water, her wet clothes stuck to her body, making it uncomfortable to walk.

They soon reached the campsite and went about rebuilding the smouldering fire, trying to get dry. Braydon pulled off his sopping wet jeans and hung them over a branch to dry. Lexi did the same.

As the couple sat by the fire, both feeling a little awkward, Lexi asked, "do you think we will ever see the children from Gracetown again?" She thought it would be a nice idea to try and trade with them. Fish for corn, or beef. "It's a shame their town is so far away from Jasper's Bay," she said, peering thoughtfully into the fire. She rubbed her hand across her brow. "I guess it's too far for the horses to travel regularly."

"Yes, unless we're rescuing someone," grinned Braydon.

Lexi laughed.

"Maybe we could meet them, half-way?" suggested Braydon reasonably. "That would halve the distance, and it wouldn't be so hard on the horses."

Lexi looked at Braydon and nodded excitedly. *That could work.* She would have to remember to suggest the idea to Jason or Ethan. They were going to have to take on a lot more of the organisation in Jasper's Bay now that she was infected. At least until she figured out how to control the rages enough to be around people for an extended period. She hoped this new batch of tonic would work just as well as the last one had.

Thinking about the tonic, Lexi stretched out her fingers and peered at the rash on her hands. It looked just the same. "Braydon," she said quietly. "Now that I have gone into a rage twice, do you think I'm going to end up like Elisha?"

Braydon turned to look at Lexi. She was sitting hunched over and staring glumly at her arms. "I'm not sure, Lexi," Braydon answered, rubbing his split lip. "I guess we all have that potential in us. I think as long as we keep drinking the tonic, we will be ok."

"Hmm. Let's hope those plants aren't seasonal," added Lexi. She dropped her arms and walked over to where Braydon had taken the pot of remedy, cooling and ready to be bottled. She leaned forward and stirred the mixture with a large slotted spoon. This time, Lexi had decided to add some of the bush basil and Lilly-Pilly berries to the brew, as Ollie had informed her that people used them to fight off infection and increase immunity. *She hoped it worked.*

As Lexi stared into the pot, she again thought about the virus. "Braydon," she said again, looking thoughtful. "The other day, when I was talking to Logan about the virus, he said something that got me thinking." Lexi paused for a moment to make sure Braydon was listening. "Logan said the mutated

KV17 virus only affects people 17 years and older because their brains are more mature and developed than younger kids."

Braydon nodded. "Yeah. It seems that way."

"What if we *all* have the virus inside of us already, lying dormant." Lexi shrugged as she walked back towards the fire and sat. "What if it only starts to develop when our brain matures," she suggested, raising her eyebrows.

"I don't know. Yeah, it's possible," agreed Braydon. He was unsure where Lexi was going with this.

"Well, what makes the virus emerge?" Lexi looked frustrated. "I get that you have to be at least seventeen before you start showing any symptoms, but I've been seventeen for a whole month and over in Gracetown was the first time I felt as though I was going to lose control. If you hadn't given me some of your tonic, I'm sure I would have completely lost it." Lexi had been angry plenty of times in the last month, particularly with Hadley; however; she had never lost control.

Braydon stared at the ground and thought about what Lexi had said. It did seem as though the virus needed some type of catalyst to bring it forth. Maybe it *was* lying inside of them all, just like a parasite waiting to *feed* off their emotions. "I think you're right. I think the virus needs a traumatic event to trigger it," suggested Braydon.

Lexi sat taller; her interest aroused.

Braydon began pacing back and forth as his idea developed in his mind. "With me, it was being stabbed by Broc," he suggested as he sat by Lexi. "Your catalyst was being kidnapped and seeing your friend Lilly die."

Lexi looked excited. "Yes. I think you're right. Once you're seventeen and you have developed the symptoms of the virus," she said as she pulled up her sleeve to expose the angry raised rash on her forearm. "Well, then it must only take a strong stimulus to bring forth the anger and rage. It has to be a strong enough event to make your *blood boil*, not your *everyday* type of argument," she murmured, looking pensive.

Lexi stared into the fire. "I really think anyone who turns seventeen or starts showing signs of the virus, should start taking some of this bush brew. Don't you?"

Braydon agreed, once more rubbing at his split lip.

Feeling restless, Lexi pushed herself up from the log she was sitting on and walked back towards the pot of bush brew. She tapped her foot on the ground. "I hope we're going to have enough," she said as she stared at the contents inside. "I'd better start filling these empty bottles."

Braydon came to help her. Both of them deep in concentration as they worked.

After a while, Lexi glanced up from the pot and noticed Braydon staring at her as if he wanted to say something. "What is it?" she laughed. "Why are you staring at me?"

Braydon reached his hand out and touched a wisp of Lexi's hair. "I really like you, Lexi. I have from the moment I saw you. Although, it may have not been in the best of circumstances." He blushed red at the thought of the night Broc and the gang terrorised Lexi and Hadley in their home.

"I've always admired your spirit and guts." He looked at her confidently. "But I want to make sure you are alright out here. I want to look after you."

Lexi listened as Braydon talked. She liked Braydon too, just not as quickly as he had liked her. In fact, she had thought him a bit of a dick at first when he had been with Broc. Now, she had a different understanding of him, and she had grown to like what she saw.

Reaching over, Lexi touched Braydon's rough stubbly chin with her fingers. Even though he had shaved it yesterday removing all traces of the scraggly beard grown from many weeks in the bush, the stubble was already regrowing. She looked into his eyes and tried to be kind, not wanting to hurt his feelings.

"Braydon, I really like you too. A great deal, but I don't need you or anyone else to *look after* me." Lexi watched Braydon's eyes drop to the floor, and she wondered if she had sounded too harsh.

"Listen, it's excellent to know you have my back though, and I've got yours, too." She smiled at him encouragingly, her green eyes crinkling at the sides. "It's not that I don't want your support, it's just that I think it's important I learn to look after myself." Lexi didn't want to feel reliant on anyone else.

"I'm really glad that we're together out here, though. It would be terrible on my own, and it's good to have a close friend." Braydon glanced back at Lexi, his eyes shining brightly.

As Lexi looked at Braydon's happy face, she felt a sudden surge of emotion and immediately leaned forward, kissing him deeply on the mouth.

Ignoring his sore lip, Braydon gently placed his hand on the back of her neck and returned her kiss. It was a tender moment that was rudely spoiled by an interruption of coughing.

At the sound of the unexpected noise, Lexi and Braydon swiftly broke away from each other. They noticed Hadley standing in front of them, her arms folded across her chest. She had Polo by her side. "I'm not interrupting anything, am I? Now I can see why you wanted to move out here with Braydon!" Hadley giggled smirking at them.

Lexi stood and hugged her sister. "Oh, Haha," Lexi replied. "Is everything alright at the farm? How are Zac and Katie?" she asked, her voice worried.

Hadley's smile fell. "They're okay, considering."

"Have you settled in, alright?" asked Lexi, hoping Hadley didn't feel too weird staying at the farm.

Hadley nodded, her face brightening. "I've moved a mattress into Katie's room, and Jason helped me bring a few of my things from the house on Rosewood Avenue, so I feel more at home.

"That's good," said Lexi smiling. "That was nice of Jason. How's Zac?" she asked, placing her hand lightly on Hadley's shoulder.

"Zac is confined to his bed, where he is supposed to be resting, but I know he hates it," giggled Hadley. "Logan has just finished re-stitching his head, so he's under strict instruction not to do any manual work for a few days."

"I suppose Logan is worried about Zac re-opening the wound or developing an infection," agreed Lexi, nodding.

"Yes. Jason and Ethan have agreed to do all Zac's jobs for him while he rests, so he finally relented," smiled Hadley. "And I've been helping with the cooking and looking after baby Sarah."

"That's great, Hadley," encouraged Lexi in a pleased tone. "I'm sure they are very thankful to have you there helping them. Especially Katie."

Hadley grinned, tapping her feet on the ground happily. She held out a large green army style bag to Lexi. "This is for you," she remarked, shaking the bag teasingly before handing it over. "While I was at Rosewood Avenue, I collected some of your things too. I brought over some of your clothes and a few of your books. Looks like you could do with some extra clothes," she said, raising her eyebrows and staring at Lexi's bare legs.

Lexi blushed. "Our clothes got wet in the creek," she declared defensively. "They're drying on the tree!" Lexi pointed to her jeans hung over the tree branch.

"Hmmm," said Hadley trying not to smirk. "Plus, I brought you a pack of UNO playing cards, just in case you get bored of kissing Braydon."

Braydon laughed loudly.

Lexi rolled her eyes but smiled appreciatively. Having some clean clothes to change into would be heavenly. She was probably already starting to stink.

"And there's more…" Continued Hadley dramatically as she opened the bag and plunged her hand inside, before pulling out a large plastic Tupperware container. "I also brought six fresh eggs courtesy of the farm chickens, four potatoes and some flour you can make damper with. How about that!" she grinned at her sister like the Cheshire cat.

Lexi clapped her hands in glee. "Wow, that's fantastic, Hadley," she exclaimed. "We can use the Wattleseeds Ollie gave us, and the flour to make Wattleseed damper!" *It would cook nicely in the coals of the fire, and they could eat it fresh and hot. Delicious!*

After thanking Hadley for her gifts, Lexi retreated to her tent to get changed out of her still damp clothes. It wouldn't do her any good to catch a cold.

Hadley found a stick and began to play a game of fetch with Polo. The little dog leapt around excitedly barking and wagging his tail. "I think you're going to love it out on the farm with me, aren't you, boy?" she exclaimed, throwing the stick into the scrub. Polo raced after it, stopping to sniff and explore all the different smells and wildlife.

After Lexi finished changing from her clothes, Braydon and Hadley helped her to pour the remaining cooled bush brew into the waiting glass bottles. Braydon had lined them up in a row along the ground.

Lexi thought this latest batch would give them a nice supply for quite a few days. She was confident that with this fresh supply of bush brew, she and Braydon would be able to be in enough control of their emotions to do their share of work at the farm. Lexi hoped that if she could manage to keep the violent mood swings of the virus under control, she could have an existence out here in the bush. It wasn't as comfortable as sleeping in a bed, plus, she still felt physically tired and suffered from terrible headaches as a result of the virus. However, at least she and Braydon weren't suffering from the effects as much as Ethan's sister Elisha, and with the tonic they could function relatively well. Lexi wondered for the second time that day where Elisha had gone.

As she sat back down by the fire, Lexi noticed that Braydon was looking decidedly uncomfortable. It had been a few hours since they had last consumed the tonic, and she was also starting to feel the effects of the virus once again. Lexi quickly grabbed one of the full bottles of brew and took a drink before offering it to Braydon who did the same. They were going to have to consume the tonic regularly and get used to carrying it around with them everywhere.

Hadley watched the two of them uncertainly. She must have seen a change in their demeanour because she looked a little frightened as though she was unsure of what might happen.

"Were okay, Hadley," said Lexi as she took Hadley's hand in hers. "We just need some more of the tonic. Want to try some?" she offered the bottle to Hadley.

Hadley took a tentative sniff of the concoction and politely refused. *It smelled revolting.*

Lexi took one look at her sister's face and burst out laughing. "It tastes even worse than it smells!"

Hadley screwed up her nose and joined in the laughter, breaking the tension building in the air. She handed the bottle back to Lexi and looked down at her feet. "Listen, Lexi," she said in a quiet voice. "I wanted to say that I'm sorry I've been such a bitch lately." She looked sheepish. "I've been worried about you, and it makes me cranky."

Lexi placed the bottle on the ground by her feet. "That's okay, Hadley. I know I've been perfect company," she grinned sarcastically, the corner of her mouth twitching. "Especially when it comes to throwing teacups at the wall!"

Hadley burst out laughing. She shook her head. "You're an idiot."

"I know," agreed Lexi, giggling. "Come on," she said, pulling Hadley to her feet. "Let me show you around our luxurious campsite."

Lexi showed Hadley the tent she was sleeping in, and they placed the books Hadley had brought for her, next to the sleeping bag. After that, the two girls made damper together using the flour, one of the eggs and Wattleseeds they had ground with a smooth river rock. Once it was ready, Lexi carefully positioned the bread, plus the potatoes into the hot coals of the fire so they could cook. Braydon busied himself with collecting firewood, giving the two sisters time to themselves.

Later that afternoon the three teenagers sat around the campfire playing the card game UNO, while they waited for the damper to cook and the potatoes to roast in the coals. There was a smell of change in the air as the fluffy white clouds of the morning were replaced by dark black, ominous ones. After months of hot, dry weather, it looked as though it might finally rain. The sounds of motorbike frogs and cicadas filled the air as though they could tell there was weather approaching.

"I hope this food finishes cooking before the rain comes," whined Hadley, poking at the potatoes with a long stick. "I wish we could microwave it!"

"No, you don't," replied Braydon, patting Hadley on the back. "Roasted potatoes are much nicer than microwaved ones," he winked. "Even if you have to wait longer for them."

Lexi peered at her UNO cards and frowned. Either the sudden change in weather, the stresses of the day or the effects of the virus had given her an intense headache. Wanting to alleviate the discomfort she felt, Lexi placed her cards on the ground and pulled some Liniment tree leaves from her pocket.

She rubbed the thin green leaves in circular movements on her temples. The smell they released was overpowering, similar to the scent of eucalyptus. Ollie had suggested using the leaves to help alleviate the headaches the virus gave her. He had instructed her that Indigenous Australians used the leaves for headaches in the past. And so far, it was helping her.

Putting the leaves back in her pocket, Lexi bent down to pick up a notebook lying by her feet. She flicked through a few pages until she found the spot she wanted. Lexi had been making notes and lists of the ingredients they were using to make the various remedies to combat the virus. Braydon, whose skill at drawing was far more accomplished than hers, had been making sketches of the bush plants, seeds and flowers. They both felt that it was essential to keep a record of what worked and what didn't. Lexi knew they wouldn't be the only ones to contract the virus and as more children turned seventeen, they too would become infected. She wanted to keep a record of their discoveries for those future kids, just in case something happened to her or Braydon. Besides, it would make life a lot easier for herself and Braydon if everyone knew what to collect from the bush. The virus left her mind a little foggy and muddled at times and having a *recipe* written down, helped.

Lexi placed the notebook in her backpack resting by her feet and looked up at Hadley who was staring intently at her UNO cards, determined to win the game. Hadley didn't like losing, especially not to her sister.

Lexi smiled. Their parents would never have believed their two daughters from Perth were sitting in the middle of the bush in front of a fire they had started themselves while waiting for a loaf of the homemade damper to cook. Lexi hardly believed it herself. They had both become so much more confident in themselves and their abilities. Learning how to make a fire, catching yabbies from the creek, growing their own food, and even hand-ploughing a field using a horse! Lexi felt particularly self-reliant. In a short time, she had seen herself grow from a shy reserved girl to a resourceful, organised leader. It wasn't always easy, in fact, most of the time, it was difficult, but she loved the challenge. She had even overcome her fear of public speaking, something Lexi never thought she would ever be able to do! *Yep, her parents would never have believed it. Two city girls making a home and a future in the harsh Australian countryside.*

"Are you going to play, Lexi or keep daydreaming!" exclaimed Hadley, fed up with waiting for her sister to take her turn.

Braydon laughed, his red curly hair shaking. "You *are* taking a long time, Lexi."

Lexi blinked rapidly, unaware that she had been daydreaming for so long. "Oh, sorry. I got lost in my thoughts," she laughed. "What number are we on?"

Hadley groaned. "Red three!" she stated, pointing to the stack of cards at their feet. "And I've only got one card left!" she teased, wiggling her card in front of Lexi's face.

"Well, I had better play this, then," Lexi giggled playing a *pick-up 4 card* and grinning gleefully.

Hadley glared at her. "What! Nooo!" she complained as her attempt to win was thwarted. Grumbling, Hadley bent forward to pick up four cards, when a movement in the distance caught her eye. Sitting up straight, she peered past Braydon, shielding her eyes from the shimmer of the sun. As she looked over Braydon's shoulder in the direction of the farm, she noticed someone walking down the long driveway towards the farmhouse.

"Who's that?!" she exclaimed not recognising the tall figure. The person seemed more thickly built than any of the kids in Jasper's Bay. *Was it a newcomer?*

Dropping her cards, Lexi stood and retrieved a pair of binoculars hanging from a pole on the outside of her tent. She held them to her eyes and peered at the figure striding towards the farmhouse. *What trouble was going to present itself now?*

Inhaling sharply in surprise, she quickly handed the binoculars to Braydon with a stunned expression on her face. "It's an adult!" she exclaimed in amazement.

"What the fuck!" cried Braydon, his eyes wide.

"But it can't be!" said Hadley feeling confused. "They all died. Didn't they?"

Lexi looked at Hadley and nodded her head. "It definitely looks like an adult," she remarked, taking the binoculars back from Braydon and Having another look, squinting her eyes. "It's difficult to judge through the binoculars, but even from this distance, I can see they're not a kid. They look about thirty!"

Lexi wasn't sure what to make of this stranger. None of them had seen an adult in over 18 months! As far as Lexi knew, every single adult had died from the virus, and yet, here one was walking determinedly towards the farm.

"But how did he survive?" asked Hadley, her face screwed up in concern. She grabbed the binoculars from Lexi and took a long look at the stranger.

"I don't know, Hadley. There's only one way to find out," said Lexi as she quickly attached a full flask of tonic to her belt. She pulled the damper and hot potatoes from the coals and shovelled sand onto the fire to extinguish it. "Lunch is going to have to wait."

Lexi had a multitude of questions she wanted to be answered. *Where had this adult come from? Were there any others? How had he survived the virus? And most of all, what did he want?*

"Come on," said Braydon grabbing Lexi's hand. "Let's go and find out who this guy is." He pulled a small folding knife from his backpack and shoved it into his back pocket, giving Lexi a knowing look. "Just in case," he whispered into her ear, not wanting Hadley to hear.

Lexi nodded in understanding. "I have one too," she whispered back, patting her jacket pocket. Lexi wasn't sure how friendly this adult was going to be, and she didn't want to be unarmed.

Taking one last look at their campsite, the three teenagers ran towards the road, determined to intercept the stranger before he reached the farmhouse. The Bailey farm was the primary source of food supply for Jasper's Bay, and Lexi was intent on protecting it. They needed to find out just who this person was before they let him in. For the umpteenth time, Lexi wished they had the use of mobile phones or even walkie talkies. It would make communication between the children of the town so much easier; however, without electricity or fresh batteries, those things were a thing of the past. She hoped that some of the kids had stayed back at the farm and that Zac wasn't there on his own with his two younger sisters.

Lexi began to run faster, the bush scrub slapping at her legs.

As they reached the farm driveway, Lexi could see the adult just ahead of them. He was now walking quite slowly, and it wouldn't take them long to catch him up.

Lexi couldn't believe she was about to speak to an adult again! She wondered what he would make of them, a town of children and teenagers. She felt both excited and nervous. Needing some reassurance, Lexi reached into her denim jacket pocket and felt the hard shape of the black pocketknife she kept there. *The town of Jasper's Bay could certainly use an adult's help, but could they trust him?* Lexi guessed they would soon find out.

The End

The story continues in the third novel.

Recipe for Australian Wattleseed Damper

Ingredients

2 cups self-raising flour
1 Tablespoon Ground Wattleseed
1 teaspoon Ground Lemon Myrtle
1/4 teaspoon salt
250ml water

Instructions

Preheat oven to 180C (or use the hot coals of a fire!)

Sift the flour and seasonings into a large bowl and make a well in the centre. Slowly pour the water into the well. Mix quickly and lightly to a soft dough. Use your hands to knead the bread until smooth. Shape dough into a round shape and place on a lightly oiled baking tray or wrap in tin foil if cooking in coals.

Bake for 30-40 minutes (it will sound hollow when tapped).

Serve hot with butter (if available!)

AUTHOR PAGE

I was born in Perth Western Australia, and as a young adult, I grew up in the small country town of Tom Price situated in the outback of Western Australia. Travelling extensively throughout Australia, I loved seeing the diverse landscapes and animals of the country. My current home is in Perth with my husband, two daughters and our cat Abby.

I have a Bachelor of Science Degree, majoring in Sports Science. My interests include watching movies, especially Sci-Fi and horror, travelling, photography and reading. I also enjoy going to the occasional comic book convention!

Like the young women in my stories, I have had the opportunity to experience many exciting adventures in my life so far, including being part of the Australian Army Reserves, climbing to Mt Everest base camp, descending into one of the pyramids at Giza in Egypt, flying in a hot air balloon over the Valley of the Kings, parachuting from a plane at 12000 feet and sitting on the edge of an active volcano on Tanna island in Vanuatu.

I am a member of the Society of Children's Book Writers and Illustrators and the Australian Society of Authors.

My first novel, *Seventeen*, is a YA dystopian adventure story that follows two sisters, Lexi and Hadley as they try to survive in the harsh Australian outback after the KV17 virus kills every adult on Earth.

Rage is the sequel in the *Seventeen Series* where Lexi, Hadley and the children of Jasper's Bay encounter more challenges as they learn to live without the help of adults or modern society.

The Pirate Princess and the Golden Locket is a children's pirate adventure story about a young orphan named Lotty and her cheeky dog, Mr Jacks.

My author website is www.Suzanneloweauthor.com

My Facebook page www.facebook.com/suzanneloweauthor/

My Instagram Page www.instagram.com/seventeentheseries/

WHY I WROTE THIS BOOK

I wanted to write a sequel to my first novel *Seventeen* as I felt the story of Lexi, Hadley and the other children of Jasper's Bay had not yet finished. Some questions needed to be answered. Did Lexi have the virus? Was anyone else immune? What happened to Braydon, Elisha and Lilly, the children who were exiled with the virus? Where did the gang of bullies go?

I also wanted to introduce a new town of children to show that others were having the same problems of survival as the children in Jasper's Bay. Eventually, the separate towns would either have to work together to survive or compete for the limited resources in the area. Similar to past history, when settlements have become either trading partners or threats.

I enjoy writing about the harsh Australian landscape, our flora and fauna and our little slang phrases that make us distinctly Australian. I would like the reader to feel that they are able to see the Australian bush as Lexi, Hadley and the other children are seeing it and get to experience it in a small way through the story.

I plan to write a third book in the *Seventeen Series* trilogy that will conclude the story of Lexi and Hadley and the other children in Jasper's Bay. If you as the reader have any questions you would like answered about the Seventeen Series or the characters in the story, please email me at **suzannelowe.author@gmail.com**

If you enjoyed this book. I'd be grateful if you'd post a short review on Goodreads, Amazon or wherever you purchased your copy. Your support really does make a difference, I read all reviews personally so I can get your feedback and make this book even better.

Thank you for taking the time to read my stories
Suzanne Lowe

Seventeen

Book one in the *Seventeen Series*

Winner of the New Apple YA horror/Sci-Fi award

Imagine a world where everything you grew up with is gone. No adults, no internet, no rules. Could you survive?

The world is facing the deadliest virus ever known.

When the KV17 virus kills everyone above the age of seventeen, life becomes a battle of survival for the children left behind. Seeking to escape the escalating violence in the city, two sisters, Lexi and Hadley flee to the Australian outback. Finding sanctuary in the small town of Jasper's Bay, they soon realise it is far from safe, as a gang of lawless teenagers terrorise the town.Caught in a bitter feud leading to betrayal, deceit and murder, the girls must quickly uncover who their enemies are, and who they can trust. In a world drastically changed from everything they once knew; can the sisters and children of Jasper's Bay learn to adapt? Can they maintain control of their town, and protect it from those who would destroy it?

www.suzanneloweauthor.com

www.silvergumpublishing.com

THE PIRATE PRINCESS AND THE GOLDEN LOCKET

Book one in the *Pirate Princess* Series.

The first thrilling tale of adventure, friendship and mystery in the Pirate Princess series.

The Pirate Princess and the Golden Locket is an exciting adventure story for 6-11-year-old children.

Meet Lotty, the brave young orphan whose life is suddenly about to change forever.

When on her twelfth birthday, Lotty is unexpectantly cast out from the Sevenoaks Home for Children, she befriends a cheeky little dog called Mr Jacks.

Her life soon becomes an exciting adventure as together they encounter lazy pirates, hidden treasure and uncover the mystery of Lotty's golden locket!

The Pirate Princess and the Golden Locket is a story full of loveable characters, swashbuckling adventures and ruthless pirates!

www.suzanneloweauthor.com

www.silvergumpublishing.com
www.facebook.com/suzanne-lowe-author